D0045080

MURDER ON
WALL STREET

Berkley Prime Crime titles by Victoria Thompson

· Gaslight Mysteries ·

MURDER ON ASTOR PLACE
MURDER ON ST. MARK'S PLACE
MURDER ON GRAMERCY PARK
MURDER ON WASHINGTON SQUARE
MURDER ON MULBERRY BEND
MURDER ON MARBLE ROW
MURDER ON LENOX HILL
MURDER IN LITTLE ITALY
MURDER IN CHINATOWN
MURDER ON BANK STREET
MURDER ON WAVERLY PLACE
MURDER ON LEXINGTON AVENUE
MURDER ON SISTERS' ROW
MURDER ON FIFTH AVENUE
MURDER IN CHELSEA
MURDER IN MURRAY HILL
MURDER ON AMSTERDAM AVENUE
MURDER ON ST. NICHOLAS AVENUE
MURDER IN MORNINGSIDE HEIGHTS
MURDER IN THE BOWERY
MURDER ON UNION SQUARE
MURDER ON TRINITY PLACE
MURDER ON PLEASANT AVENUE
MURDER ON WALL STREET

· Counterfeit Lady Novels ·

CITY OF LIES
CITY OF SECRETS
CITY OF SCOUNDRELS
CITY OF SCHEMES

MURDER ON WALL STREET

A Gaslight Mystery

Victoria Thompson

BERKLEY PRIME CRIME
NEW YORK

BERKLEY PRIME CRIME
Published by Berkley
An imprint of Penguin Random House LLC
penguinrandomhouse.com

Copyright © 2021 by Victoria Thompson
The Edgar® name is a registered service mark of the Mystery Writers of America, Inc.
Penguin Random House supports copyright. Copyright fuels creativity,
encourages diverse voices, promotes free speech, and creates a vibrant culture.
Thank you for buying an authorized edition of this book and for complying with
copyright laws by not reproducing, scanning, or distributing any part of it in
any form without permission. You are supporting writers and allowing
Penguin Random House to continue to publish books for every reader.

BERKLEY and the BERKLEY & B colophon are registered trademarks and
BERKLEY PRIME CRIME is a trademark of Penguin Random House LLC.

Library of Congress Cataloging-in-Publication Data

Names: Thompson, Victoria (Victoria E.), author.
Title: Murder on Wall Street / Victoria Thompson.
Description: New York: Berkley Prime Crime, [2021] | Series: A gaslight mystery
Identifiers: LCCN 2020046439 (print) | LCCN 2020046440 (ebook) |
ISBN 9781984805775 (hardcover) | ISBN 9781984805799 (ebook)
Subjects: GSAFD: Mystery fiction.
Classification: LCC PS3570.H6442 M8797 2021 (print) |
LCC PS3570.H6442 (ebook) | DDC 813/.54—dc23
LC record available at https://lccn.loc.gov/2020046439
LC ebook record available at https://lccn.loc.gov/2020046440

Printed in the United States of America

1st Printing

This is a work of fiction. Names, characters, places, and incidents
either are the product of the author's imagination or are used fictitiously,
and any resemblance to actual persons, living or dead, business
establishments, events, or locales is entirely coincidental.

To my daughter Lisa and her lost diamond earrings.

Murder on
Wall Street

I

T<small>HE BABY SEEMS TO BE IN THE RIGHT POSITION, BUT YOU</small> haven't dropped yet, so I think you have a while still to go."

Sarah Malloy managed a smile. No woman in the last month of her pregnancy wanted to hear she still had a while to go, especially in July.

"How long is a *while*?" Jocelyn Robinson asked crossly as she sat up in her bed and rearranged her clothing after Sarah's examination. They were in Jocelyn's bedroom, which she obviously had newly decorated with the most stylish furnishings.

"No one can say for certain. Babies come when they're ready."

"But . . . I thought it would be easy to figure out since I know exactly when . . . when the baby got started," Jocelyn said with a frown.

By which Jocelyn meant that she knew the exact day when she had been raped by a young man whom she'd had no reason to suspect would do such a thing.

Sarah's reassuring smile held. "That does make it easier, but even still, we can't predict exactly when the baby will come. You could give birth tomorrow and prove I have no idea what I'm talking about."

"I don't want to insult you," Jocelyn said with a rueful grin, "but I'd be very happy to give birth tomorrow. Or even today." She wrinkled her nose hopefully. "Don't you know some midwife trick to hurry things along?"

Sarah laughed at that. "I know a dozen, but none of them really work. About all they accomplish is giving the expectant mother something to do while she's waiting."

Jocelyn sighed and reached out in a silent request for Sarah to help her up from the bed. When she was on her feet, after some effort from both women, Jocelyn invited Sarah to join her downstairs for some cool lemonade.

The parlor—like the bedroom and most of the rest of the house—had been redecorated since Jocelyn had married Jack Robinson in January. The dark, heavy velvet furnishings favored by the house's original owner—and left undisturbed after Jack had acquired the house—had been replaced by lighter, more fashionable damask, showing Jocelyn's excellent taste. Today the parlor windows were open to what little breeze was available, and the lemonade was a welcome treat.

When the maid who had served them withdrew, Sarah said, "How are things going with you and Jack?"

Jocelyn sighed, making Sarah a little fearful of what her

answer would be. Sarah had, after all, played matchmaker for the couple, who hadn't even known each other until a few weeks before they wed. "I can't believe how kind Jack has been to me. From the very first day, he's been so thoughtful about everything."

"I noticed that you are sharing the bedroom," Sarah said. The little signs of Jack's presence had been everywhere.

Jocelyn smiled shyly at that, and the color blossomed in her cheeks. "Yes, we have been, almost from the beginning. Jack is . . ." She gestured helplessly.

Sarah was sure she understood. Jack had set out to completely charm his bride, and he had obviously succeeded. "So that part of your marriage is good," Sarah guessed.

Jocelyn sighed again. "Better than good."

"But something isn't right," Sarah guessed again, wondering if she dared offer advice or even if she would have any to give.

"Not really. It's just that . . ." Sarah waited, giving Jocelyn time to choose her words. "I can't help wondering if Jack will be able to accept the baby."

"Has he said anything to make you think he won't?"

"No, he hasn't, but he doesn't speak of the baby much at all. Neither do I, come to that. I think we're both a little . . . self-conscious about it."

"He did understand that the baby is part of the bargain you made with him when you chose to marry," Sarah said. "I know some people think Jack Robinson is an immoral man because of the way he made his living, but he does have his own moral code. Keeping his word is important to him."

"Oh, I know he'll keep his word, but providing for a child and accepting it as your own are two very different things."

"Ah yes, I see what you mean. I can't speak for Jack, of course, but I do know that it's very possible to come to love someone else's child as much as you would your own."

"How could you know that?" Jocelyn scoffed.

"Because neither of my children is mine by birth."

"What?" Jocelyn asked, thoroughly shocked. "What do you mean?"

"Brian is Malloy's son with his first wife. She died when . . . when he was a baby." No sense telling a pregnant woman that Malloy's first wife had died in childbirth. "And Catherine was a foundling. I took her in, and when Malloy and I married, we adopted her. I adopted Brian at the same time."

"And you . . . you love them?"

"As if they were my own flesh and blood. Malloy already loved Brian, of course, but he's come to love Catherine just as much. So you see, families can be made as well as born, and let's not forget we're talking about a baby here. Nothing is cuter or easier to love than an infant."

"Even for a man?" Jocelyn asked with a worried frown.

"Especially for a man," Sarah said with a knowing smile, "because he doesn't have to get up with it in the middle of the night or change its diapers or do all the unpleasant parts of parenting."

Jocelyn finally smiled at that. "I see what you mean. I hadn't thought of that."

"Just give Jack a chance. If you expect him to accept the baby, he probably will. He might not be as excited as he would be if he were the baby's father, but let him know you expect him to be the father in every way from now on, and he will probably rise to the occasion."

Jocelyn's sigh was more relief than worry this time, and she rubbed her rounded stomach possessively.

"Do you feel a little better now?" Sarah asked.

"A little. I'll just be glad when the baby is born and I know how he's going to react."

"Speaking of knowing, have you spoken to your parents?"

"Oh my, didn't I tell you? Well, I think I did tell you that I wrote to them right after the wedding so they would know where I was and why I'd left the clinic." When they originally found out she was pregnant, Jocelyn's parents had sent her to the maternity clinic that Sarah had opened on the Lower East Side. They had wanted to keep her out of sight so she could give birth in secret, put the baby up for adoption, and resume her place in society.

"Yes, you told me that. I'm sure they were quite surprised."

"They always assumed I'd been lying about being raped, of course. When I married Jack, they decided that I'd just been ashamed of being seduced by a gangster and made up the whole rape story."

"That's probably just as well, since that's what you and Jack expected people to believe anyway."

"Yes, well . . . It hurt when they didn't believe me, and I don't think I can ever forgive them for that, but seeing their faces when they met Jack almost made up for it."

"They've met him, then?" Sarah asked in delight.

"Oh yes. I had invited them to dinner. They didn't respond at first, not for months, in fact. I wasn't surprised. They must have been thoroughly shocked that I would dare defy them like that and marry without getting their permission, much less without them even knowing. Then, about a month ago, my mother wrote me a note saying they would be happy to meet Jack. We had put an announcement in the newspapers, of course, and we had already entertained some of my friends who were anxious to meet my notorious new husband. I guess my parents' friends were asking all sorts of questions about their new son-in-law, and how could they admit they'd never met him?"

"That would be difficult. Even if you'd eloped against their wishes, they'd eventually be reconciled."

"And so they were. I'd done all the redecorating of the house by then. Jack was so generous. He told me to buy whatever I wanted."

"And you did a marvelous job."

"Thank you," Jocelyn said with a modest smile. "My parents were shocked, though. I don't know if they expected to find me living in a hovel or what, but they were obviously impressed by the house. And they were terrified of Jack!"

"Terrified? Why?" Sarah asked, amazed.

"His reputation, I suppose. And I'd also like to think they felt at least a little guilty for sending me to the clinic."

"Maybe they thought Jack would want revenge or something," Sarah said.

"Maybe," Jocelyn agreed. She was really smiling now. "Anyway, they were so nervous, they could hardly have a conversation. I have to admit, my mother did seem to have been worried about me. She told me privately that she'd wanted to visit me right away, but Father wouldn't let her come."

"How did Jack treat them?"

"That's the really funny part. Even though they were obviously frightened of him, he treated them with complete respect. I think that upset them more than anything."

"Because they'd been expecting him to be angry, I suppose."

"Or uncouth. Jack said he was nervous about meeting them, but you never would have known. He was the perfect host."

"I'm sure Jack has been in much more stressful situations. Your parents probably weren't carrying weapons, for example," she said with a grin. "Have they invited you to dine with them in return?"

"Yes, but I'm too far along to be out in public, so I had to decline."

"Are you serious?" Sarah asked.

"Oh yes. Jack doesn't want me to leave the house for fear I'll go into labor, and even if I wanted to defy him, my *servants* wouldn't permit it."

"And by *servants*, I assume you mean Tom and Marie O'Day," Sarah said with an amused smile. Sarah knew Jocelyn's butler and cook well from a case she and Malloy had worked on. Jack Robinson had hired the O'Days to help him with his new, respectable persona.

"Exactly. Marie has been making sure I eat well every single day, and Tom guards me like I was some rare treasure entrusted to his care. They only relax their vigilance when Jack is at home."

"And is he frequently at home?"

"More so of late. He has been divesting himself of almost all his illegal businesses. He said they kept him out in the evenings when he preferred to be home with me." Jocelyn gave her another modest smile.

"How very sweet of him."

"I thought so."

"What business is he in now?"

"He's buying real estate, or so he says. He calls it *investing*."

"How respectable."

"That's what I told him. He seems quite pleased with himself, although I do worry about him. Businessmen can be rather unscrupulous. I hope no one is taking advantage of him."

"Oh, Jocelyn," Sarah said, shaking her head. "If I were you, I'd worry about Jack taking advantage of other people. That's far more likely!"

The next morning, Frank looked up with pleasure when Jack Robinson entered the modest offices of Frank Malloy, Confidential Inquiries. Maeve Smith, his part-time secretary who also served as nanny to his children, was at home taking care of the children this summer morning, and his partner was still recuperating from a particularly troublesome case, so Frank was holding down the fort alone.

After the two men had greeted each other and observed the usual pleasantries—Jocelyn was doing well, as Sarah had already reported to Frank at dinner last night—and Frank had escorted Jack into his private office, the men settled back into their chairs. Frank said, "Now tell me what brings you here."

"Hayden Norcross is dead."

Frank frowned as he tried to remember where he had heard the name. "Is that the fellow who was shot in his Wall Street office the other day?"

"The very one."

Frank considered this information for a moment and found nothing of interest in it. "I saw it in the newspapers, but why do you care?"

"Don't you know who Norcross is?" Jack asked, a bit puzzled.

"Some rich society fellow who made his living by cheating other rich society fellows, I'd guess."

"He's . . ." Jack looked away and for the first time in the year since Frank had known Jack Robinson, he looked disturbed. But only for a moment. When he turned back to Frank, he was resolute again. "He's the man who . . . attacked Jocelyn."

By which he meant Norcross was the erstwhile suitor who had raped Jocelyn and gotten her with child. Then he had denied it and refused to marry her. Jack must hate Norcross with a passion, and he certainly had good reason to want him dead, and now Norcross really was dead. "I see," Frank said, afraid that he saw all too clearly. "And you need to hire a private investigator to help you."

To Frank's amazement, Jack smiled at that. "Yes, but not for the reason you obviously think. You think I killed him, don't you?"

"The thought crossed my mind," Frank admitted. "Did you?"

"No, I did not, although I will always regret missing my opportunity. I had other plans for Norcross, though, plans that involved humiliating him and ruining the rest of his miserable life, but I didn't kill him."

"Then why do you need my services?"

"Because the death will be investigated, *thoroughly investigated*, will it not?"

"By the police? It probably will since the victim was rich and the newspapers will be interested." Frank had been a detective sergeant for the New York City Police for a number of years, and he could easily imagine the amount of pressure the chief of detectives would put on his men to find the killer of such a prominent citizen. A generous reward from the family would also motivate the detective squad.

Jack shifted uncomfortably in his chair. "Normally, I wouldn't care how much they investigated, of course, but you see, I have a connection to Norcross."

"What kind of connection?"

Jack shifted again. He crossed his legs and cleared his throat. "A business connection."

"Did you sell him one of your saloons? Or a gambling hell, by chance?" Frank asked. Sarah had told him Jack was divesting himself of those.

Jack smiled in spite of himself. "I should have tried that. No, my association with Norcross was all completely legal. He worked for his father's investment bank, and he was putting a deal together for which I was an investor."

"Wait." Frank held up a hand as if to stop him. "What is an *investment* bank?"

"As you obviously understand, it's not like a regular bank. It's . . . You can't just walk in and open an account. You have to deposit at least fifty thousand dollars with them before they'll even do business with you."

Frank whistled his appreciation. "And then what kind of business do they do?"

"They arrange financing for various enterprises. Railroad mergers or company expansions or anything that requires a large investment of capital, really, and promises a generous return."

"So only rich clients need apply."

"Yes, rich clients who can afford to lose a few hundred thousand now and then while most of the time they can double their money in a matter of weeks."

"I guess that kind of thing would appeal to a gambler like you."

But Jack shook his head. "I owned gambling houses, but I never gambled. Only a fool risks his money like that because, as I know only too well, the house always wins."

"But you were investing with Norcross anyway. I gather that was part of the plan you mentioned."

"Yes, it was."

Frank settled back in his chair. "Maybe you should explain your plan to me and how you were going to ruin Norcross with it."

"I would be happy to. It's rather ingenious, if I do say so myself."

"I'll be the judge of that," Frank told him with a grin.

Jack nodded his agreement. "First you need to under-stand a bit about how the investment banks work. There are large banks and smaller banks. The smaller ones are called second-rank houses, and Norcross's father owns one of them. But being a second-rank house doesn't mean being *second rate*. It just means that you're a bit smaller, and instead of owning a bunch of corporations, your clients own a bunch of factories."

"Or a bunch of saloons," Frank offered.

"I don't actually own any saloons anymore," Jack re-ported with a hint of pride. "At any rate, it didn't matter to me what size house Norcross was, because I wanted to do business with him, no matter what."

"I see. Go on."

"When the investment bankers put their deals together, things sometimes move rather quickly. The investors may only have a matter of days to decide whether to invest, so they don't have time to do any research into the deal or the business they'll be financing."

"That sounds dangerous."

"It can be, so the clients must trust the investment bank-ers to do the research for them. If a deal goes bad, the banker will be blamed, and he will lose the confidence of his clients."

"Which means they won't do business with him any-more," Frank said.

"Exactly, and the firm must dismiss an untrustworthy banker or risk being forever tainted by his carelessness."

"Let me guess," Frank said. "You were planning to taint Hayden Norcross."

Jack smiled ruefully. "It did take me some time to figure out how the whole thing works and then to learn enough about Norcross to find his weakness. That part was surprisingly easy. His weakness was in not being overly careful about investigating the deals that were brought to him."

"You mean he's been wrong before?"

"I won't say he was incompetent, but he's had some failures. His father had to cover for him more than once to prevent the clients from finding out."

"But you were going to involve him in a deal that failed and make sure his father couldn't cover up for him."

"It was all rather clever, actually. Norcross was so cocky that fooling him was child's play."

"But would a father truly dismiss his son, even if he really was incompetent?"

Jack shrugged. "If the old man dismissed him, Norcross would be ruined, and if he didn't, they would all be ruined. It didn't matter to me which one happened."

Frank nodded his understanding. "And how close were you to achieving your goal?"

"Weeks away, but now . . . Well, now it no longer matters except that I do have this connection to Norcross that could be discovered if someone looks for it."

"Did anyone else know about your plans?"

"No, no one, not even Jocelyn."

Frank could understand why he wouldn't tell his pregnant wife about his plans to ruin her rapist. "I don't pretend to understand all this investment banking business, but would someone be able to figure out that your deal was purposely doomed to failure?"

"I don't think so, although I suppose it's possible, but that's not really what worries me. You see, Norcross knew that I married Jocelyn."

"Did you tell him who you were?"

"I didn't have to. He knew who I was when he met me, but I pretended I didn't know what he had done. He tested me with a few snide remarks, but I have a lot of experience not letting my true feelings show, which has kept me in good stead for a long time."

"I'm sure it has."

"So he may have suspected that I knew, but I never confirmed it."

"But if Norcross knew who you were, he might have suspected your motives anyway."

"Yes, but it wouldn't have mattered, because whoever I was, Norcross thought he was going to outsmart and swindle me, not the other way around. It only matters now because from what Jocelyn told me, her father had confronted Norcross and demanded that he marry her, so it's possible his family knew as well."

"Then his father might also suspect your reasons for coming to their bank."

"And tell the police that I had a personal motive for wanting Norcross dead."

Frank nodded his understanding. "I don't suppose you have an alibi for the night Norcross was killed. What night was it?"

"Tuesday. I was at home with Jocelyn. We had a quiet dinner and played a game of chess. She won."

"Not exactly ironclad. How unfortunate that you didn't have a party that night with a dozen guests."

"If I had known, I would have."

"So you've come to me with this, but you haven't said anything about how you think I can help you."

"I thought it would be obvious," Jack said. "I need you to find the real murderer before anyone figures out that I would be a good suspect."

You do realize how dangerous this situation is for Jocelyn," Sarah said when Malloy had finished telling her about Jack Robinson's predicament. She had been surprised when he telephoned to let her know he would be home for lunch, but now that she knew the danger their friends were in, it made perfect sense that he'd want her to know immediately. She'd asked Maeve to take the children to the park after they had eaten their own lunch so she and Malloy could speak freely.

"I imagine there would be a scandal of sorts," Malloy said, pushing his empty plate aside. They were dining in the breakfast room, which was far more comfortable for two than the enormous formal dining room. The cheerful room overlooked the backyard, where flowers struggled to bloom in the anemic city sunlight.

"Oh, it's far worse than just a scandal," Sarah said, the remains of her own lunch now forgotten. "Even Jocelyn's own parents didn't believe that Norcross really raped her.

They assumed she'd somehow invited his attentions or even consented to them. In any case, they blamed her for the attack, and if the news of her pregnancy had become public, everyone else would have done the same. She would have been branded as immoral, and no decent man would ever have married her."

"Which is why they tried to hush it up by sending her to your clinic and demanding that she give the baby up."

"But things like that are so difficult to keep secret, and rumors would have followed her simply because she had disappeared for months. Even if they had managed to carry out their original plan for Jocelyn, her chances of making a good marriage were slim."

"Which is why you arranged for her to meet Jack. I know all this."

"But you need to understand how *important* this is, Malloy, and what the consequences of failure would be for them. Their elopement gave the impression that Jack was the baby's father, and while that makes for a tasty bit of gossip, it isn't the first time a society couple has needed to make a hasty marriage and it won't be the last. If anything, it made them more interesting and more likely to be included in social events."

"Which was what Jack wanted out of the marriage in the first place."

"But if the truth were to come out that Jack had married her after another man had gotten her with child, then she is once again disgraced and Jack is a joke. Even worse, the newspapers will have a field day with it, making up all kinds of salacious lies and creating new scandals we can't even imagine while also accusing Jack of murder. We simply can't let that happen."

"*We?*" Malloy echoed with some amusement.

"Yes, *we*, because you can't hope to solve this case without help."

"I had no idea you were an expert on the workings of Wall Street, Mrs. Malloy."

"I'm not, of course, but neither is Gino, even if he were available to help you." Malloy's partner, Gino Donatelli, had been through a harrowing ordeal last Saturday, and Malloy had insisted he take some time off.

"Oh, didn't I mention it? He came in today. He said his mother was driving him crazy, fussing over him, and he was perfectly fine and ready to come back."

"Maeve will be happy to hear that."

"Will she? With Maeve, it's hard to tell."

It wasn't hard for Sarah to tell, so she'd make a point of questioning Maeve later when she brought Catherine and Brian home from the park. In the meantime: "Getting back to Jack Robinson, I may not know anything about the workings of Wall Street, but I do know the workings of society, and that's the most likely place to start if you want to know who had a reason to kill Hayden Norcross."

Malloy sipped his coffee thoughtfully. "You're probably right. But I do need to know more about the workings of Wall Street, too."

"My father could probably help with that. He advised you about investing your money, didn't he?"

After making a career of working for the New York City Police Department, Malloy had inherited a rather large sum of money. That had enabled him to marry Sarah, the daughter of one of the old Knickerbocker families in the city, and to make a home for them and their family. "He is *still* advising me. I don't think I'll ever figure it all out. You need to be trained from birth to deal with money, I think."

"Then he'll be thrilled to have you ask for his advice on this, too."

"And what about your mother? She does hate to be left out."

Sarah sighed. "Father thinks she takes too great an interest in your cases, but she is an expert on New York society, while I have been avoiding it for years."

"Do you suppose they are free this evening to consult with us?"

Sarah smiled. "If they aren't, I'm sure they'll cancel their engagement if I tell them we need their help."

As it happened, Sarah's parents were at home that evening, and they insisted Frank and Sarah have dinner with them when they learned their assistance was needed. Felix Decker believed that the dinner table was no place to discuss a murder investigation, so they chatted amiably about the children and the hot weather and Theodore Roosevelt's recent nomination as vice president and what it would mean for him when McKinley was reelected.

"Not much," Sarah's father predicted. "Everyone knows the vice president has no powers or duties. He'll be stuck in Washington City for four years with nothing to do and everyone will forget about him. The New York politicians just want to get Teddy out of the governor's mansion so they can be rid of him once and for all."

"His efforts at reform haven't been any more popular in the rest of the state than they were when he was police commissioner here in the city," Malloy said.

"Or any more successful," Sarah's mother said.

"Which is why he's made so many enemies," her father said, "and why they finagled to get him nominated as vice president. McKinley is bound to get reelected and poor Teddy's promising political career will grind to a halt."

They lamented Theodore's fate for a few more minutes before adjourning to the family parlor for coffee. The family parlor was the room used every day. The furniture here was more comfortable and the atmosphere far less formal than the front parlor.

Sarah sat down next to her mother on a sofa while her father and Malloy went to the sideboard, where her father poured them each an after-dinner drink. Her mother, she noticed, looked particularly animated this evening, which indicated how happy she was that her daughter and son-in-law had come to them for help. Her father was right, Elizabeth Decker really did take far too great an interest in their cases.

Sarah glanced over at the men and noticed her father chuckling at something Malloy had said. How comfortable they were with each other now after such a rocky start several years ago. As an Irish police detective, Malloy had been a pariah to a man like her father. Felix Decker's respect had been hard won, but Sarah was happy to know it had been won long before Malloy inherited the money that allowed him to rise socially as well.

"Now tell us why you've come," her mother said impatiently when she'd poured coffee for them both.

Her father and her husband joined them, taking the chairs opposite the sofa. "It's about Hayden Norcross's murder," Malloy said.

"I thought it might be," her father said.

"I *hoped* it would be," her mother said. "Such an unpleasant young man. It's a wonder someone hasn't shot him long before now."

"Elizabeth!" her husband scolded.

"It's the truth, and Frank and Sarah need to know all about him, don't you?"

"Yes, we do," Sarah said with a reassuring smile. "How much do you know about him?"

"Far too much, I'm sure. He is often the subject of gossip."

Sarah's father winced. "Is it really necessary to go into all that?"

"I'm afraid so," Malloy said. "I have been hired to find his killer, so I need to know of any reason someone might have borne him a grudge."

Her mother didn't actually rub her hands together in glee, but Sarah was sure that's how she felt. "Well, then, let's start with his recent marriage."

"He's married?" Sarah asked in surprise.

"Oh yes, although by all accounts, he was a rather reluctant bridegroom. He married Violet Andriessen."

"Why was he reluctant?" Sarah asked.

"Because he didn't want to marry at all, apparently," her mother said. "He was enjoying his bachelorhood far too much."

"What changed his mind?" Malloy asked.

"The Andriessens are quite wealthy," Sarah guessed.

"So are the Norcrosses," her father said, his pinched expression stating quite vividly how much he hated gossiping. "So it wasn't that. It had more to do with the *power* the Andriessens wield. Some threats were made against the Norcross's bank, I understand."

"To harm its reputation, you mean?" Malloy asked. "So they would lose business."

"Exactly," her father said, surprised Malloy would know that. "The Andriessens are an old family, and people trust their opinion."

"But why were they so anxious to marry Violet to Hayden Norcross, especially with his reputation?" Sarah asked.

"Violet is in a family way," her mother said, "and Hayden is responsible."

Sarah and Malloy exchanged a look. Jocelyn wasn't Hayden Norcross's only victim. Was this what people meant when they said Norcross was *enjoying* his bachelorhood?

Even more disturbing was the realization that if Jocelyn's father had been more influential, she might have been forced to marry Norcross herself. The very thought made Sarah shudder.

"It's possible that Violet wasn't the only young woman Norcross violated," Sarah said. "Mother, do you think we could find out who else might have been victimized?"

"Certainly," her mother said. "Hayden's murder was the main topic of conversation at the luncheon I attended today. I imagine people will be talking of little else in the coming days."

Her father turned to Malloy. "I hope you don't expect me to report gossip to you, too."

"Not at all," Malloy said with a teasing smile. "I know that Norcross had lost money on some of his deals recently, though. I just need to find out who the investors were and if they were angry enough to shoot him over it."

"Well, if it's business you want to talk about, that's not a problem. You can come with me to my club. The men there will be happy to tell you anything you want to know."

Sarah took a sip of her coffee to cover a smile. Her father had been trying to get Malloy to join his club for a long time.

"But isn't that gossip, too?" her mother asked with feigned innocence.

"Not if it's business," her father informed her. "If it's business, it's just information."

Her mother shook her head in dismay. "Men," she muttered. "Frank, can you at least tell us who hired you to find Hayden's killer? I'm assuming it's his parents."

"I'm afraid that's confidential, Mother Decker."

She turned to Sarah, who could only shake her head. "But it's someone who deserves the effort, Mother."

"Then we will make that effort, won't we, Felix?"

He could only agree.

II

I'M WONDERING WHY YOU DIDN'T DRIVE YOUR MOTORCAR," Felix Decker said to Frank after his carriage driver had dropped Sarah off at the Malloy house later that evening. Mr. Decker had convinced Frank to go with him to his club, where the members tended to gather after supper and stay late into the night, so this would be the perfect time to engage them in speculation about Hayden Norcross's death.

"I noticed that none of the other millionaires in town drive their own motorcars, so I leave the driving to Gino." Frank wouldn't mention that although even Maeve had learned to drive, Frank had not completely mastered the skill.

"Ah, that makes sense, although I doubt Mr. Donatelli would appreciate being taken for a chauffeur."

"He doesn't wear a uniform, so that helps."

"I suppose it does. At any rate, I don't expect this mania for motorcars to last. They're an interesting novelty, but nothing will ever replace horses."

Frank hoped he was right. "I understand that Hayden Norcross worked for his father's bank."

"That's right. Bram Norcross has a second-rank investment bank a few blocks from the stock exchange."

"Do you do business with him?"

"I have occasionally."

"Why only *occasionally*?"

"Because I'm not as wealthy as some of his clients, and I don't like taking unnecessary risks with my money."

Frank had thought the Deckers were extremely wealthy when he'd first met them, but since then he'd learned there were degrees of wealth and that only wealthy people really understood them. "Is Norcross's bank unreliable?"

Mr. Decker braced himself as the carriage rounded a corner a little faster than was prudent. "Not unreliable, although I wouldn't have trusted *Hayden's* advice. I just prefer to have my money invested more safely."

"Is that why you've never mentioned investment banks to me before?"

Mr. Decker smiled at that. "I didn't think you'd feel comfortable with the risks involved, and besides, I was thinking about my daughter's future."

Frank could appreciate that. He didn't want to squander the money that had been entrusted to him, especially when he was expected to use it to provide for his own daughter. If he didn't want to squander it, he certainly didn't want to lose it in a foolish investment. "How eager do you think Norcross's father will be to find his son's killer?"

"That's an odd question," Mr. Decker said. "Shouldn't every father be eager to do that?"

"They should, but they aren't always, as I'm sure you realize. I just need to know where Mr. Norcross falls on the question."

"I'd expect him to want justice, but . . ."

Frank gave him all the time he needed to choose his words.

Finally, Mr. Decker said, "A scandal would be very bad for his business."

"And would that be more important to the father than justice for his son?"

"I imagine it would depend on how bad the scandal was," Mr. Decker said. "I'm guessing from your questions that Bram Norcross is not the person who hired you to find Hayden's killer."

Frank ignored the implied question. "I don't suppose Mr. Norcross is a member of your club."

"Unfortunately, no, but that also means the members will be speaking freely since they won't have to worry about offending him."

"What kind of a man is Bram Norcross?"

Reading Mr. Decker's expression in the dark cab was difficult, but Frank had just proven Norcross senior was not his client and Mr. Decker knew it. "He's a proud man. Some would probably say arrogant. He's been successful and his clients trust him. He had high hopes for his son but spoiled him, I'm afraid."

"Does he have other children?"

"He had a daughter, but she died in childhood. A tragic accident, if I recall."

"So the son was his only child. Tell me about the girl Hayden married. You said her family was very powerful."

"I should have said *influential*. This is America, after all. We don't have a class of powerful aristocrats."

"Some would argue with that, but I won't bother. How are they influential?"

"Some men simply command respect, and Thomas Andriessen is one of them. I think Elizabeth mentioned they are one of the old Knickerbocker families, but that alone wouldn't explain it. My family is as well, but I don't have the same influence that Thomas does."

"And he would be protective of his daughter."

"I'm not sure *protective* is the word I would use. He did marry her off to Hayden Norcross, after all."

"I take it Hayden has a reputation."

"Have you heard things about him other than what Elizabeth and I told you?"

Frank considered his reply and decided to trust his father-in-law with the truth. "The girl he married isn't the only one he got in a family way."

Mr. Decker swore. "I can't believe he would be tolerated if he goes around seducing girls from good families."

"I don't think there was much seduction involved. He apparently relies on force."

Mr. Decker swore again, obviously outraged. "How could a man like Hayden get away with that?"

"Probably because the young ladies involved didn't dare accuse him because their own reputations would be ruined."

"You're right, of course. What kind of a world do we live in that doesn't protect innocent girls?" Mr. Decker demanded.

Frank had no answer for that, so the cab fell silent as both men considered the unthinkable.

"I suppose if there were others, one of them might have gotten revenge by shooting him," Mr. Decker finally said.

"I was thinking a father or a brother might have done it."

"That's certainly possible, perhaps even probable, but how will you find them? No one speaks of these things, and the girls probably don't tell anyone at all, so they don't even become a matter of gossip."

He was right, of course. "I don't know, and if that's the case, I might not find the killer, but if Norcross was that kind of man, he probably had other enemies as well, for completely different reasons."

"I'm sure he did. And here we are at the club, so let's see if we can find out what they might be."

The Knickerbocker Club was one of the newer men's clubs in the city, but no less exclusive for all of that. Barely thirty years old, it had been founded when members of the much older and more venerable Union Club decided the membership standards there had fallen too far. They formed the Knickerbocker Club in response. Although you had to be rich to belong, wealth alone was not enough to qualify a man for membership. He also had to belong to what everyone— except perhaps Mr. Decker—recognized as the American aristocracy, which meant they were descended from one of the old Knickerbocker families who originally settled New York, hence the name for the club. Later they expanded their membership to other elite members of society as well, but those judged to be "new money" need not apply.

No one had newer money than an Irish Catholic ex-policeman who hadn't even earned his fortune. Since its founding, the Knickerbocker Club had actually accepted some Jews as members, but Frank was certain they wouldn't extend that exception for an Irish Catholic, no matter whose daughter he married.

Frank followed Mr. Decker up the front steps and waited for the butler to answer their knock. The fellow greeted Mr. Decker by name, and to Frank's surprise, he bowed and said, "It's a pleasure to have you visit us again, Mr. Malloy."

Frank blinked in surprise, although he probably should have expected to be recognized. He'd been here before, when he solved the murder of one of the members who had died in the club's library. That had been a long time ago, though. This fellow had a good memory.

"Would you enter Mr. Malloy as my guest, please, Ralph?" Mr. Decker asked.

"I would be happy to do so, Mr. Decker." He took their hats and ushered them into the main gathering room.

Mr. Decker proceeded to make his way around the room with Frank in his wake, greeting and being greeted by the members sitting in small groups. The cigar smoke was thick and the liquor was flowing freely. Mr. Decker made sure to introduce Malloy to those who didn't know him from the murder case. If some of them raised their eyebrows at the mention of an Irish surname, Mr. Decker didn't appear to notice and Frank pretended not to.

"Ah, this is the group we need to see," Mr. Decker whispered to him as they approached three men sitting off by themselves. Mr. Decker greeted them and made the introductions.

The three men, Frank saw at once, were not only obviously wealthy—their bespoke suits gave them away—but also obviously drunk. Rich people got drunk differently from poor people, though, Frank had observed. Poor people drank to oblivion, to forget the futility and the constant struggle of their lives. Rich people drank to relax. Talking to a drunk poor person was a waste of time, but talking to a drunk rich person could be very enlightening indeed.

These three were just intoxicated enough to tell him whatever he wanted to know—if they happened to know it in the first place.

"May we join you?" Mr. Decker asked. His reply was enthusiastically affirmed and followed by the summoning of a waiter to move some chairs over for them.

When they were settled and the waiter had taken their drink orders, Mr. Decker said, "Have you heard anything more about the Norcross boy's death?"

"We've hardly heard about anything else," George Vanderslice said. Like Mr. Decker, he was slender and elegant. Even his voice sounded like money. "Phillip here was just saying it must be one of those anarchists. They want to kill all of us, don't they?"

"Is that what the police think?" Frank asked with mild interest.

"The police?" Phillip Sonders scoffed. Sonders had obviously enjoyed his privileged position in life a little too much. His bloated stomach strained the buttons of his finely tailored vest, and the broken veins in his bulbous nose told of too many evenings spent sipping a glass of whiskey, exactly what he was doing this evening. "The police will think what Bram Norcross tells them to, won't they?" Which was probably true.

The third man in the group, Michael Washburn, nudged Sonders with his elbow and nodded at Frank. "You remember our guest is with the police, don't you?" Washburn was neither fat nor slender but his eyes had a crafty expression that even alcohol hadn't dimmed.

"Not anymore," Frank said with a smile. "Which is why I asked. I'm sure they'd love to blame the anarchists, though. They could even hang a few for good measure."

"And let poor Hayden's killer go free," Sonders said with obvious disapproval.

"*Poor* Hayden?" Vanderslice echoed in amazement. "Are we talking about the same person?"

"Poor *Bram* is more like it," Washburn said. "He's got a real mess to clean up now, and after all the other trouble he's had . . ."

"What other trouble?" Mr. Decker said, saving Frank from appearing too interested.

"Didn't you hear? He had to let one of his partners go. What was the boy's name?"

"Tarleton, wasn't it?" Sonders offered.

"That's right, Wendell Tarleton," Washburn said.

"You called him a boy, but you said he was a partner,"

Frank said, frowning with apparent confusion. *Boys* didn't usually rise to power on Wall Street.

"A prodigy," Washburn said, "at least according to Bram. Brought him into the company and moved him right up to partner after a year or two. Couldn't stop bragging about how good he was."

"Better than Hayden?" Mr. Decker asked archly.

"Everyone was better than Hayden, but the boy was pretty good. He put a deal together for me. Made everyone a bundle. I was impressed."

"Why did Norcross let him go, then?" Frank asked.

Washburn shrugged. "A deal went wrong for him. Turned out the money went to finance a revolution or something. Every cent disappeared."

"I thought the investment banker was supposed to check out these people," Frank said.

"He did, and there was a bad report, but Tarleton claimed he never saw it. Somebody had to take the blame to save the bank, so Bram had to let Tarleton go."

"Near broke Bram's heart," Sonders said with all the melancholy that whiskey could induce.

"I suppose the investors were upset as well," Frank said.

But Vanderslice was shaking his head. "If you think one of them shot Hayden over that, you're wrong. Hayden wasn't even involved. Besides, if investors shot their bankers every time they lost money, Wall Street would be knee-deep in gore."

That seemed to strike all three of the men as hilarious and they roared with laughter. Frank smiled politely, and Mr. Decker just shook his head.

"Who do people think did shoot Hayden, then?" Mr. Decker asked when they'd sobered again.

"Some jealous husband, no doubt," Washburn said.

"Oh no, he preferred maidens," Sonders said. "Everyone knows that."

Frank actually winced.

"An angry father, then," Washburn guessed.

"Or an angry maiden," Sonders offered.

"Would a woman have brought a gun to his office, though?" Mr. Decker asked with credible innocence.

"Nobody brought it. It was Hayden's gun," Washburn said quite confidently. "The newspapers didn't mention it, but that's what everyone is saying. He must have been worried about those angry fathers, because he kept it in his desk."

"Shot with his own gun. That's irony," Vanderslice said.

"Or justice," Frank murmured. No one seemed to notice.

"What I don't understand," Mr. Decker said without even a glance at Frank to give away their plan, "is what he was doing in his office so late."

"Not working," Vanderslice said. "That boy never worked a minute longer than he had to."

"Meeting somebody, probably," Washburn said. "Maybe a liaison."

"In his office?" Sonders scoffed.

"A client, then," Washburn insisted.

"But why so late?" Vanderslice argued.

Plainly, none of them could think of a reason.

"Could somebody have snuck into the office without him knowing?" Frank asked.

The men exchanged puzzled glances.

"It's possible, I guess," Sonders allowed.

"That's how an anarchist would've gotten in," Washburn pointed out.

"But doesn't the bank have a night watchman?" Mr. Decker asked.

"I suppose they do," Vanderslice said.

Someone Frank would need to question.

"So was the watchman bribed or something?" Sonders asked.

"Or maybe Hayden told him to let his visitor in," Frank suggested.

"An anarchist?" Sonders scoffed. "Not likely."

"But maybe a maiden," Washburn said with a lascivious grin.

After that, the conversation became an incoherent and inconclusive argument about who Hayden Norcross's visitor might have been. When it got too loud, one of the other club members came over to distract them, and Frank and Mr. Decker took their leave.

"Did you find out anything useful?" Mr. Decker asked.

"I found out who I need to talk to next. Any idea where I can find this Wendell Tarleton?"

I SHOULD DYE MY HAIR," MAEVE SAID THE NEXT MORN-ing, after Sarah had told her what they knew about Hayden Norcross's murder. They had taken advantage of a few spare moments to talk while the children were playing upstairs.

"Why would you dye your hair?" Sarah asked, thoroughly confused.

Maeve touched her auburn locks. "Because everyone thinks I'm Irish, but if I had black hair, I could pretend to be a society girl. Then I could go with you to investigate all these rich people."

Sarah knew it would take more than changing her hair color for Maeve to convince people she was a society girl, but she didn't bother to explain. "You are far more useful to Malloy and Gino as yourself, I'm sure."

"Oh, I know! I could drive you and your mother in the motorcar." Gino had taught her to drive, and she was quite good at it.

"I'm not sure my mother would be happy about that. She's not too fond of motorcars. Besides, no one employs a female chauffeur."

"I'm not a chauffeur!"

"Of course you aren't, which is why my mother and I will just rely on cabs, and you will stay home and watch the children."

"Watching the children is boring."

Sarah shook her head in feigned dismay. "I told Malloy he should never have let you help with investigations."

"I didn't really mean it was *boring*," Maeve hastily assured her. "I just meant it's not as much fun as investigating."

"Maybe Gino will come over and help you entertain the children," Sarah suggested with a knowing grin.

To Sarah's delight, Maeve's cheeks reddened. "Why would he do that?"

"Maybe because you invited him. I just thought you might like to see him." Something had happened between

Maeve and Gino during the last case they'd worked on, changing their relationship. Neither of them was giving anything away, though, so Sarah would just have to figure it out for herself.

Maeve sniffed. "Why would I want to see him?"

Just then, the children came running down the stairs. Brian was signing madly, his fingers flying, and Catherine was both signing—for Brian's benefit—and babbling that Maeve and Sarah had to come up and see something they had built, effectively ending their conversation.

Sarah was pleased to note that she had understood almost everything Brian was signing. Having him home for the summer was giving all of them a chance to really practice their American Sign Language. Both children whined piteously when she left for her mother's a couple hours later, trying to make her feel guilty, even though she knew they would be fine the moment she was out of sight. She walked over to Ninth Avenue and took the elevated train uptown. She hadn't lied to Maeve about the cabs, but it was much faster to take the El to her mother's neighborhood, faster even than the motorcar, which had to stop for traffic.

When the maid showed her into her mother's back parlor, Elizabeth Decker was ready and waiting, having thought of nothing else all morning except their upcoming condolence call on Mrs. Hayden Norcross.

"I've been thinking and thinking about how we should approach this," her mother said, not even bothering to greet her. "I know her mother, so I'm just going to lie and pretend she suggested I pay her a visit. Oh, what's that? Have you brought your medical bag with you?"

Sarah smiled. "Yes. I thought and thought about this, too, and I realized I could mention that I'm a midwife and would be happy to check Mrs. Norcross's health. You did say she was expecting."

"That's what I heard, so your approach might be a better one."

"I think we can combine them. You felt you needed to pay her a call, and you asked me to come along in my professional capacity."

Her mother nodded, seeing the wisdom of this. "You're so very clever, Sarah. I'm sure you get it from me."

"I'm sure I do. Have you found out where Mrs. Norcross lives?"

"Yes. They weren't married long enough to be in the City Directory, much less the Social Register, but I only had to telephone the people who manage the Social Register. They keep track of everyone."

Armed with the address, Sarah and her mother found a cab and soon arrived at the new town house. The row of homes had been built for the successful New Yorkers moving uptown and seeking more luxurious accommodations. The black mourning wreath on the door told them they were in the right place.

Sarah's mother obviously impressed the maid with her confidence and sense of entitlement, so she ushered them into the small receiving room to wait while she took the engraved visiting card up to her mistress.

The maid returned with an apologetic expression. "Mrs. Norcross isn't receiving, but Mr. Andriessen will see you."

Sarah and her mother exchanged a puzzled glance, then

followed the maid upstairs to the lavishly furnished front parlor, where a man awaited them. He was much younger than Sarah had expected. This gentleman appeared to be on the sunny side of thirty, although he met them with the self-assurance of someone much older.

"Mrs. Decker," he said by way of greeting. Then he gave Sarah a curious glance, obviously expecting an explanation for her presence.

"This is my daughter, Mrs. Malloy." Which was all the information her mother thought he would need. "How are you, Louis? When the maid said Mr. Andriessen, I expected to see your father."

"Yes, I . . . Well, my parents are meeting with Mr. Norcross about arrangements for, uh, the funeral tomorrow, but they didn't want to leave Violet alone."

"I'm sure she's very upset. How awful for her. May we sit down?" Sarah's mother added, as if she were merely curious and not reminding the young man he was violating all sorts of social etiquette by keeping his visitors standing.

"Oh yes, I'm sorry. I suppose I'm rather upset myself. Please forgive my manners. May I offer you some refreshment?"

He rang for the maid and asked her to bring the ladies something to drink. When the maid had gone, Sarah caught him eyeing her medical bag, which she had set beside her on the floor. She and her mother were sitting on a sofa while Mr. Andriessen had chosen a chair opposite them.

"It's very kind of you to call," he said after a moment of awkward silence.

"Nonsense," her mother said. "It was the least I could do. Your mother is one of my oldest friends." A slight exaggeration, but who would argue? "When we last spoke, well . . . we thought it would be a good idea to call on poor Violet to see if we could help in any way." Had she given the impression that Mrs. Andriessen had influenced their decision to come? Sarah was sure that she had.

"I'll tell Violet you called. She will be grateful."

"The maid said she isn't receiving. I hope she's not unwell."

"She is, uh, prostrate with grief," Andriessen claimed.

"Really?" her mother said with just the right amount of concern. "Because I've never actually known anyone to be *truly* prostrate. If that is indeed the case, perhaps her grief isn't the only cause. I know Violet is with child, and a shock like this could be a serious strain."

Andriessen stirred uncomfortably. Men and women who weren't intimately related didn't usually discuss pregnancy. "We are well aware that—"

"Which is why I brought Sarah along with me," her mother continued, ignoring his interruption. "You see, she is a midwife."

"A midwife?" Andriessen's astonishment was almost comical. He would be shocked to learn that Felix Decker's daughter practiced a trade, of course, and he would certainly be shocked to learn she intended to practice it on his sister. "I . . . I see, but . . . Violet won't need a midwife for many months."

"Sarah also cares for women during their confinement. She could, for instance, examine Violet to make sure her health or the child's was not in danger as a result of the shock of Hayden's unfortunate death."

"That really isn't necessary," he tried, glancing uneasily at Sarah. "I mean, Violet isn't . . . she's not . . . I mean . . ."

"Is she truly ill?" Sarah asked. "Because if she is, it could be something very serious."

Plainly, he hadn't considered this. He sighed. "I don't know if she's truly ill or not. She's taken to her bed and won't speak to anyone."

"Perhaps I could try," Sarah said. "I have a lot of experience talking to expectant mothers."

Andriessen sighed again, this time in despair. "That's just it, you see. She refuses to . . . She doesn't want to admit that there's a baby at all."

"Oh dear," her mother said.

Oh dear, indeed. Sarah tried a reassuring smile. "Then it's very important that I speak to her. I might be able to help her accept her condition, and if she's ill, she definitely needs care."

The maid brought in the tray just then, and when she had served them, Andriessen instructed her to take Sarah upstairs to see Mrs. Norcross. Sarah could tell just how serious the situation was by the expression on the maid's face, but she did as she was instructed.

"Aren't you going with her?" Andriessen asked her mother as Sarah followed the maid.

"Oh my, no. I wouldn't be the slightest bit of help. I'll just keep you company while we wait."

Sarah bit back a smile. Hopefully, her mother would be able to get some information from Louis while she examined Violet Norcross. When she and the maid had started up the stairs and were out of earshot, Sarah said, "Do you know how ill Mrs. Norcross is?"

The maid stopped dead and turned to face Sarah, her eyes wide with concern. "I wouldn't like to say, ma'am."

"It's very important. I'm a nurse, you see, and I'm going to try to help her."

"She's . . . she's in pain, I know. I hear her crying, but she won't let anybody help her, not even her personal maid."

Sarah nodded, her own alarm growing. The maid stopped outside one of the closed doors along the upstairs corridor and knocked. "Mrs. Norcross?"

Sarah heard nothing, and apparently the maid did as well. "Let me," Sarah said, gently guiding the girl out of the way. Then she simply opened the door, ignoring the maid's gasp of dismay.

The room was stifling, with all the drapes drawn to create a twilight glow. A figure had been curled on the bed, and it bolted up into a sitting position with a terrified yelp.

"I'm sorry, Mrs. Norcross," Sarah said hastily, hurrying over to reassure her. "I didn't mean to startle you. I'm Sarah Malloy. I'm a nurse."

But the woman—who was really no more than a girl—wasn't even looking at her. She looked past Sarah with terrified eyes to the door that still stood open. "Is he here? Is he coming?"

"Your brother?" Sarah asked, confused.

"No, *him*. Hayden!" she cried.

"No, no one is coming," Sarah assured her, truly alarmed now. "No one except me, and I'm here to help you."

"Close the door," she cried. "He might see me!"

Behind her Sarah heard the door close with a definitive snick, probably the maid making her exit.

"There's nothing to be frightened of," Sarah assured her, setting her bag down in case it was disturbing in some way.

"Who are you? Did he send you?" Sarah could see now that Mrs. Norcross wore only her nightdress. Her long hair hung in a hopeless tangle, wet around her face, which glowed from perspiration in the thick heat.

"Your brother sent me," Sarah said.

"Louis? Why would he send you?"

"He's worried about you."

"He's the only one who is, then," she said bitterly, dashing her hair out of her face impatiently. "My parents, they gave me to Hayden and then they forgot all about me."

"I'm sure they didn't forget. Your parents were here earlier. They just went out to . . . to make the funeral arrangements."

"What funeral arrangement? Who's dead?" she demanded, newly terrified.

Oh dear, could she possibly not know? "Your husband's dead," Sarah said gently.

"No, you're lying. He's lying. He's trying to trick me. He does that, you know. He plays evil tricks on me to make me cry."

"This isn't a trick. He's really dead. Someone shot him."

Mrs. Norcross stared at Sarah. Her lovely blue eyes—Sarah could see now that she really was a beautiful young woman—were uncertain and full of doubt. "Did he pay you to say that?"

"No, he didn't. I never met your husband and now I

never will because he's dead. He's really dead and he's never coming back, and you don't need to be afraid of him ever again."

Those lovely blue eyes slowly filled with tears that soon overflowed and ran down her cheeks, although she didn't make the slightest sound.

"Would it be all right if I opened the drapes? It's a little warm in here, and I wouldn't want you to get overheated."

When Mrs. Norcross didn't respond, Sarah walked slowly over to one of the windows and pulled back the drapes. The window was closed, so she opened it, allowing what little breeze there was to enter. She glanced back to see if Mrs. Norcross had any objections, but she was still staring off into space, tears continuing to roll down her cheeks. Sarah quickly opened the remaining two windows, letting in both air and light, and when she looked back, she saw Mrs. Norcross still hadn't moved.

Sarah walked back to the bed, smiling what she hoped was a reassuring smile. Now that she could see clearly, she noticed Mrs. Norcross's nightdress was damp with sweat and yellowed around the neck, as if she'd worn it for several days. Her hair hadn't been brushed in a while, and her face was nearly crimson from the heat and whatever emotions she was experiencing.

But maybe also from a fever.

"How are you feeling?" Sarah asked.

"I . . . I don't know."

"Have you eaten anything today?"

She was painfully thin, the bones of her face almost visible through her translucent skin. "I . . . I don't remember."

"Have you been nauseated? Because of the baby?"

Mrs. Norcross's head jerked around at that. "What baby?"

"I thought you were expecting a baby."

The fear flared in her eyes again. "No." She shook her head frantically. "No, I'm not expecting anything at all."

"I must have been mistaken," Sarah said. "But you have been ill. That's why you're in bed, isn't it?"

Mrs. Norcross's lovely face crumpled and she began to weep in earnest, with great gulping sobs. She raised both hands to cover her face, and the sleeves of her nightdress slipped down, revealing forearms covered with bruises.

III

Hayden's death must have come as quite a shock," Elizabeth Decker repeated to recapture Mr. Andriessen's attention. For several minutes he'd made no attempt to be social as he stared with apparent apprehension at the doorway through which Sarah had gone.

"What? Oh yes, quite a shock."

"Do they have any idea who might have shot him?"

Andriessen blinked in surprise at the question, probably because it had come from a respectable society matron who should not be concerned with such things. "I don't . . . No, not that I know of."

"I gather he was a difficult man." Elizabeth smiled benignly to take the sting out of her words.

"*Difficult?* That's one way to describe him." He sounded bitter.

"I'm not one to listen to gossip, of course," she lied, "but I know he had offended a lot of people."

"So it would seem."

"Are you one of them?"

He blinked again, although he looked more angry than surprised this time. "Certainly not."

"Not even after the way he treated your sister? By refusing to marry her, I mean."

"How do you know?"

Elizabeth smiled sympathetically.

He sighed in defeat. "I suppose everyone knows."

"News like that can never be a secret."

Andriessen shook his head. "They should have just sent Violet away. Even if people had found out, it couldn't have been worse than giving her to that monster."

"Do you think he mistreated her?"

"I know he did. He was furious when his father told him he had to marry her. He even threatened to run away to Europe, but Mr. Norcross promised to cut him off without a cent if he did, so he had no choice."

"And he took his anger out on Violet."

Andriessen's young face tightened with disgust. "She begged our parents to let her leave him and come home, but they wouldn't hear of it. The scandal, they said. A woman's place is with her husband and all that nonsense. She was just a nervous young bride and would get used to being married. They sent her back to him even though she was obviously terrified."

"I'm so sorry. Parents can be . . . I'm sure they thought they were doing the right thing." Elizabeth remembered a terrible time she had been sure of that herself, only to learn how very wrong one could be.

"I wish I shared your confidence, Mrs. Decker. At any rate, I'm glad Norcross is dead. At least he can't hurt my sister anymore."

"That is something to be thankful for, at least."

They sat in silence for a long moment while Elizabeth remembered the daughter she'd lost and Andriessen kept his own counsel. Finally, he said, "Do you think Violet could really be ill?"

"Women in her condition are susceptible to any number of ailments, and if Norcross really was abusing her, she could also be injured. But my daughter is highly skilled," she added hastily, seeing Andriessen's dismay, "and I'm sure she will see that Violet gets the very best care. I understand that Mr. Norcross worked for his father's investment bank," Elizabeth said to distract him with a change of subject. "I assume Violet and her child will be well provided for."

That was hardly a topic one would be discussing under the circumstances, but Elizabeth had already violated several rules of etiquette just by barging into Violet Norcross's home, so in for a penny . . .

Andriessen seemed to realize she was simply being nosy, if his shocked expression was any indication. But he also was not used to dealing with society matrons determined to get information, so he apparently had no idea how to respond except to answer her question. "I . . . Hayden probably never thought about such things, but I'm positive his father will make sure his only grandchild is secure."

Which might mean he'd want to take possession of the

child, but Elizabeth wouldn't mention that. If Violet wanted to raise her child, her father could certainly make sure she did. "Do you suppose someone at Norcross's office could have killed Hayden?" she asked.

Plainly, he hadn't even considered that. "I can't imagine anyone there liked him very much, but businessmen don't typically shoot each other, do they?"

"Not typically, no," she had to agree.

"It was surely one of those anarchists. They're always trying to murder someone, aren't they?"

Elizabeth had no idea. "How odd that they'd kill Norcross and not his father, though. Wouldn't they want to cut the head off the snake, so to speak?"

He smiled grimly at her analogy. "I hadn't thought of Norcross as a snake, but you're right, his father is the important one in that bank."

"Unless they simply wanted to cause Mr. Norcross pain by killing his only son."

"Losing Hayden wouldn't cause the old man much pain. He knew exactly what Hayden was, and besides . . ." He seemed to catch himself, straightening in his chair.

"Besides what?" she asked.

"Nothing. I'm not going to spread any more gossip." He looked around as if seeking some escape. "I wonder how your daughter is doing with Violet. Perhaps you should go see."

"Perhaps you could ring for a maid and ask her to check," Elizabeth countered, having no desire to interrupt Sarah's ministrations.

The speed with which Andriessen jumped up to give the

bellpull a jerk was a little insulting, but Elizabeth managed to bear up. When the maid appeared, he couldn't seem to verbalize what he wanted. "Would you, uh, go up and, uh . . ."

"Ask Mrs. Malloy if she needs anything," Elizabeth supplied.

"Yes, do that," he said gratefully.

The girl scurried out, leaving them alone again in their awkward silence.

"Don't worry, Mr. Andriessen. I have no intention of gossiping about your sister. She has endured quite enough in her short life, and she deserves some peace."

He returned to his chair and slumped down into it. "I'll just never understand why Violet was attracted to him in the first place."

"What makes you think she was?" Elizabeth asked.

He looked at her as if she were insane. "It's obvious. The child."

Elizabeth returned the look tenfold. "Do you think she gave herself willingly to a man like Hayden Norcross?"

Elizabeth was gratified to see realizing the truth drained all the color from his face. "But I . . . I just assumed . . ."

"And your parents didn't care that he'd forced himself on her, did they?" Elizabeth guessed. "All they cared about was getting her married to avoid a scandal, even if it meant sacrificing their daughter's future happiness and perhaps even her very life."

"Dear heaven," he murmured.

Before Elizabeth could think of a suitable reply, the maid returned.

"Yes, what is it?" Andriessen snapped when the girl didn't speak.

"Mrs. Malloy says she will be attending to Mrs. Norcross for most of the afternoon. She suggested that you not wait for her, Mrs. Decker."

"The rest of the afternoon?" Andriessen echoed. "What on earth is wrong with her?"

"She . . ." The maid looked desperately between him and Elizabeth and back again.

"It's all right," Elizabeth assured her.

"She . . . Mrs. Norcross needed a bath and Mrs. Malloy told us to prepare some food for her and—"

"That's enough. Thank you, Sally," Andriessen said, dismissing her. When they were alone again, he said, "Thank you for coming, Mrs. Decker, and I suppose I should be grateful you brought your daughter."

"I just hope Sarah is able to help. This is a difficult situation for everyone."

"But mostly for Violet, I'm afraid," he said. "Please allow me to see you out."

Is anybody going to believe I'm a potential client?" Frank asked his father-in-law as they approached the front door of the Norcross and Son Investment Bank. The building was impressive, with a marble front and pillars holding up the imitation Greek arch over the door. Only a small brass plaque identified the business inside.

A doorman in a uniform adorned with yards of gold braid greeted them, calling Mr. Decker by name. He gave Frank the fish-eyed look he'd been expecting but held the door open for them.

A young man sitting at a rolltop desk just inside the door jumped up to greet them. Frank noticed he wore a black armband, probably in deference to Hayden Norcross's death. "Did you have an appointment, Mr. Decker?"

"I'm afraid I did not," Decker admitted with feigned chagrin, "but my son-in-law expressed an interest in a project I was doing with Mr. Norcross, so I thought I would stop by to see if someone could speak with us."

"Your son-in-law," the young man echoed, eyeing Frank with newly born interest. "I see. Well, you must know that we are all in mourning, and Mr. Norcross isn't here, of course."

"I didn't expect he would be, but perhaps one of the other partners could help."

"I, uh, I'll see if someone is available," he said. He invited them to have a seat in the comfortably furnished waiting area while he went in search of someone. Frank looked around, impressed in spite of himself. The ornate and gilded lobby reminded him of most banks except instead of cages for the tellers, there were over a dozen rolltop desks where other young men were working, adding up columns of figures or writing furiously. All of them, he noted, wore black armbands.

A few minutes passed, and the young man who had greeted them returned with another young man. This fellow also wore a black armband, but he was smiling as if he didn't have a care in the world. Frank immediately noticed his bespoke suit and had an urge to ask the name of his tailor.

He was also quite striking-looking, with even features and strong, white teeth. His dark eyes seemed to see more deeply than average, and his hair was even more impressive. Frank prided himself on having a good head of hair, but his was merely black. This fellow's hair was chestnut brown with golden streaks here and there where the light caught it. He wore it brushed straight back from his broad forehead, emphasizing his impressive widow's peak.

"May I present Wendell Tarleton," the young man who had greeted them said. "He is one of our partners, and he will be happy to assist you."

Sarah had just finished tucking a newly bathed Violet Norcross into her freshly remade bed when the maid arrived with a bed tray. Sarah stepped back as the maid set the tray over Violet's lap.

"Oh, I couldn't possibly eat anything," Violet protested.

"Perhaps just a little tea and toast," Sarah said, sending the maid away with a nod of her head.

She had already managed to get Violet out of bed, stripped off her sweat-stiffened nightdress, and into a bath while the maids changed her sheets. Sarah had gently washed the poor girl, examining her as she did so. Fortunately, most of her injuries were only bruises of varying shades that betrayed their differing ages and illustrated quite plainly that Hayden Norcross had beaten his wife at regular intervals. It was a miracle she hadn't lost the child, although Sarah knew it could still happen. Women under the kind of strain Violet had endured in her marriage often miscarried.

"Have you had much morning sickness?" Sarah asked.

Violet winced. "At first. That's how my mother found out."

It had taken nearly an hour of talking, with Violet clutching the sour bedclothes to her chest while apprehensively watching the door, for Sarah to convince Violet she was safe and get her to admit she was pregnant. "But you haven't been eating much lately. Your maid told me."

"I . . . My stomach hurts all the time."

"I think you'll start feeling better very soon, once your mind convinces your stomach that you'll never see your husband again."

Violet stared at her in surprise. "Can I make that happen?"

"Yes. In fact, you may have already done it. Try drinking some tea."

Violet obediently picked up her cup and took a sip. With Sarah coaxing her for nearly every bite and sip, she was eventually able to eat more than half of the food on the tray. Then she laid down her fork and sank back against her pillows with a sigh. "I can't eat any more."

"That's fine. You did very well. The important thing is to keep eating. If you starve yourself, it will only hurt you, because the baby will take what it needs from you. That's why women lose teeth when they're pregnant."

Violet covered her mouth with both hands, as if she could protect hers.

Sarah smiled reassuringly. "Don't worry, I don't think you're in any danger yet."

Violet lowered her hands. "What will happen now?"

"With the baby?"

"No, I mean with . . . with me. With my life."

"Oh, I see. I imagine there will be a funeral tomorrow. I believe your parents have gone to discuss the arrangements."

Violet shook her head. "Mr. Norcross will make the real arrangements. He arranged everything else in Hayden's life."

Sarah thought she might be right. "And then I assume you'll decide where you want to live."

"Won't I have to stay here?"

"Not if you don't want to. Widows have much more freedom than wives do."

Violet brightened visibly at this. "I hadn't thought of that. I don't want to stay in this house. I hate it."

"You'll have to find out your financial situation, of course."

"I don't care if I have to live in a rented room. I'm not staying here."

"Your life from now on will depend on what decisions you make, but I'm sure you will choose wisely, for yourself and your child."

Violet frowned, and Sarah wondered what she was thinking. She plainly wasn't happy about the child and perhaps she never would be, but there was still time for her to come around. Sarah thought of Jocelyn, who had married a man she barely knew so she could keep her child. Sarah hoped Violet could at least reconcile herself enough to love her baby.

Sarah removed the bed tray and set it by the door. Then she got a fresh towel. "Let me try rubbing your hair again. I think it's almost dry now."

Violet leaned forward so Sarah could blot the remaining moisture from her long hair. Sarah had managed to get out most of the knots, and now that it was clean, Violet's maid should be able to manage the rest. Violet would be a beautiful girl once she got some color back in her cheeks and the terror had faded from her eyes.

"Did they tell you how Hayden died?" Sarah asked.

Violet frowned and twisted her head so she could see Sarah's face. "No, they didn't. They said it would be too upsetting. I think that may have been why I didn't believe them."

"Someone shot him," Sarah told her again, more firmly this time because obviously Violet hadn't believed her the first time.

"With a gun, you mean? Like in a dime novel?"

Sarah couldn't help smiling at that. "Do you read dime novels, Mrs. Norcross?"

Violet actually smiled back, the first time she had done so, and the sight of it warmed Sarah's heart. "My brother did. I used to sneak them out of his room."

"I see. Yes, he was shot like in a dime novel. I'm told he was shot with his own gun, too. Did you know he had a pistol?"

"I knew he owned guns. He liked to hunt." She shivered.

"You don't use a pistol to hunt, and he kept this one at his office."

"Why would he need a gun at his office?"

"For protection, perhaps. Do you know if anyone had threatened him?"

Violet's smile had faded and now she frowned again. "He never talked about things like that to me. He complained about his father a lot, but his father wouldn't have shot him. He was too important to the future of Norcross and Son."

Sarah clearly heard the bitterness in her voice. "Why did he complain about his father?" Sarah asked idly.

"He thought Mr. Norcross liked one of the other partners more than he liked Hayden."

Sarah tried to imagine a man preferring someone else over his own son, even a son like Hayden, and why would Mr. Norcross prefer a partner in his bank? Those men tended to be middle-aged and portly and not at all likable. "How odd. Who was this partner?"

"Someone named Wendell Tarleton."

WENDELL TARLETON LED FRANK AND MR. DECKER upstairs to his office, which was a well-appointed room with a commanding view of Wall Street. His enormous desk dominated the space and a thick carpet muffled their footsteps.

"Please have a seat," Tarleton said, gesturing to the two club chairs positioned in front of his desk. "May I get you something? Coffee or lemonade or perhaps something stronger?"

They settled on lemonade and Tarleton asked his clerk to fetch it for them.

"I was very sorry to hear about Hayden's death," Mr. Decker said. "I realize this is not the best time to be calling."

"Thank you, but you don't need to apologize for bringing

us business. Hayden's death was a shock, of course, but he would have wanted us to keep the bank going. Mr. Norcross is taking some time to grieve but the rest of us are at your service."

"Is it true that Hayden was shot in his own office?" Mr. Decker asked. Frank was impressed by how perfect his tone of voice was. Frank would have sounded as if he were interrogating Tarleton, which he would have been, but Mr. Decker just sounded curious, and not even rudely curious but politely curious. It was amazing.

"I'm afraid so," Tarleton said, his expression strained. "Now, what—?"

"But who could it have been? And how could someone get in without being noticed?" Mr. Decker continued, ignoring Tarleton's attempt to take control of the conversation. "Surely, he wouldn't have gotten past your doorman."

"It was after hours," Tarleton said patiently. "Everyone had gone home."

"Don't you have a night watchman?" Frank asked in amazement.

Plainly, Tarleton didn't like the questions, but he wasn't going to create more interest by refusing to answer. "Of course we do, but he never saw anyone. We believe Hayden admitted his visitor himself through the back door."

"So it was someone known to him," Mr. Decker marveled.

"I'm not sure we can assume that." Which meant that the company wasn't going to admit that one of their customers or employees might have killed the boss's son. "But Hayden did have many friends who were . . . well, shall we say, of questionable character."

"And you think one of them came to visit him at his office after hours?" Frank said, not bothering to keep the disbelief out of his voice.

Tarleton was growing annoyed, but he covered it moderately well. "I don't think any other explanation makes sense."

"You're probably right," Frank said. "He wasn't likely to have invited an anarchist in, was he?"

"An anarchist? What do you mean by that?" Tarleton asked in alarm.

"That's what people are saying," Mr. Decker explained. "They think an anarchist assassinated him."

"That's ridiculous. As you said yourself, Hayden wasn't likely to let someone like that into the building. Now, as I'm sure you can understand, discussing Hayden's death is quite distressing, so perhaps we could talk about why you are here instead." His smile was professionally gracious and they could hardly refuse the request.

"Of course. Forgive me," Mr. Decker said. "You must think me a ghoul for being so interested."

"Not at all. It's perfectly natural to be curious. Now, what can I help you with today?"

"Tarleton," Frank mused before Mr. Decker could reply. "Now I remember where I heard your name before." He turned to Mr. Decker. "At the club."

"Oh yes," Mr. Decker said, nodding. "I thought . . . that is, we heard you had left the firm."

Tarleton did a good job of pretending the question didn't

rattle him, but he couldn't stop the color that rose in his neck. "Yes, well, it was a misunderstanding. These things happen in business, but Mr. Norcross himself made amends and invited me back, so how could I refuse?"

How indeed? And exactly when had Tarleton returned? Before or after Hayden Norcross's death? How very interesting. Tarleton wouldn't thank them for asking that question, though, and Frank could probably find the answer elsewhere, so he just nodded.

"I'm sure Bram is glad to have you back," Mr. Decker said generously. "And as to why we're here, I'm trying to interest my son-in-law in investing with you."

They spent almost an hour while Tarleton explained some of his investment opportunities to Frank, who found all of them terrifyingly vague and unlikely to produce a profit. In the end, he had to inform Tarleton that he would consider the possibilities and get back with him. Tarleton seemed more relieved than disappointed when they left without making a decision, and Frank supposed he was. He had certainly been uncomfortable discussing Hayden's murder and even more uncomfortable discussing his recent dismissal and reinstatement.

The two men didn't speak until they were safely in a cab heading back uptown. "Your friends at the club said that Tarleton had been fired after his investors got cheated on some deal," Frank said.

"Yes, they did, and I'm sure they were correct. I'd heard the same rumblings myself."

"Then why is he back at work?"

"Probably because Bram Norcross wants him back."

Mr. Decker knew something, and Frank shifted a little in his seat to get a better look at him. "Why would he want Tarleton back if he'd caused some investors to lose money and thereby caused a scandal that could ruin the whole company?"

"Maybe Tarleton didn't really cause it."

"Then who—?" But Frank didn't need to finish the question. The answer was obvious. "Hayden caused it."

"Perhaps he did."

Frank hardly heard him. He was too busy putting all the pieces together. "Hayden did it but Norcross couldn't blame his own son, so he blamed Tarleton, but with Hayden dead . . ."

"Or—and I'm only guessing here—" Mr. Decker said, "Bram wasn't sure who was responsible, so he let the blame fall on Tarleton because he couldn't accuse his son and heir."

"But Bram Norcross must have known it was Hayden. Otherwise why would he have hired Tarleton back so quickly?"

Mr. Decker got a look on his face that Frank recognized because he'd seen it on Sarah's lovely face many times. It was a smug, self-satisfied look that told him he was going to hear something very interesting. "I think Bram Norcross had a very good reason for hiring Tarleton back."

"And what would that be?" Frank asked, confident his father-in-law knew the answer.

"You've not met Bram Norcross yet, have you?" he said instead.

"No, I haven't."

"If you had, you wouldn't even have to ask. Bram is rather well-known for his most outstanding feature, his hair. It is a rich chestnut brown, and he has a prominent widow's peak."

It could be a coincidence," Sarah said when Malloy had finished telling them what he had learned from his visit to Norcross and Son today. They'd had to wait to discuss it until after dinner, when the children were safely tucked into bed, and now they had all gathered in the parlor.

Malloy's partner, Gino Donatelli, had joined them for dinner, and they had waited until Maeve had put the children down for the night. Even Mother Malloy was there, quietly knitting by the fading light by the front window, while the rest of them had gathered on the sofa and chairs in front of the cold fireplace.

"You don't really think it's a coincidence, do you?" Maeve scoffed. "How many men do you know with widow's peaks?"

"She's just playing devil's advocate," Gino said with a grin. Sarah was so glad to see him back in their family group. They'd come very close to losing him only a week ago. "This Tarleton is certainly Norcross's illegitimate son."

"Which would explain why he rose so quickly in the company," Malloy said. "And why Norcross took him back in spite of the trouble."

"And if Tarleton is Mr. Norcross's son, it would explain why Hayden Norcross complained to his wife that his father preferred Tarleton to Hayden," Sarah said, surprising them all.

"Did Mrs. Norcross tell you that?" Maeve marveled.

"Yes. I spent quite a long afternoon with her, and we talked about a lot of things."

Malloy sat back in his chair and folded his hands across his stomach expectantly. "And what other things did you discuss?"

"Her husband, of course. He beat her, you know."

Everyone gasped, even Mother Malloy.

"Did she tell you that?" Maeve asked, furious.

"She didn't have to. I helped her bathe. The poor girl was covered with bruises. And she was still terrified of Hayden, even though she'd been told more than once that he was dead. Apparently, he used to play cruel tricks on her as well. She thought this was another one and that as soon as she believed it, he'd suddenly appear and terrorize her again."

"How horrible," Maeve said. She glanced at Gino, who looked suitably appalled as well. They were sitting together on the sofa, although they had left a respectable distance between them, as if they were merely friends or business associates.

Sarah wondered whom they were trying to fool. "Yes, it took me a long time to convince her. She of course had no idea why Hayden had a gun in his office. She said he liked to hunt and owned other guns, but presumably they would be rifles or shotguns."

"And did your mother do any detecting today?" Malloy asked with a twinkle. "I know she went with you."

"As a matter of fact, she learned that Violet Norcross's brother, Louis Andriessen, is quite devoted to her. It seems Violet had begged her parents to let her leave Hayden and return home, but they refused."

"How awful!" Maeve said. "Why on earth would they refuse?"

"Fear of scandal, it seems. They'd only barely managed to get Hayden to marry Violet. Louis told Mother that Hayden had threatened to run away to Europe to escape, but his father would have cut him off if he did."

"So," Gino said, having listened attentively to everything so far, "it seems that quite a few people had a good reason to hate Hayden Norcross."

"I suppose you're going to list them for us," Maeve said.

"I have to earn my keep as Mr. Malloy's partner," he informed her. "He hasn't let me do a single thing on this case yet, and I need to catch up."

"All right," Malloy said with a grin. "Tell us who you think killed Norcross."

"Oh, I don't pretend to know who did it, but I can list a few people who might have hated him enough. Wendell Tarleton is an obvious choice."

"That one is easy. The bastard boy who could never be acknowledged," Maeve teased. "It's like a penny dreadful."

"But it's also possible," Malloy said. "Suppose Hayden Norcross arranged the business deal that went wrong and made sure Tarleton took the blame."

"That would make *me* want to kill him," Gino said.

"Or any other man," Sarah agreed.

"Or woman," Mother Malloy said from her place by the window. She didn't even look up from her knitting.

Gino and Maeve covered smiles while Sarah exchanged a knowing glance with Malloy. Mother Malloy often contributed to their discussions.

"Who else is on your list?" Maeve challenge Gino.

"Louis Andriessen. If he knew how Hayden was abusing Violet and that she had no other hope of escaping, he might have taken matters into his own hands."

"But murdering someone like that?" Maeve said. "Not many people could do it."

"We don't know what happened, though," Malloy pointed out. "Hayden was shot with his own gun, which he presumably kept hidden somewhere in the office."

Sarah nodded. "Which means the killer didn't come with his own gun—"

"Or *her* own gun," Maeve corrected her with a glance at Mrs. Malloy, who pretended not to hear her.

"Yes, or *her* own gun," Sarah said with a patient smile. "The killer may have just come to meet with Hayden about something."

"Like confronting him about the way he was abusing Violet," Gino said.

"Possibly," Sarah said. "Whatever they were discussing must have grown heated enough that Hayden took out his gun from wherever he kept it."

"And the killer somehow got possession of it and shot him," Maeve finished for her.

"If there was a struggle for the gun, the killer must have been a man. Hayden could have overpowered a female," Sarah said.

"And what if there wasn't a struggle," Malloy said. "What if the killer knew where the gun was and simply got it."

"How do we figure that out?" Maeve asked with a frown.

"I suppose I'll have to find out if they did an autopsy on

him or at least take a look at the body before they bury him. If Hayden was in a fight, he'd have bruises."

"You'd better hurry," Sarah said. "The funeral is tomorrow."

"I don't suppose Violet mentioned what funeral home they were using," Malloy asked.

"She did not."

"But we're detectives," Gino reminded all of them gleefully. "We can find out."

"Did you have anyone else on your list?" Maeve asked.

"I was going to say Violet's father might have done it, if he found out Hayden was abusing Violet, but now I'm wondering if he would even care."

"Because he wouldn't let Violet leave Hayden, you mean," Sarah said.

"Yes. He doesn't sound like the sentimental type."

"No, he doesn't," Sarah said. "It's also unlikely that Hayden's own father would have killed him."

"But can you be sure?" Maeve said with a grin. "Maybe he was furious at what Hayden had done to Tarleton, the son he actually liked best."

"Maeve makes a good argument," Gino said.

"And aren't we forgetting that Hayden probably made some enemies outside of his family?" Malloy asked. "According to what I hear, he caused some people to lose a lot of money."

"I thought his clients were all millionaires, though," Gino said.

"Even millionaires don't like losing money," Malloy assured him. Since Malloy was one himself, Gino couldn't argue.

"You boys have no imagination."

They all turned to where Mother Malloy sat, still knitting as if she hadn't just insulted half the people in the room.

"What does that mean?" Malloy asked, winking at Sarah.

"It means if this Hayden what's-his-name was so awful to women, it's likely that one killed him."

IV

FRANK ROSE EARLY THE NEXT MORNING TO SEE IF HE
could find out where Hayden Norcross's body was and if
there had been an autopsy. He started at Doc Haynes's office at Bellevue. Doc Haynes did many of the police autop-
sies, and he and Frank had always had a good working
relationship when Frank was a cop. Frank wasn't surprised
to find the doc at work on a Saturday morning. His desk
was piled high with folders, some of them teetering danger-
ously.

Doc greeted Frank and they exchanged pleasantries.
When the formalities were over, Doc said, "Whose murder
are you investigating?"

"Hayden Norcross. He was shot in his office on Wall
Street on Tuesday night."

"Oh yes. Such a young man."

"Did you do his autopsy?"

"Yes. The family didn't want one, but the police insisted, because it was a murder." Doc shuffled through one of his piles and pulled out a file folder. He flipped it open and glanced over the papers there. "Not much to see, though. Somebody shot him in the head, so the cause of death was pretty easy to determine."

"Was he shot from behind?"

"Oh no. Right in the forehead. I'd say right between the eyes, but it was higher up than that." Haynes touched a spot in the middle of his own forehead.

"From close range?"

"No powder burns, so not real close, but not far away either. Around arm's length, I'd say."

"Did he have any other injuries?"

Haynes frowned. "Why? What do you think happened to him?"

"I don't know, but the gun belonged to him, so how did the killer get it away from him? If there was a struggle, he might've had bruises or something."

Haynes shook his head. "Not a mark on him. If the killer took the gun from him, he didn't put up much of a fight. I'd say whoever shot him got the gun some other way."

So Sarah's theory that the killer couldn't be a woman was wrong, because if the killer hadn't fought Norcross for the gun, anyone could be the killer.

I SEE THEIR CARRIAGE," SARAH TOLD MALLOY. THEY'D been waiting for her parents to pick them up on the way to

Hayden Norcross's funeral, and she'd just peered out the front window at the sound of wheels on the cobblestone street.

"I hate funerals," Malloy said, rising from his chair.

"This one should be especially grim since I doubt anyone will be able to say a kind word about the deceased."

"Nobody ever tells the truth at a funeral, though. Maybe someone will manage to make Norcross sound like a saint."

"I hope not. I'm not sure I could bear it," Sarah said, thinking of how much more difficult that would be for Violet Norcross. "It's funny they didn't have a viewing."

"Doc Haynes said he was shot in the face."

"Oh." No other explanation was necessary.

The Deckers' carriage had stopped out front.

"Quick, before the children figure out that we're leaving," Malloy said with a grin. Maeve had taken them upstairs to play.

"I already told them their grandparents will come for a visit later."

"That won't stop them from howling if they see us leaving without them." He opened the front door and shooed her quickly out.

The footman held the carriage door for them, and her parents greeted them warmly. When they were on their way, her mother said, "What should we be looking for during the funeral?"

"*Elizabeth*," her father said in exasperation. "You shouldn't be looking for anything. You should just be sitting still and looking solemn."

"I can look solemn and still look around," she argued.

"Don't worry about the funeral itself," Malloy said to end their disagreement. "It will be at the funeral repast that we might learn something."

"Yes," her mother confirmed. "A lot of gossip is exchanged at those events. That's when you find out what people really thought of the deceased."

"It will be interesting to see how Wendell Tarleton is received, too," Sarah said.

"Who is Wendell Tarleton?" her mother asked.

Her father raised his hand to stop her when Sarah would have explained. "Let's see if she can guess who he is when she meets him."

Sarah and Malloy exchanged a grin, while her mother watched, mystified. "Now I can hardly wait for the repast."

"And let me know if you see someone who is a little drunk," Malloy said. "People tend to be less discreet when they've had too much to drink."

"You don't really think people get drunk at funerals, do you?" her mother asked.

"People get drunk anywhere alcohol is served, my dear," her father said patiently. "They just tend to be less boisterous at a funeral."

Sarah wasn't sure what she expected, but their carriage had to wait in line in front of the church. The crowd was probably more a testament to the senior Mr. Norcross's position rather than respect for Hayden, but at least the church pews wouldn't be empty. Nothing was sadder than a funeral with no mourners.

They found seats near the back so they could see everyone. People filed in but no one went forward to the casket, which was covered with a blanket of flowers but closed tightly. The front pew was empty, which meant the family either hadn't arrived yet or were waiting somewhere for the service to begin.

"Most of these men are Bram Norcross's partners and business associates," her mother reported. "I assume the younger ones work for the firm."

The organ music discouraged further conversation, so they were simply waiting until everyone was seated. The very last person to enter the church was a middle-aged man wearing a checked suit so loud that Sarah had to blink. Since virtually everyone else in the church wore black, this made him doubly noticeable, but he didn't seem to care. He stopped in the middle of the aisle and looked around, removing his straw boater only as an afterthought. Many people were staring now, and Sarah felt sure the organ music was covering a lot of whispered questions about his identity. After a long moment, the man walked purposefully toward a pew with empty space. The couple sitting there instantly slid over to make room and continued to stare at him in alarm, but he made no move to speak to them or even glance at them again.

Sarah turned to Malloy, who was frowning. "Do you know him?"

He nodded. "Never expected to see him here, though."

Before Sarah could ask anything else, a side door opened and the family filed into the church, distracting everyone from the strangely dressed guest. First an older man and a woman wearing a veil over her face came in. Then Violet, also veiled, but Sarah recognized her slender form. She was clutching her brother's arm for support. Behind them came another older couple, and that woman was not veiled. One of the older men had a remarkable head of hair combed back to accentuate his widow's peak, which may have been even more dramatic because his hair was thinning. This must be Mr. Norcross and the veiled woman with him would be his wife. The other couple was probably Violet's parents. They took their seats in the front pew.

The music ceased at last and the minister strode up to the pulpit, his robes swirling about him as he moved. They sang some hymns, and the minister read scripture about eternal life and the glories of heaven. The sermon was short and simple, a reassurance that death was not the end of life but merely a passage to something far better. He did say Hayden's name once or twice and offered sympathy to his parents and his wife, but he made no mention of Hayden's contributions to the world or how much he would be missed. Then they were standing for the final hymn.

Sarah's mother leaned over to her and whispered, "Not even a eulogy."

Had Hayden Norcross not had one friend to say kind words about him?

When the hymn ended, the minister invited them to the cemetery and then to the Norcrosses' home for a reception.

They waited then for six young men to hoist the casket and carry it out of the church. The one in the front on the side nearest them had a magnificent head of hair that immediately caught Sarah's eye.

It must have caught her mother's, too. "Is that Tarleton?" she asked her husband in a whisper.

"Yes, it is."

Her mother turned to her. "He's Bram's son, isn't he?"

Sarah nodded. That couldn't be a coincidence.

As they made their way out of the church, Sarah's mother said, "What a strange service. Hardly a word said about Hayden. We could have been burying anyone at all."

"Perhaps the less said, the better, my dear," Sarah's father said.

Sarah had to agree.

So who was he?" Sarah asked when the four of them were safely in the Deckers' carriage and on their way to the cemetery.

"The man in that awful suit, you mean?" her mother asked a little too eagerly, which made her father frown.

Frank managed not to wince, but he couldn't refuse to answer. "Charlie Quinn."

"I take it from your expression that you've arrested him at some point," Mr. Decker said with a tiny smile.

"As a matter of fact, he's too smart to get himself arrested. His men do all the dirty work."

"But he's a criminal?" Mrs. Decker asked, still too eagerly.

"He runs a lot of illegal businesses and does a lot of illegal things, yes."

"Then what was he doing at Hayden Norcross's funeral?" Sarah asked.

"That is what we will have to find out," Frank said.

. . .

CHARLIE QUINN DID NOT ATTEND THE BRIEF GRAVESIDE service, so they had no opportunity to observe him further. Sarah was disappointed, thinking they would have no other chance to question him, but when they arrived at the Norcrosses' home, they found him ensconced there, along with the other mourners who had chosen to forgo the cemetery.

"Do you see him?" Sarah said as the butler took Frank's hat.

"Yes. I'll take care of him myself."

She smiled sweetly. She had no intention of tackling a gangster. "I need to check on Violet."

He nodded and she hurried off in search of the widow. Sarah found her in the rear parlor, where none of the other guests had yet ventured. Louis had seated her in a comfortable chair and hovered over her helplessly.

"Mrs. Malloy," he said with obvious relief when he saw her approaching. "Thank God you're here."

"Are you not feeling well, Mrs. Norcross?" Sarah said.

Violet didn't answer. She just looked up at Sarah with dull eyes, as if she'd never seen her before. Her face was white.

"Mr. Andriessen, it's such a warm day, perhaps you'd fetch your sister something cool to drink?"

"What? Oh yes, of course." He hurried off obediently.

Violet had pulled back her veil but still wore the heavy hat. "Let's take this off, shall we?" Sarah said, removing the hatpin and lifting the hat carefully so as not to disturb Violet's hair.

"Mrs. Malloy?" Violet asked, as if she'd just noticed Sarah's presence.

"Yes. How are you feeling?"

"I don't know," she said with a puzzled frown. "I don't seem to feel anything at all."

"It's been a trying day, I'm sure. Perhaps—"

"There you are, Violet," a woman's strident voice announced. Sarah looked up to see one of the women who had been sitting in the family pew with Violet, the one who had not been wearing a veil. She had once been handsome, but time had hardened her features and now she simply looked unhappy. "You should be greeting your guests, not hiding in here."

"I'm not hiding, Mother, and they aren't my guests. This is Mrs. Norcross's house."

Her mother blinked in surprise, obviously not used to having Violet answer back. "But it's your husband's funeral. You have responsibilities."

"I don't think Mrs. Norcross is feeling well," Sarah said.

If she had expected that information to arouse Mrs. Andriessen's maternal instincts, she was disappointed. "And who are you, if I may ask?"

Sarah opened her mouth to reply, but Louis Andriessen beat her to it. "That's Mrs. Malloy, Mother. You remember, I told you she called on Violet." He was carrying two glasses of lemonade, and he gave one to Violet and one to Sarah.

"Oh yes, Elizabeth Decker's daughter." She sounded affronted, although Sarah couldn't imagine why.

"So nice to meet you," Sarah said, rising to her feet so she wouldn't be at a disadvantage. "Mrs. Norcross was just telling me she doesn't feel well."

"Of course she doesn't feel well. She's just attended her husband's funeral. None of us feel well, but we have responsibilities." Mrs. Andriessen obviously thought she had made her point and turned to Violet, silently dismissing Sarah.

"Are you going to endanger her health—and her child's—just to fulfill some imaginary social obligations?" Sarah asked with what she hoped was total innocence.

Color bloomed in Mrs. Andriessen's face, and Sarah couldn't tell if she was angry or simply embarrassed by her own thoughtlessness. Whichever it was, she chose to blame Sarah. "And what makes you an expert on my daughter's health?"

"I told you," Louis said with more than a hint of disgust. "She's a nurse."

"And a midwife," Sarah said. "I would strongly recommend that Mrs. Norcross return to her home immediately. This has been an exhausting day, and considering her condition, I'm sure everyone will understand that she needs to rest."

"I'll call for our carriage, Mother." Louis hurried off without waiting to see if she would agree or not.

Plainly, Mrs. Andriessen was not accustomed to being defied. "Really, this is none of your business, Mrs. . . ."

"Malloy," Sarah reminded her. "And it certainly is my business to see that Mrs. Norcross's health is protected. If anything happened to her or her child, I would never forgive myself. I'm sure you must feel the same way."

Now Mrs. Andriessen's face was scarlet, and Sarah had

no problem deciding she was simply angry. "I don't need to be instructed on how to care for my own child."

"I'm happy to hear it," Sarah said.

Mrs. Andriessen glared at Sarah for a long moment. "I suppose you think I should accompany Violet home."

Sarah glanced at Violet, whose expression betrayed her true feelings on the matter. "I'm sure you have obligations here. Perhaps your son will go with her to make sure she arrives safely."

"Yes, Louis will go with me, I'm sure," Violet said. "You stay here, Mother, and take care of the guests." Was that a note of sarcasm? Sarah didn't dare meet Violet's eye to find out.

Mrs. Andriessen made a strangled sound and left without another word.

Sarah finally turned back to Violet to find she had finished all her lemonade. Sarah plucked the glass from her hand and gave her the second one.

"But . . ." she protested.

"Drink it. I can get another. Do you want me to go home with you?"

"Oh no, I just need to rest. I hardly slept at all last night. I kept thinking about how awful this day would be. Thank you for rescuing me."

"I'm happy to help. You are fortunate that your brother looks out for you."

"As much as he can."

"Violet," Louis said, coming back into the room. "Are you all right?"

"I think she will be if you take her home," Sarah said.

"I'll be only too glad to. I was dreading this afternoon, listening to condolences for that monster. Come along, Violet. They're bringing the carriage around."

"Let's put your hat back on. The veil will give you a little privacy, at least," Sarah said. Getting the hat back on took a few moments, and then Violet was ready.

"Make sure she gets something to eat," Sarah said as Louis escorted his sister out.

Sarah sighed when they were gone. Now she needed to get to work.

WHEN SARAH DISAPPEARED DOWN THE HALL, ELIZABETH Decker took her husband's arm and they made their way to the front parlor, where the Norcrosses were greeting guests and accepting condolences. Bram Norcross looked grim, but then he usually did, even in the best of circumstances. He managed to mutter a cool "thank you" when Elizabeth said how sorry she was, and then he turned to Felix, silently dismissing her.

Greta Norcross looked remarkably composed for a woman who had just buried her only surviving child, but then Elizabeth had no idea if this was her usual behavior or not. Greta was somewhat of a recluse, and Elizabeth realized she hardly knew her, even though they had been acquainted for decades. Greta never entertained and seldom attended social functions. One occasionally saw her at the theater or a concert, but those events provided little opportunity for conversation. Bram would excuse her absences by vague references to "her health" in a tone that hinted at female troubles and discouraged further inquiries.

"Greta, I'm so very sorry," Elizabeth said.

"Thank you. Did you know Hayden?" she asked in a way that indicated Greta sincerely doubted that she did.

"No, but Isabel Andriessen is an old friend, and my daughter knows Violet." Not a lie at all, even though Sarah and Violet had just met.

A flicker of some emotion crossed Greta's face but was instantly gone. "Violet is such a lovely girl."

"Yes, she is," Elizabeth said, having no idea if it was true or not. "This must be difficult for all of you."

"'In the midst of life, we are in death,'" she said, quoting a common prayer.

Before Elizabeth could think of a suitable reply to such an odd statement, Felix had turned to Greta and expressed his own feigned sorrow at the loss of Hayden Norcross. This time Greta gave him only a simple "thank you" and turned to the next person in line.

"Oh my," Elizabeth said when they had stepped out into the massive entry hall again and were out of earshot.

"She looks remarkably calm," Felix observed. "Even Bram appeared to be grieving, at least a bit."

"Perhaps she knew what her son was."

"I thought mothers refused to think badly of their children, no matter how awful they were."

"That is often the case, I'm sure, but . . . I don't know. Perhaps Greta is simply a deeply private person who never lets her true feelings show."

"Or perhaps she took some laudanum this morning," Felix said with a wink.

Elizabeth resisted the urge to swat him, since they were approaching a group of her friends who had gathered near the impressive staircase that swept up an additional two stories. As expected, Felix changed direction and drifted off into the dining room, where he was sure to find some friends of his own to chat with. Elizabeth in turn greeted the other ladies and exchanged pleasantries.

"Have you seen the widow?" her friend Mary asked. All three of them were wearing black, since every well-dressed woman owned at least one "mourning" dress to be used when attending funerals and in the event of a sudden family death. Mary looked a bit like a sausage in her finery, however, with her large bosom and equally large bottom separated by a tightly cinched waist. Her pudgy face was lit with avid interest.

"No, I haven't seen her," Elizabeth said. "I'm sure she's overwhelmed by all of this, and in her condition . . ."

"What condition is that?" Gertrude asked with equally avid interest. She was a tall, gaunt woman who, to Elizabeth's constant annoyance, never seemed to gain an ounce no matter how much she ate. Her dark eyes were quite prominent and seemed to offer a challenge even when she wasn't speaking.

"You don't mean she's in a *delicate* condition, do you?" Blanche asked with a frown. True to her name, she was a pale creature with hair gone prematurely white. Her blue eyes were the only color on her face and they were peering at Elizabeth with renewed curiosity. "They were only married a little over a month."

"Really?" Elizabeth said, refusing to be scandalized. "I may have misunderstood or perhaps jumped to a conclusion."

"I wouldn't doubt it, though," Gertrude said wisely. "Hayden had a reputation for seduction."

"How foolish young girls can be," lamented Mary. "I suppose Violet was unlucky enough to get caught."

"I suppose that's how the Andriessens were finally able to bring Hayden up to scratch," Blanche said. "Heaven knows, he's managed to keep his freedom much longer than anyone could have expected."

Elizabeth had to bite back the reply she wanted to make. "I can't believe a girl like Violet would be attracted to a man like Hayden Norcross, though."

"Some women like rogues," Blanche said wisely. "I don't understand it, of course, but Hayden did have his admirers, even after all those stories about him."

"What stories?" Elizabeth asked.

"Yes, what stories?" Gertrude asked.

Mary widened her eyes in feigned astonishment. "You mean you haven't heard them?"

"Let me tell," Blanche said, and continued without waiting for Mary to agree. "They say he killed his little sister."

Gertrude shook her head. "I remember when she died, but the poor child simply fell down the stairs."

"That's what they claimed," Mary hastened to say before Blanche could speak.

"But Hayden hated poor little Susie," Blanche said. "She was about five years younger than he was and such a darling child. Small for her age and delicate. She would have been a beauty."

"Everyone fawned over her," Mary said. "Hayden hated that. Then one day, they found poor little Susie right there." She pointed to a spot at the bottom of the large, sweeping staircase.

All of the women looked down at the spot and then up to where the stairs ended, two stories above.

"They say that Hayden pushed her," Mary said. "That's why she fell all the way down and so hard. Her little neck was broken."

"Good heavens," Gertrude said. "But children get up to all kinds of mischief. Anything is possible, and how can you even think a boy would do that to his sibling?"

"I'm just telling you what I heard," Blanche said.

"I'm surprised a story like that hasn't followed Hayden all of his life, and yet Gertrude and I have never heard it," Elizabeth said.

"It may have just been conjecture, after all. As I said, most people didn't believe it," Blanche said.

"I don't remember you saying that," Elizabeth said with a smile to soften the accusation.

"Well, most people didn't," Blanche insisted.

"But he did grow into a disagreeable young man," Mary added.

If they only knew.

Frank had no trouble at all engaging Charlie Quinn in conversation, since no one else at the repast was going to deign to even speak to him. Frank found him examining the buffet table as if trying to decide if the food was good enough to eat.

"I didn't expect to see another Mick here," Quinn said when Frank approached him. "You look familiar. Where do I know you from?"

"New York City Police," Frank said.

Quinn took in Frank's suit with an appraising glance. "I thought I knew all the bigwigs in the department."

Indeed, a mere detective sergeant couldn't afford the suit Frank was wearing. "I'm retired. Frank Malloy." The two men shook hands. "Were you a friend of the deceased?" Frank asked.

Quinn actually laughed at that, earning glares from the guests standing nearby. He didn't seem to notice. "Not likely. That son of a—" He caught himself. "I guess I shouldn't speak ill of the dead, but with Hayden Norcross, it's hard to think of anything good."

"If you aren't a friend, why come to his funeral?"

"Just to make sure he's dead, I guess. And to remind the old man that I'm still here."

"You know Bram Norcross, too?" Frank managed not to sound too surprised.

"I'm one of his clients. Or at least I was until—"

"Mr. Malloy," Wendell Tarleton said a little too heartily, coming up beside Quinn and sticking out his hand for Frank to shake. Frank obliged. "How kind of you to come."

"My wife is a friend of Mrs. Norcross," Frank said absently. His attention was focused on Quinn's reaction to Tarleton.

Quinn glared at the young man.

Tarleton pretended not to notice. "Mr. Quinn, I must say it was generous of you to pay your respects today."

"Is that what you think I'm doing?"

Tarleton's phony smile never wavered. "I believe that is how most people would interpret your attendance at a funeral."

"And yet you know how I really feel about Hayden Norcross. I wouldn't have spit on him if he was on fire."

"You probably feel the same way about me, I suppose," Tarleton said, his smile slipping away.

"Oh no, Mr. Tarleton. I know you're just another victim in all of this, but I see you're back at Norcross now. Has all been forgiven?" Quinn asked archly.

Tarleton didn't even blink. "Mr. Norcross was kind enough to invite me back, yes."

"To fill his son's spot, I guess." Quinn's dark eyes were knowing, and Tarleton reddened in response.

"Yes, to fill Hayden's spot," Tarleton said tightly.

Frank decided to rescue him. "Mr. Tarleton is trying to interest me in investing with his firm."

"Is he?" Quinn said with interest. "Are you going to?"

"I haven't decided yet. I'm new to all of this, and it seems a bit too much like gambling to me."

"I was new to it, too, when Hayden convinced me it was a sure thing. I don't get taken in very easily, but Hayden was a good talker."

"I'm sorry you had such a bad experience, Mr. Quinn," Tarleton said. "If you give us another chance, however, I'm sure—"

"Another chance?" Quinn echoed in amazement. "Do I look like a sucker to you? Well, maybe I did to Hayden, and he proved I was, but I don't fall for the same trick twice."

"But you must understand that Hayden purposely scuttled that deal to ruin me," Tarleton said, lowering his voice so as not to be overheard, although Frank noticed the other mourners were giving them a wide berth. "You just happened to be one of the unlucky investors." No one who saw Tarleton's face could doubt he was telling the truth.

"If you believe that, you're a bigger fool than I took you for, Tarleton," Quinn said. "He picked the investors pretty carefully, too. He didn't dare cheat any of his father's loyal clients. Oh no, all of us were nobodies, people who didn't matter to him or the old man. He thought we couldn't possibly hurt him if we tried to raise a stink about what happened because we aren't in his social class."

Plainly, this had not occurred to Tarleton. "But . . . I'm sure you're wrong. It was just a coincidence that—"

"No, it wasn't a coincidence," Quinn insisted. "He cheated us because he thought we couldn't hurt him in return, but he was very wrong about that."

"What do you mean?" Tarleton asked, clearly shaken.

Quinn laughed mirthlessly, earning more glares from the other mourners. "He's dead, isn't he?"

SARAH STROLLED DOWN THE ENTRANCE HALL, GLANCING into each room as she passed to see if she could locate someone she could speak to. Her mother was engaged in conversation with several of her friends and didn't even notice when Sarah passed, so Sarah left her to it. Hopefully, she was hearing some useful gossip. At last she reached the front parlor. She and Malloy had skipped the receiving line, so she had not expressed her condolences to the Norcrosses yet. The line was gone now, all the guests having arrived and dispersed to other rooms. Several groups of people were chatting in the parlor, but Mrs. Norcross was sitting all alone in the far corner.

She looked up with what might have been resignation and certainly wasn't a welcome as Sarah approached. She was still a lovely woman with hardly any gray in her light brown hair. Her face might have been carved of marble, so still and white was it. Pain had etched its lines there, and Sarah recalled that she had lost another child years ago.

She almost felt guilty about intruding on Mrs. Norcross's solitude, but she wanted to explain Violet's absence, at least.

"Mrs. Norcross, I'm Sarah Malloy, Felix and Elizabeth Decker's daughter."

Mrs. Norcross's expression instantly softened. "Your mother said you are a friend of Violet's."

"I like to think so," Sarah said.

"Do you know where she is? I haven't seen her since we got back from the cemetery. Bram thought she should be with us to greet the mourners, but I said she needed to rest."

"She did need that. She was exhausted, and her mother insisted that Louis take her home." A little white lie, but Mrs. Andriessen was hardly going to deny being concerned about her daughter's health.

"That's a relief. I wouldn't want anything to happen to her or the child."

Sarah nodded. "May I sit with you for a while or do you prefer to be alone?"

"Usually, I prefer to be alone, but please join me."

Sarah concentrated on not looking victorious in her determination to question Mrs. Norcross and took the empty chair beside her. "I'm very sorry about Hayden."

"Did you know him?" she asked. It was almost a challenge.

"Not well," she said, which was true. "I think we attended some events together when I came out, but I'm afraid I was rather rebellious, and I stopped attending those parties very early in life."

"Oh yes, I remember now. You took up a trade, didn't you?"

"I'm a midwife."

Her gaze brightened. "You're the one who helped Violet yesterday."

"Yes, I am."

"Thank you. I didn't know what we were going to do with her. She wouldn't eat or even leave her bed, and she even refused to admit she was with child."

"I'm glad I was able to help. She's still very fragile, though."

"Of course. Her mother isn't much help either, but I will make sure she's looked after. It's the least I can do."

What an odd thing to say, but perhaps Mrs. Norcross felt responsible for Hayden having been such a terrible person. "I'm sure she will appreciate it."

"Do you have children, Mrs. Malloy?"

"Yes, a boy and a girl." How good it felt to say that.

But a shadow flitted across Mrs. Norcross's face. "I had a boy and a girl, too."

Sarah could not imagine how painful it must be for her

to have lost both her children, even if Hayden had not been worthy of his mother's love. "I haven't lost a child, thank heaven, but I lost my sister, so I can understand a little of what you must be feeling."

"Can you?" Mrs. Norcross smiled grimly. "I certainly hope not."

V

FRANK WAS MORE THAN HAPPY TO LEAVE WHEN SARAH found him a little while later. Her parents had already summoned their carriage, and the four of them had an interesting ride back to the Malloy house. Frank, Sarah, and her mother shared the things they had learned. None of it showed Hayden Norcross in a very good light, but it did give them at least one new suspect in his murder: Charlie Quinn.

"And did you hear anything of interest, Felix?" Mrs. Decker asked him.

"I did indeed, and I may even have some information that will be helpful to Frank in his investigation."

The three other occupants of the carriage immediately gave him their full attention.

"Do tell, Felix," Mrs. Decker said.

"Let me first say that I'm impressed with the work the three of you have done, although I think we can safely assume that Greta Norcross did not sneak out to her son's office and shoot him in the face with his own gun."

"But if Hayden really did kill his younger sister . . ." Mrs. Decker tried.

"Even if he did—and we only have a vicious rumor to rely on for that—it's been nearly twenty-five years since it happened. That is a very long time to wait for revenge."

"Father is right," Sarah said. "Even if his mother knew what a cruel person Hayden was and if we could convince ourselves that a mother would kill her own son for any reason at all, why would she suddenly choose to kill him now, after all these years?"

"Thank you, Sarah," he said. "And I must admit that Charles Quinn makes an excellent candidate for the role of killer for many reasons, and he may well be guilty, but I learned some information about the actual facts of Hayden's death that are very interesting."

"Then stop teasing and tell us," Mrs. Decker said in exasperation.

Mr. Decker allowed himself a small smile. "I found Paul Undermeyer nursing what was obviously not his first glass of whiskey."

"Isn't he one of Bram Norcross's partners?" Mrs. Decker asked.

"Indeed he is. I told him I couldn't understand how someone got into their offices after hours, and he was only too happy to confirm my suspicions that all of the remaining partners were just as baffled. They have a night watchman, you see, who makes regular rounds, checking all the offices and making sure the doors and windows are secure."

"Which is what night watchmen usually do, I assume," Sarah said.

"Exactly," her father confirmed. "But, you see, it has long been a concern because Hayden frequently goes to his office late in the evening, and he doesn't use the front door."

"How does he get in, then?" Frank asked, thinking Mr. Decker may have discovered something interesting.

"Remember Tarleton told us there's a back door? It's in the alley. All the partners have their own keys, in case they need something from their offices after hours or a client is visiting from out of town and can only meet them in the evening or whatever."

"But we know Hayden didn't meet clients," Sarah said. "Or at least, no one believed he was working that night."

"He did meet people in his office, however," Mr. Decker said. "He had some rather unsavory friends, and they would call on him when no one else was around."

"What kind of unsavory friends?" Frank asked. "You mean people like Charlie Quinn?"

"Mr. Quinn is apparently considered respectable compared to the individuals who called on Hayden in the evening."

"Oh my," Mrs. Decker said, more thrilled than appalled. "But surely he wasn't doing business with people like that."

"Not investment business," Mr. Decker said. "Hayden had some rather curious tastes and interests. The people who called on him supplied him with . . . with what he needed."

"Is this something you will explain to me later, Felix?" his wife asked.

"Absolutely not, although I think Frank has some idea of what I mean."

"I do, although I don't need to know the particulars. Did they find anything in Hayden's office to indicate who he might have been meeting that night?"

"That is another issue. You see, Paul told me that they didn't find Hayden's body until the next morning."

"You mean the night watchman didn't hear the shot?" Frank asked in amazement.

"He swears he didn't. The building is rather solidly built, and he might have been far enough away at the time that he didn't notice it. At any rate, whoever found the body summoned Bram Norcross immediately, and Bram spent a goodly amount of time going through the entire office, removing things, before summoning the police."

"So any real evidence is gone," Sarah said with a frown.

"Unless Bram cares to share it," Mr. Decker said.

"Maybe he gave it to the police," Frank said.

"Oh please," Mrs. Decker said. "Even I don't believe that. Bram isn't going to tell the police that his son was an opium addict or whatever it is that Felix thinks I'm too delicate to know about."

Mr. Decker frowned, but his wife ignored him, and Sarah bit back a smile.

Meanwhile, Frank was thinking. "I don't suppose Mr. Norcross would talk to me about what he found."

"We could try," Mr. Decker said.

"I wouldn't want you to ruin your friendship with Norcross over this," Frank protested.

"I appreciate that, but he definitely isn't going to speak to you unless I intercede. Even then, there's no guarantee."

"Don't you think he wants his son's killer found?" Sarah asked.

Her father considered his reply for a long moment. "I really don't know."

"The fact that he cleaned up Hayden's office indicates that he might not be too interested," Mrs. Decker said.

"Yes," Frank mused. "I was thinking he'd be happy to learn it was a stranger, but maybe not."

"Not if identifying that stranger caused a brand-new scandal," Mr. Decker said.

"Sometimes not knowing can be a blessing," Mrs. Decker said.

"Only if Norcross is satisfied with not knowing," Frank said. "But he might be willing to cast blame on an innocent party to protect his family from scandal, and that is what my client is concerned about."

"But surely Bram wouldn't falsely accuse an innocent person," Mrs. Decker said.

"Perhaps not formally," Sarah said, "but even if the police never charge anyone, the family could start a rumor that distracted people from the truth."

"And hurt someone irreparably," Mr. Decker concluded. "Now I understand your interest in the case."

"And why it's so important to find the actual killer," his wife said. "But what if finding the true killer makes things even worse?"

"That is a real concern," Frank said, "but we won't know how much of a concern it is until we find the killer."

CATHERINE AND BRIAN WERE OVERJOYED TO SEE THEIR grandparents. Sarah was pleased to notice Brian eagerly greeting her father, whose natural reserve usually kept even adults at arm's length. Brian was signing to him eagerly, even though he knew her father wouldn't know what he was saying, but to her surprise, her father signed back.

It was a simple message, just that he was glad to see Brian, but Brian's shock was wonderous to behold. He started signing furiously, making her father laugh. He made the sign for slow, and Brian giggled in reply, clapping his hands with pleasure before continuing to sign very slowly.

"I think he wants me to see something," her father said, never taking his eyes off Brian's fingers.

"He wants you to see his motorcar, Grandfather," Catherine said, signing along for Brian's benefit. "Papa got him a toy that looks just like his real one."

Brian started nodding violently and grabbed his grandfather's hand.

"I suppose I have no choice," Sarah's father said with a grin, allowing Brian to pull him toward the steps.

"Grandmother, you have to come, too," Catherine decreed. "I need to show you how I rearranged my dollhouse."

"Are you crying?" Malloy asked Sarah as the children escorted her parents upstairs to the nursery.

"Just a little," Sarah admitted, dashing a tear away. "Mother told me he was trying to learn to sign, but . . ."

"It is amazing. He never ceases to surprise me."

"He told her that there was no use in having a grandson if he couldn't talk to him," Sarah said.

Malloy gaped at her. "He called Brian his grandson?"

Sarah shrugged, smiling in spite of the tears still gathering in her eyes. "Brian is my son now, so he's my father's grandson, too."

"Legally yes, but . . ."

"More than legally, it would seem. I think this means we are officially a family now."

"Of course you're a family," Mother Malloy said from where she had been lurking. "Did you think Sarah's parents wouldn't be excited over grandchildren?"

They hadn't known what to expect, but Sarah didn't bother to explain that to Mother Malloy, who knew perfectly well how unlikely it had been that Sarah's family would ever accept an Irish Catholic ex-policeman as a son-in-law. Equally unlikely was the possibility that Mother Malloy would accept Sarah as her daughter-in-law. Yet here they all were on a Saturday afternoon, prepared to enjoy the rest of the day together. It was something like a miracle.

"Should we go up and see how they're doing?" Malloy asked.

"Let them have their time with the children," Mother Malloy said. "They'll come down when they get worn out."

As if to prove her right, Maeve came down the stairs, a look of wonder on her pretty face. "Did you know Mr. Decker could sign?"

"We do now," Sarah said. "Did you leave them alone and unprotected from the children?"

"They told me to go downstairs. They said you had some things to tell me about the case."

"Indeed we do," Sarah said. "Come into the parlor and we'll explain everything."

Sarah pretended not to notice that Mother Malloy followed them, prepared to listen to every word.

SUNDAY PASSED UNEVENTFULLY, BUT FRANK HAD SENT Jack Robinson a message arranging to meet him at Frank's office on Monday morning. Frank had just finished filling Gino in on everything they had learned when Jack arrived.

"Where is your lovely secretary?" Jack asked when they had greeted him.

"She's doing her other job, which is looking after my children," Frank said. "Summer just started, but I think she's already wishing them back at school. I may have to hire a new nanny soon so she can devote herself full-time to the business. How is Jocelyn doing?"

"She's complaining a lot, but still nothing is happening. You know she'll send for your wife the moment something does."

"I'm sure she will. In the meantime, come into my office and I'll fill you in on what we've learned so far."

"I don't suppose you're going to tell me who killed Hayden Norcross," Jack said, following Frank and taking the client chair Frank indicated.

"Unfortunately, we don't know that yet, but we do have

a lot more information than we did before. I'm going to need your help to follow up on some of it, though." Frank moved to sit behind his desk, and Gino took the other client chair, a tablet in his lap for taking notes.

Frank briefly explained what they had learned.

"Charlie Quinn, eh?" Jack mused. "He's not someone you'd mess with if you had any sense."

"How do you suppose he got involved with Norcross?" Frank asked.

Jack gave this some thought. "He might be trying to become legitimate, too. Or maybe he just thought he'd make some easy money with Hayden."

"How would he have met Norcross in the first place?" Gino asked.

Jack smiled at this. "Hayden had many bad habits. Gambling, women, drinking, and opium dens. Any one of them could have him crossing paths with Charlie."

Opium dens. So the rumor was true. "But you didn't know Hayden before . . . before you sought him out, did you?" Frank asked.

"I'd heard of him, of course. A man with money who likes to go slumming gets to be well known in certain circles, but my places were too tame for his tastes, apparently. And of course, I never tolerated drugs."

"Hayden did use opium, then?"

"So I'm told, although it took some digging to find that out when I was doing my research on him."

Frank nodded. "What do you know about the deal where Quinn lost his money and Tarleton got fired?"

"Not much. I just know that it happened and people blamed Tarleton for not investigating the project better, although rumor had it that Hayden had also been involved and his father covered it up."

"Do you know who the other investors were? Because Quinn said they had been carefully chosen to be people like him rather than the regular clients Norcross would have picked."

"People like him?" Jack asked with a frown.

"People who aren't high society. As Quinn himself said, people whose opinion wouldn't matter. He thought Hayden had chosen them specifically, because if they got cheated and told their friends, no one who normally did business with Norcross would care very much."

"But the fact that the deal went bad would tarnish Tarleton enough to get him fired," Jack concluded. "Sounds like Hayden wasn't quite as big a fool as I thought. But why did he want to get Tarleton fired?"

Frank and Gino exchanged a glance. "Rumor has it that Tarleton is old man Norcross's bastard son."

"Could it be true?" Jack asked.

"The physical resemblance is remarkable," Frank said.

"I see, and if true, it could explain Hayden's resentment, although usually it is the bastard child who resents the legitimate heir."

"In fairy tales, but in this case, it seems the bastard was the favored child."

"You mean the old man liked him better?"

"Yes, in business at least, probably because he did a better job than Hayden, who apparently didn't do much at all. I haven't met anyone who had a good word to say about Hayden."

"But Hayden would know enough about the business to implicate his father's other son in a deal gone wrong. Do you think the old man realized what happened?"

"He hired Tarleton back as soon as Hayden was dead," Frank said.

"He didn't even wait for the funeral," Gino added.

"How interesting."

"We thought so," Frank said.

"All right, you said you needed my help, but I haven't heard anything I can help with yet."

"I was hoping you'd help me make an appointment to see Charlie Quinn."

Jack grinned at this. "From what you told me, I thought you and he were good friends now."

"Hardly," Frank said, returning the grin. "I also need to ask him some questions that he probably won't like, so I was hoping you'd go along as protection."

"If you're going to ask him if he killed Hayden Norcross, I'm afraid I won't be much protection. Nobody would."

"I know better than to do that, but I'm hoping he'll at least have an idea who might have been visiting Hayden the night he was murdered and what Hayden's father was trying to hide."

"I'll see what I can do."

"Remember, you're the one who hired me and it's your neck I'm trying to save."

"I do remember that, but even still, I can't make any promises where Charlie Quinn is concerned."

. . .

Hᴀʏᴅᴇɴ Nᴏʀᴄʀᴏss ɪs ᴅᴇᴀᴅ," Jᴏᴄᴇʟʏɴ Rᴏʙɪɴsᴏɴ ɪɴ-formed Sarah the moment the maid who had escorted Sarah into the Robinsons' parlor had closed the door behind her.

"I know, dear," Sarah said, taking a seat beside her on the sofa.

"Do you know who he is?" Jocelyn asked almost desperately. "Do you know he's the one who—"

"Yes, I know. We know. Jack told Malloy."

"Why would he do that?" Jocelyn looked far more upset than Sarah liked to see a woman in her last month of pregnancy. When Jocelyn had telephoned, she'd made sure that Sarah knew she was not in labor but that she needed to see her immediately, and now Sarah knew why.

"Hasn't Jack mentioned any of this to you?" Sarah asked, thinking someone should slap some sense into him.

"Of course not. He's determined not to upset me, so I didn't bother to mention it to him either and telephoned you instead."

"How did you find out Norcross was dead, then?"

"I read the obituaries. You never know when a person of your acquaintance might die, and I don't really have much else to do at the moment."

Of course she didn't. "I haven't seen his obituary. Did they mention that he was murdered?"

"Murdered? Good heavens, no. I think it said he died suddenly, which could mean anything from a fall in the bathtub to suicide. I was hoping it was suicide."

"Someone shot him, in his office, with his own gun."

Jocelyn's hand, which had been absently rubbing her rounded stomach, stopped dead. "Shot? Oh no. Is that why Jack told Mr. Malloy about it? Did he shoot Hayden Norcross?"

"No," Sarah hastily assured her. "Of course he didn't. Jack would never do anything that foolish."

"Are you sure? Oh, Sarah, I never should have told Jack who the man was. I didn't think about him wanting revenge. He was so calm and reasonable when he asked me to tell him the man's name. He said he just needed to know in case they ever met. He didn't want to be caught off guard."

"That does seem reasonable," Sarah agreed.

"But I should have known. Jack isn't a gentleman, not deep down. He's become very good at pretending to be one, but part of him is still that wild boy who grew up on the streets, fighting for every scrap of bread. That boy wouldn't be a bit reasonable."

"That boy wouldn't shoot a man down in cold blood either," Sarah assured her.

"Then why did he tell Mr. Malloy about it?"

"Because he is innocent, but he was afraid someone might find out he had a good reason to want Hayden dead and accuse him of the crime."

"But if he's innocent, why would someone accuse him of it?"

"Innocent people get accused of things all the time, and the story would make an excellent scandal that would sell thousands of newspapers. Jack asked Malloy to find the real killer to spare you that."

"To spare *me*? Why would . . . ?"

Sarah sighed, hating everything about this. "The story would be about Hayden and you and a baby."

"Oh no. Jack did it to protect me, to protect my reputation," she said with renewed horror at the realization.

"He must love you very much."

"Oh, Sarah, do you really think so?"

"He has shown every sign of it. I think I can safely say that your well-being was his primary concern in all of this."

"He's never said he loves me."

"I imagine a confession like that would be very difficult for a man like Jack. Have you told him you love him?"

"I . . . I've been afraid to."

"Ah, then you do love him."

"How could I not? He . . . he's wonderful."

"So wonderful that you were afraid he'd committed murder for you," Sarah said with a smile.

Jocelyn sighed. "That does sound ridiculous, doesn't it? But rather brave and heroic, too."

"He actually loves you too much to commit murder, which is probably a solution he would have seriously considered in his checkered past."

"This is a very unusual conversation, Sarah. I don't think I ever expected to be discussing my husband's propensity to commit murder with anyone."

"I'm sure you didn't, but I hope I've put your mind at ease."

"A bit, but there is still the problem of who did murder Hayden Norcross."

"Do you have any idea who might have wanted to? Anyone who might have wanted to avenge your honor, perhaps?"

Jocelyn smiled sadly. "I wish I could say my father was a suspect, but he never believed that Hayden forced me. He thought I'd done something to encourage him."

"I'm sorry for that."

"My mother was just as bad—worse, in fact. She couldn't understand how I'd let such a thing happen. I was almost glad when they sent me to the maternity hospital. At least I didn't have to listen to them berating me anymore."

"Hayden got married a little over a month ago. Did you know?"

"I'd seen the announcement in the newspapers."

"Do you know Violet Andriessen?"

"A little. She's a few years younger than I, so she hasn't been out very long."

"Norcross raped her, too."

"Oh no!"

"Yes, and she's also expecting."

"But Hayden married her," Jocelyn said with a frown.

"Her family is apparently very influential and her father threatened to ruin the Norcross family business if he didn't."

"Thank heaven my father didn't think of that," Jocelyn said with feeling.

"And if you ever imagine for a moment that you should have married Norcross yourself, he was very cruel to Violet and violent as well."

"You mean he hit her?" she asked, horrified.

"I'd say from the bruises that he beat her repeatedly. She was terrified of him."

Jocelyn laid a hand over her heart. "Thank heaven I was

saved from that, at least. Now I have to be doubly grateful to Jack."

"I don't think he wants your gratitude, Jocelyn, but he would definitely like to know that you have come to love him."

"Then I shall have to screw up my courage to tell him. Wait, you asked me if I knew anyone who might want to avenge my honor. Is there someone who might have wanted to end Violet's suffering?"

"I don't think her parents would have. She told me she had begged them to let her leave Hayden and return home, but they absolutely refused."

"Oh yes, divorce is such a scandal," Jocelyn said sarcastically. "So much worse than being beaten by your husband."

"Yes, well, that was their concern. She does have a brother who cares for her, but he is such a nice young man, I hate to think of him as a killer."

"I remember Louis. I imagine he would want to protect his little sister, but if he did shoot Hayden Norcross, I'd also hate to see him punished for it."

"And that," Sarah said resignedly, "is the problem. The person who shot Hayden Norcross saved the world a lot of suffering and I don't think *anyone* is going to want to see him punished."

FRANK WAS BEGINNING TO WONDER WHY HE HAD AL-lowed Gino to convince him they should use the motorcar to pick up Mr. Decker and travel down to Wall Street to see

Mr. Norcross. He'd already had to grab hold of his seat three times to keep from being ejected from the vehicle when Gino careened around corners going at least ten miles per hour, and they hadn't even reached the Decker house yet.

Surely Frank wasn't the only man in the country who realized how dangerous motorcars were. He only hoped the craze for them died quickly, before they wiped out the human race.

Mr. Decker's expression was a little hard to read when he stepped out of the house and saw them parked in front. Was it terror or excitement? Surely not excitement.

Frank got out of his seat beside Gino and opened the door to the tonneau for Mr. Decker, who climbed up carefully into the rear seat.

"I'll sit back here with you," Frank said, thinking the backseat might be safer in the event that Gino ran into something.

"This is rather a nice view from up here," Mr. Decker said. The tonneau was about a foot higher than the front seat. "And it's nice to be able to see everything. Riding in a carriage is a bit confining."

"Hold on to your hat. It can get a little windy," Frank advised as Gino shifted the gears and slammed down on the gas to send them lurching forward.

Fortunately, they didn't need to make many turns on their way downtown, and the traffic on Broadway wasn't too bad. Gino seemed to be driving a little more carefully now that Mr. Decker was with them, so Frank relaxed a little.

"What exactly do you want to learn from Bram Norcross?" Mr. Decker asked.

"As much as he'll tell me about Hayden's secret vices and whether anyone from that world might have wanted to kill him or at least have been driven to it."

"Perhaps he doesn't know much about that part of Hayden's life. I certainly wouldn't want to, if I were Hayden's father."

"Then he won't have much to tell me, but I'm hoping he'll be open to at least helping identify his son's killer."

"And I suppose you want to know what he took from Hayden's office before he called the police."

"I don't imagine he'll tell me, but it's worth asking. And feel free to ask him anything you think of. You know more about his business than I do."

"I'm afraid I'm not used to interrogating people," Mr. Decker said with a sheepish grin.

"You just have to be interested. Ask questions about things you want to know."

"You make it sound easy."

"Not easy but not hard either. If you can learn American Sign Language, you can do this," Frank added with a smile.

To his surprise, Mr. Decker's face turned pink. "I hope you approve of that."

"Of course. Why wouldn't I? And Brian is thrilled. He keeps asking when Grandfather is coming for another visit."

"Does he?" Mr. Decker seemed inordinately pleased by that bit of news. "Well, we can't disappoint the boy, can we?"

Gino pulled up in front of the Wall Street office of Norcross and Son, a sign that Frank realized didn't even need to be changed if Bram Norcross decided to publicly recognize his illegitimate son. The uniformed doorman hurried out to open the motor's door for them and to help Mr. Decker down. Gino told them he would find a place to park and wait for them in a nearby café.

This time when the young man at the front desk greeted them, Mr. Decker was able to say that they had an appointment, even though it had been made only that morning when Mr. Decker had called to schedule it.

Mr. Norcross's assistant came down to escort them to the senior partner's office, and Bram Norcross stood up and came around his desk to shake their hands. Mr. Decker introduced Frank, who hadn't actually met Mr. Norcross at the funeral.

When they were seated in the comfortable client chairs and Norcross had returned to his own seat behind his desk, he said, "I understand you met with Wendell Tarleton last week."

"Yes, we did," Mr. Decker said. "What an impressive young man. He seems quite knowledgeable for one so young."

"Like father, like son, do you mean, Felix?" Norcross asked with a twisted smile.

"I'm not sure I know his father, Bram," Mr. Decker replied ingenuously.

"Of course you do. Everyone who meets him sees the resemblance. Not that I ever had any intention of denying him, but such things can be embarrassing for the family, can't they?"

"Somehow I can't imagine Hayden being embarrassed by anything," Mr. Decker said with a smile to soften the words.

Norcross grew solemn. "Yes, well, perhaps *embarrassment* was the wrong word."

"Brothers do have a tendency toward rivalry, I'm told," Mr. Decker said. "That is probably doubly true in this case."

"Because Wendell was illegitimate, you mean," Norcross said bitterly. "He is no less my son for all of that."

"No, he isn't," Mr. Decker agreed. "And I must say, it's unusual for a man in your position to be so generous to an illegitimate child."

"When his mother must have been a tart, you mean," Norcross said, angry now.

"I meant no such thing," Mr. Decker hastily assured him.

"But she must have been, mustn't she, to take up with a married man?" Norcross challenged.

"People can be very judgmental," Mr. Decker said with the utmost diplomacy. Frank could only marvel. "You must have . . . cared for her," he added a bit lamely.

"I did and I still do. I would have married her if I could, but of course Greta would never give me a divorce. But enough of my family skeletons," Norcross added, obviously realizing he had said too much. "What brings you here today?"

Mr. Decker turned to Frank, silently giving him permission to take over the conversation.

"Mr. Norcross," he began, "I'm a private investigator, and I have been hired to find your son's killer."

Color flooded Norcross's face, and his hands clenched in fury. "How dare you?"

"You seem angry, Bram," Mr. Decker said in his cultured, perfectly reasonable voice with just the right amount of amazement. "Why would you be angry that someone wants to find Hayden's killer?"

Plainly, Norcross had no answer for that. His eyes darted

between Frank and Mr. Decker several times before he finally managed to say, "Of course I want to find Hayden's killer, but that is a matter for the police."

"Have the police made any progress?" Mr. Decker asked, still perfectly reasonable and slightly amazed.

"They don't keep me informed," Norcross admitted, then turned to Frank with narrowed eyes. "You said you'd been hired. Who hired you?"

"That is confidential, I'm afraid."

"Well, I didn't hire you, and I can't imagine the Andriessens even care, so who was it? Not Violet. She wouldn't even know what a private investigator is."

"You may be underestimating your daughter-in-law," Frank said, "but in any case, my client is very interested in seeing justice done. I assumed you would be, too, so I asked Mr. Decker to introduce us so I could ask you some questions."

"Of course I want to see justice done. Why wouldn't I?" Norcross asked, still furious.

"I can't think of any reason," Frank lied.

"And if you don't want to answer Frank's questions, you don't have to," Mr. Decker said calmly. "But I'm sure your answers will help him find Hayden's killer. That's what we all want, isn't it?"

Norcross needed to think about that for a moment, and he leaned back in his chair and purposely unclenched his fists. "Yes, of course. What is it you want to know?"

VI

Frst of all," Frank began, "can you tell me about the night Hayden was killed?"

"I don't know anything about that. I wasn't even here," Norcross insisted.

"But you must know some basic things. Did Hayden often work late?"

"He . . ." Norcross took a deep breath, either to calm himself or gather himself. Frank couldn't be sure. "He was often in the office at odd hours."

"Did he see clients?"

Now the color was rising in Norcross's scrawny neck, but he kept his voice even. "He would receive *visitors*, yes."

"Did the night watchman admit them?"

"I understand that Hayden would admit them himself

through the back door." Now Norcross seemed to be grinding his teeth.

"Do you know who these *visitors* were?" Frank put special emphasis on *visitors* because obviously they weren't clients and Norcross knew it.

Before Norcross could refuse, Mr. Decker said, "One of them may have killed Hayden, you know. It would be a minor scandal, but one that would quickly die."

Frank could actually see the worry lines on Norcross's forehead relax. It would indeed be a scandal if some lowlife had murdered Hayden, but not as much of a scandal if someone like Wendell Tarleton had done it. Plainly, Norcross realized this. He cleared his throat. "Hayden had several vices that were . . . unpleasant."

"I'm sure this is very painful for you, Mr. Norcross," Frank said, trying for a little of Mr. Decker's diplomacy, "but the more you can tell me, the more likely it is that I'll be able to find the culprit. Do you have any idea who the people were who came to see Hayden?"

"None at all, I'm afraid, but it might not be too difficult to find them. I'm sure they've bragged to someone about how they freely come and go here," he said.

"Then if you wouldn't mind telling me what Hayden's vices were, I can attempt to identify the people involved."

"He . . ." Norcross swallowed. "Opium."

Frank pretended to be surprised. He didn't check to see Mr. Decker's reaction. "Did he frequent opium dens?"

"No," Norcross said quite firmly. "He'd been seen going into one a year or so ago, and word got back to me. I warned him I would disown him if he was ever caught in one again."

"But he was still smoking it?"

"He said he couldn't quit, no matter how hard he tried, and to tell you the truth, he was impossible to deal with when he couldn't get it. Fortunately, he could afford to have it delivered to him here at night."

"Do you know anything about the people delivering it?"

"I never saw them, of course," Norcross said, his lip curling in distaste. "But I was told it was a female."

"A woman?" Frank said in genuine surprise this time.

Norcross's gaze was icy cold. "I told you, Hayden had unpleasant vices. Another of them was whores."

"Was it always the same woman?" Frank asked.

"How should I know? I made a point of pretending none of this was happening. The less I knew, the less I had to ignore."

"Until someone found Hayden dead," Frank said. "Then you had to clean up his mess."

Once again Mr. Decker jumped in before Norcross could rage back at Frank's challenge. "It must have been awful for you to see what he had been doing."

A spasm of pain flickered over Norcross's face. "He was naked. Sprawled on his sofa with that . . . *paraphernalia* spread out on a table beside him. And all that blood . . . I had to dress him and . . ." His voice broke and he ran a hand down his face.

"I'm so sorry, Bram," Mr. Decker said quite sincerely.

Even Frank felt pity for him. No one should have to see their child like that, no matter who that child was.

After a few moments, Norcross cleared his throat again and continued. "Wendell helped me. I couldn't face it alone, so I sent for him. He was the only one I could trust, you see. We got his clothes back on him and sat him up. Then we gathered up all those *things* and carried them away. I don't know what Wendell did with them. He told me not to worry about it. He'd take care of everything."

"And you didn't mention any of this to the police," Frank confirmed.

"Of course not," Norcross snapped. "Why bother to remove everything otherwise?"

So true. "Did anyone see who came to him that night?"

"I have no idea. I didn't question anyone, and if the police did, I haven't heard anything about it. They were Chinese, though."

"Who was?" Frank asked.

"The women who brought the opium. Or woman. I don't know if there was more than one."

A Chinese woman? How strange. And now that Frank knew how Hayden had really died, the case had just become much more interesting.

WHEN THEY'D GOTTEN ALL THE INFORMATION BRAM Norcross would or could give them, they took their leave. They found Gino in a café nearby and ordered some ice cream to reward themselves for enduring such a distasteful interview. While they ate, Frank told Gino what they'd learned.

Gino gave a low whistle. "That gives us a whole new direction to look for Hayden's killer, doesn't it?"

"I should say so," Mr. Decker said with what might have

been enthusiasm, although he was too well-bred to actually act excited over a murder investigation.

"Except why would a prostitute kill him?" Frank asked. "Especially one who was also selling him drugs? Seems like it would be bad business to murder such a good customer."

"But Hayden wasn't very nice to women," Gino reminded him. "Maybe he managed to frighten her or offend her in some way."

"I can imagine him making a woman angry enough to shoot him, but how would she get his gun?" Frank challenged.

"If she's been coming to see him regularly, maybe she found it somehow."

"Yes," Mr. Decker said, getting into the spirit, "Hayden might have threatened her with it at some point, perhaps even that night. He probably wouldn't think twice about killing a prostitute, so she would be justified in feeling threatened."

"It shouldn't be too hard to find this woman either," Gino said. "There aren't many Chinese women in the city."

The law had long forbidden Chinese females from emigrating to the United States. America had needed the Chinese men for labor on the railroads, but the government's intention had always been that they would return home when the work was done. By forbidding Chinese men from bringing their women with them, the authorities had thought to guarantee they would eventually leave. The plan had not worked, however. The Chinese men had stayed and married American women instead.

"Sarah knows some Chinese families," Frank recalled.

"Maybe they can help us figure out who this woman might be."

"You know what else occurs to me," Mr. Decker said. "The night watchman might know more than he admitted. I wonder if anyone has spoken to him."

GINO IS RIGHT," SARAH SAID LATER THAT AFTERNOON when Malloy had told her about the meeting with Mr. Norcross. "There are only a handful of Chinese women in Chinatown and all of them are married to rich Chinese men. The woman might be half-Chinese, someone who was born here, but even that seems far-fetched. The Chinese are so careful with their children that I can't believe one of them would become a prostitute."

"I thought it sounded strange, too," Malloy admitted. They were upstairs in their private sitting room, where they could speak without being overheard by their own children. "But if she really is Chinese, people in Chinatown would know her, wouldn't they?"

"I'm sure they would. It's a small community, and gossip spreads quickly there. I assume you want me to find out if anyone knows who this woman might be."

"Could you? I know you've delivered babies in Chinatown."

"And we solved some murders there, too," she reminded him.

"So people might still be grateful enough to share their gossip with you."

"Then I'll go there tomorrow to see what I can find out. What are you planning to do?"

"I'm planning to go back down to Wall Street first thing in the morning to see what the night watchman has to say for himself."

Frank found a very sleepy hansom cab driver to take him down to Wall Street just as dawn was breaking. He watched the building carefully, noting when the elaborately dressed doorman arrived and observing that he did not enter through the front door but went down an alley and found what was probably the back door that Mr. Norcross had mentioned. Frank waited in the alley, thinking how much more pleasant alleys were on Wall Street than they were in the Lower East Side, until he saw a middle-aged man in a workman's uniform exit the building.

Frank accosted him, and the man stopped, giving Frank a once-over, making note of his fine suit.

"Clients go in through the front door, mister."

"I'm not a client. I'm investigating Hayden Norcross's murder."

The man actually winced. "I already told you coppers, I don't know nothing about that."

"I have a hard time believing that. I think you know more than you realize."

"I'm telling you I don't know nothing. Now I gotta be going."

"Do you have another engagement?" Frank scoffed, since

he'd be unlikely to have plans this early in the morning after working all night. "If you talk to me, I'll buy you breakfast."

"I've got to go, I tell you. I've got to get to work."

He started to step around Frank, but Frank grabbed his arm. "What do you mean, you've got to get to work. You just worked here all night, didn't you?"

The man glared at him and tried to shake loose, but Frank didn't release him. His years as a cop had taught him how to hold on to a suspect. "I've got another job, and they don't like it if I'm late."

"Then how about if I walk with you to this other job and ask my questions. I'll make it worth your while." Frank pulled out a silver dollar and held it up enticingly. This would probably be a day's wages for the watchman, for at least one of his jobs. The man reached for the dollar but Frank held it away. "Not until you answer my questions."

"All right, you can ask, but don't blame me if I don't know the answers." This time Frank let him shake free of his grip, and Frank fell into step beside him as he hurried out of the alley.

"How can you work a job all day after you've been awake all night?" was Frank's first question.

The man gave him a sidelong glare that also gave him the answer to his question.

"You sleep at the bank, don't you?"

"Nothing ever happens there. Nobody tries to break in. What would be the point? They hardly keep any cash there at all. The money comes in by wire and goes out by wire or some such thing. I don't know how it works, but I do know there's nothing in there worth stealing."

"And that explains why you didn't see or hear anything the night Norcross was killed. You were asleep."

"I learned a long time ago to steer clear of young Norcross when he's there. He brings his women in and does whatever he does with them and then they leave." They had reached the corner and stopped, waiting for a break in the traffic so they could safely dash across the street.

When they had made it to the other side, Frank said, "Except he didn't leave last Tuesday night, did he?"

"No, but I didn't know that, did I? He's got his own keys, and I mind my own business. I never heard no gunshot either. I've got a comfortable little hidey-hole as far from Norcross's office as I can get."

"Did you ever see the people he meets?"

"Like I said, I steer clear."

"You must have seen something over the years. What about the woman?"

He sighed. "You heard about her, huh? I didn't think the old man knew about her."

"So you have seen her."

"A glimpse now and then. Young Mr. Norcross didn't like to be spied on."

"Was it always the same woman?"

They'd reached another corner, and the watchman turned to Frank and shrugged. "The few times I saw her, it seemed like the same one."

"What did she look like? Would you recognize her if you saw her again?"

"No. I never really saw her face. It was dark, and she was hurrying by, ducking her head like she knew I was watching. She was Chinese, though." He judged there was room to make it across the street and he charged out with Frank in his wake.

"How do you know she was Chinese if you didn't see her face?" Frank asked when they reached the other corner.

"Her dress. She was wearing one of them shiny dresses with flowers all over. It's hard to miss that."

"And did this Chinese woman visit Norcross the night he died?"

"I didn't see her, but I reckon she did. They say young Tarleton found him with his layout still on the table."

Frank looked at him in surprise. *Layout* was the word used to describe the collection of instruments needed to prepare and smoke opium. "How did you know he smoked opium?"

"You can smell it, can't you? I never could figure out why he smoked it at his office, though. If you have a layout, you can buy opium at any drugstore and cook it up yourself. He could've done it at home, or if he wanted to be fancy, just go to an opium den like all the other swells."

But Frank knew why Norcross couldn't be seen going to an opium den, and if he lived at home with his parents, they wouldn't have tolerated it there either. Once he'd married, he could have smoked in the privacy of his own home, but he'd been married only a little over a month, so maybe he hadn't thought of that yet. Or maybe he'd come to enjoy the woman who delivered his drug as much as he enjoyed the drug. A man could hardly entertain a prostitute in the same house as his wife, no matter how browbeaten the wife might have been.

"Did you know Mr. Norcross kept a gun in his office?"

"How would I know that? My job was to make sure nobody broke in, not search everybody's office. They could have a whole arsenal in their desks, for all I know."

He was right, of course, although it sounded as if there was no good reason for the employees of Norcross and Son to be concerned about their personal safety, at least during regular business hours.

"Is that all you wanted to know?" the watchman asked impatiently when Frank hadn't asked another question.

"I appreciate your time," Frank said, fishing the dollar back out of his pocket along with one of his business cards. "Let me know if you think of anything else that might be helpful. I'll be even more generous, and I'm especially interested in talking to that woman."

"I can't help you with her." The night watchman snatched the dollar and the card, and Frank let him disappear into the crowd of pedestrians on their way to their various jobs.

Maybe Sarah would have better luck in Chinatown.

MALLOY STOPPED BY THE HOUSE TO TELL SARAH ABOUT his conversation with the night watchman before heading to his office. Then Sarah made sure Maeve knew where she would be in case Jocelyn Robinson needed her, and she headed down to Chinatown.

Chinatown wasn't an actual town, marked off by a wall or a fence or any other boundary. Its streets ran on into other neighborhoods and people could freely walk through it on their way to other places. No one had ever officially defined the limits of Chinatown or even prescribed who would live there, but like every other group of immigrants who had settled in the city, the Chinese had chosen to live close to the others who spoke their language and practiced their customs. The place they had chosen was just south of another, equally ethnic stronghold, Little Italy, but the city was full of neighborhoods inhabited mainly by one group or another: the Germans, the Irish, the Negroes, the Russians, and the Jews all had their own defined communities. The only difference between Chinatown and the other neighborhoods was that the women were not the same ethnicity as the men.

Sarah had delivered babies for several of those women, and she'd kept in touch with one of them. Cora Lee lived in a well-maintained apartment building in a city where most ethnic groups lived in filthy tenements. Cora had come to America from Ireland as a young girl with high hopes, and she had done well for herself, marrying a successful Chinese businessman who provided well for her and allowed her independence.

Cora was thrilled to see Sarah and invited her in for a cool drink and a long chat.

"You're expecting again," Sarah was pleased to note. Cora was a buxom woman and her pregnancy wasn't showing much yet, so Sarah had needed a few minutes to notice.

"Yes. Daniel is three now, so it's about time. I was beginning to give up hope that I'd ever have another." At the sound of his name, Daniel looked up from where he was playing with the top Sarah had brought him. He smiled broadly, and Sarah was in love. He was a beautiful child, with his father's raven black hair and dark eyes and his mother's chubby face.

"I think I once told you that babies come when they want," Sarah said with a smile.

"I thought that only meant when they were born, not when they got started. George is thrilled. He'd been teasing me that he'd take another wife if I didn't give him more sons."

"I hope you reminded him that he's in America now and we only allow one wife per customer."

"He knows that, and he knows what I'd do to him if he even tried to take another wife, but he does like teasing me."

"I'm glad you made such a good marriage," Sarah said, thinking of Violet Norcross. Society must have thought she'd done well for herself and would look down on Cora Lee for marrying a Chinese man. How wrong they would have been about both women.

"I wish . . . Well, it doesn't do any good wishing, does it? But it makes me mad sometimes that people feel sorry for us. The wives, I mean. The Irish girls who married Chinese men. You can't blame the men for wanting a wife and a family, and the government won't even allow any Chinese women into the country, so what are they supposed to do?"

"It's a cruel law, and I guess we both know why it was made."

"Yes, to keep the Chinese from settling here, but it didn't work, did it? And what about us? The Irish girls, I mean. Most of us came here alone because our families were dead in the famine. With no family to look after us, we had to make our own way, but who were we supposed to marry? Everybody knows Irishmen don't make the best husbands.

They can't get work even if they want it. I didn't like the idea of taking in laundry for the rest of my life to support myself, so instead I married a man who *owns* a laundry."

"I have to disagree with you, since my husband is Irish and he's wonderful, but you don't have to explain to me. I know you did well for yourself, Cora. You should be very proud."

Sarah asked after the other members of Cora's family whom Sarah had come to know when she and Malloy had worked on a murder case here three years ago. Then Sarah had explained that she and Malloy were now married. Cora thought that was great news, but she was sorry to learn Sarah was no longer working as a midwife. Sarah told her about the maternity clinic she had opened on the Lower East Side, but of course Cora wouldn't have need of such a place.

When they had finished bringing each other up to date, Cora said, "If you aren't a midwife anymore, why are you in Chinatown?"

"I was hoping you might be able to help us with a new case we're working on."

"I thought Mr. Malloy wasn't a policeman anymore."

"He's working as a private investigator now. He got too bored with nothing to do."

"And is he working on a case in Chinatown?"

"Not exactly, but he's learned that the man who was murdered was an opium user."

"And that man came to the opium dens here," she guessed.

"As a matter of fact, his father had forbidden him from being seen at an opium den because of the possible scandal, but someone was apparently delivering opium to him at his office on Wall Street in the late evening."

"Someone from Chinatown?" Cora asked with a puzzled frown.

"We aren't sure, but a man who saw this person said it was a Chinese woman."

But Cora was already shaking her head. "That's impossible."

"I agree, but please explain to me why you think so, because this man was very sure."

"It's impossible because I know every Chinese woman in New York. There are only three of them and all of them are married to wealthy men and would never dream of being involved with delivering opium to a white man."

"What about the girls who are half-Chinese and were born here?"

Cora shook her head even harder. "No family would allow their daughter out alone at night like that. Those girls are precious to them. This makes no sense. Did he actually see her? She was really Chinese?"

"He didn't see her face, but she was apparently wearing a dress that looked Chinese to him."

"A cheongsam, you mean?"

"I don't know the official name, but he described it as shiny with flowers all over it and he thought it was Chinese."

Now Cora was really confused. "This makes even less sense. We wives don't wear those dresses, and the daughters only wear them for special occasions. Why would a woman be walking around the city in one?"

"I have no idea. Maybe the man was lying, but that's an odd lie to make up, isn't it?"

"It is," Cora mused. "This woman, do you know anything else about her?"

"I . . . Well, she visited the man who was killed quite often and when he was found—when his body was found—he was naked," Sarah admitted reluctantly.

But to Sarah's relief, Cora was not offended. In fact, she brightened noticeably. "She was a whore."

"We don't know that for sure, but—"

"But what other explanation could there be? And I think I've heard . . . Well, first let me say that the respectable wives of Chinese businessmen would never go to an opium den."

"Of course not," Sarah said.

"But we also can't help seeing the people who do, since they walk through our neighborhood to get to them."

"That would be completely understandable."

"And I have to admit that we gossip about them *a lot*," Cora confided with a touch of glee.

"I can't tell you how pleased I am to hear it," Sarah assured her. "Am I right to think you have a theory about this woman?"

"More than a theory, I think. Lots of different kinds of people go to the dens, you know."

"I do know. The man who was murdered used to go to them, and he was the son of a very successful banker."

"Yes, rich men in fancy suits go there. They don't even bother to hide their faces. And ladies who arrive in private carriages wear veils so no one will know who they are. But then there are the prostitutes. They walk right in, not even caring who sees them."

"How do you know they are prostitutes?" Sarah asked.

"Oh, you can tell by the way they dress. The brazen way they walk, too. But it's sad. I could never understand how a woman could do that, sell herself to any man with money in his pocket, no matter who or what he was. So when I saw them going into the dens, I realized that's how they stand it. Some drink, I guess, and others use hop. It helps them forget or something."

Sarah had known that respectable ladies and gentlemen frequented the opium dens. She'd even delivered a baby for a woman who had been addicted to opium, but she'd never thought about who the other customers might be. "So the gentlemen in their fancy suits might be mingling with prostitutes."

"But not Chinese prostitutes, because I don't think there are any, at least not in this city."

"So who would this woman be if she's not Chinese?"

"I think she's a woman I've seen around. She's not Chinese, but she's got dark black hair, and she has a cheongsam that she wears sometimes to the dens."

"Why would she do that?"

Cora shrugged. "Who knows? The wives think she does it to get customers. Because you hardly ever see a Chinese woman, they're mysterious and exotic, so she might pretend to be Chinese."

"Do you have any idea where this woman lives or what her name is?"

"Of course not, and I can't imagine any of the other wives do either, but I can ask around."

"That would be such a help. How can I ever repay you?"

"Promise you'll deliver this baby when the time comes," Cora said with a grin.

SARAH HAD MISSED LUNCH WITH MAEVE AND THE CHILdren, but Velvet, her cook, had kept a plate for her. Malloy and Gino, whom Malloy had brought home with him for lunch so they could consult with Sarah, sat at the breakfast room table and watched her eat while she told them what Cora Lee had said about the mysterious Chinese woman.

Malloy nodded sagely when she had finished. "Well, Gino, you've been wondering what you could do to help with this case, and here's your chance."

"Where's my chance?" Gino asked with a frown, certain he was being tricked into something, which of course he was.

"We need to find this woman, so you can go down to Chinatown and mention that you're in the market for a Chinese prostitute."

Sarah didn't even bother to cover her smile when she saw Gino's pained reaction. "I can't do that."

"You're the perfect one to do that," Malloy said. "You look so young and innocent nobody will bat an eye when you make a fool of yourself."

"But that's the part I don't want to do," Gino said, glowering now.

"They must get a lot of fools in Chinatown," Malloy said. "No one will think badly of you."

"And what am I supposed to do if I find this woman?" Gino asked unhappily.

"Find out who she is and where she lives," Sarah said before Malloy could make any indiscreet suggestions.

"Or at least ask her a few questions and find out if she's the one who delivered Hayden Norcross's opium," Malloy added.

"But won't she expect me to, uh, do something?" Gino asked with obvious dismay.

"You can be disgusted to discover that she really isn't Chinese," Malloy suggested. "You can even demand your money back."

Gino still didn't look convinced. "Are we sure she really isn't Chinese?"

"According to my source," Sarah said, "it is impossible."

"All right, but . . ." Gino glanced uneasily at the door. "Don't tell Maeve, all right?" Maeve was upstairs with the children or at least that's where she should have been.

Sarah exchanged a meaningful glance with Malloy.

"I mean it," Gino said. "Not a word."

"Of course," Sarah said. "I'm sure she'd tease you unmercifully."

Gino wasn't satisfied, though. He glared at Malloy until he said, "I won't tell her."

"Swear it."

Malloy rolled his eyes, but he raised his hand and said, "I swear."

"All right, then. I guess I should go tonight."

"That seems like a good time," Malloy said.

"Are we sure he'll be safe by himself?" Sarah asked with a worried frown.

Malloy grinned. "Maybe one of your brothers would go with you."

Gino groaned. "They'd all go if I told them what I was doing."

"I'd feel much better if you didn't go alone," Sarah said.

"I'm not too worried about a bunch of hopheads attacking me," Gino scoffed.

"The woman probably doesn't work in Chinatown, though," Malloy said. "There's no telling where you'll have to go to find her."

Gino sighed. "All right, but what if we can't find this woman?"

"We'll worry about that if it happens," Malloy said. "In the meantime, I think we also need to speak to Wendell Tarleton. He's the one who found Hayden's body. He might have seen something that Mr. Norcross didn't tell us about."

"I wonder if Hayden knew that Wendell was his half brother," Sarah said.

"You saw Wendell," Malloy said. "How could he not know?"

"People have a way of only seeing what they want to see," Sarah said. "If Hayden didn't want to know, he wouldn't have noticed the resemblance."

"But people have told us they were rivals, so Hayden must have at least guessed," Malloy said.

"Or maybe he just knew instinctively that his father favored Wendell, for whatever reason, and that was enough to make him insanely jealous," Sarah said.

"Just knowing his father favored Wendell would've been hard for him," Gino said. "My parents really try not to have favorites, but we still fight for their attention."

"Everyone wants their parents to love them unconditionally," Sarah said, then turned to Malloy. "But I thought you and my father already met with Wendell Tarleton."

"We've learned a lot more about Hayden since then," Malloy said. "I'd like to find out just how much Tarleton knew about Hayden's bad habits. He might even know something about this mysterious woman."

"Are you going back to his office, then?" Gino asked. "If so, I'd like to go with you this time."

But Malloy shook his head. "I think I'd like to speak with Mr. Tarleton away from his office. Can we find out where he lives?"

"If he's in the City Directory," Sarah said. "I doubt he's in the Social Register, though."

"No, he wouldn't be, even if Bram Norcross is his father."

Sarah had finished her lunch. "Let's go look, shall we?"

Velvet came to clear the table while they made their way to the small room where Sarah had her writing desk. She pulled the directory down from the shelf and flipped through it. "Is Tarleton married?"

"I don't know," Malloy said. "Why do you ask?"

"Because there's a Pamela Tarleton at the same address as Wendell."

"I haven't heard anything about a wife, but I suppose it's possible," Malloy said.

"Or maybe it's his mother," Sarah said. "Didn't you tell me that Bram Norcross indicated he was still in love with her? That means she's still alive and presumably living somewhere."

"And where else would she live but with her only son?" Gino said with a grin.

"Well, wife or mother, I'm thinking it would be a good idea if you and I both called on the Tarletons, Mrs. Malloy," Malloy said with a grin.

"This evening?" she asked.

"The sooner the better."

"Evening is such an awkward time to call on people, but I suppose this is a special case," Sarah said, searching for a pencil with which to write down the address.

"Would you like me to drive you to the Tarletons' on my way to Chinatown?" Gino asked.

Sarah held up the paper on which she had written the address. "It's not really on the way."

"Do you think he minds that?" Malloy asked. "Yes, Gino, you can drop us off on your way to impress the good people of Chinatown with my flashy motorcar."

VII

"WHICH BROTHER ARE YOU TAKING WITH YOU?" SARAH asked Gino as he drove them uptown to the apartment building where the Tarletons were listed as living. She had to shout to be heard from the tonneau where she and Malloy were sitting. Malloy, it seemed, preferred to sit in the back with her, although Sarah thought it had more to do with Gino's driving than with wanting to sit with her.

"Enzo, if he's home." Gino had five brothers. "You didn't say anything to Maeve, did you?"

"Not a word," Sarah said. She glanced at Malloy, who was managing to look totally innocent, too.

"Enzo should enjoy himself," Malloy said.

"He doesn't get much excitement working at Pop's shop, and I owe him a favor for the way he helped Maeve."

Sarah smiled at the way Gino had phrased Enzo's contribution to the efforts that had saved Gino's life. Men could be so sensitive about their masculinity.

The Tarletons lived in a fairly new apartment building in the Lenox Hill neighborhood. It wasn't particularly luxurious or showy, but it had a doorman to regulate who entered the building. Frank telephoned the Tarleton apartment and obtained permission for them to go up. From the expression on his face, the permission had been given rather reluctantly.

Sarah was ready with a smile for whoever opened the door, and it seemed to surprise the woman who did. She was a slightly plump matron, probably in her forties, although she was very well kept. She wore a simple brown skirt and a cream-colored shirtwaist, but the waist was rather elaborate, with lace trim and too many ruffles to be practical for an ordinary housewife. Her brown hair showed no trace of gray and was pinned up neatly in a most flattering style.

"Mrs. Tarleton," Sarah said with as much enthusiasm as she could muster, "thank you so much for seeing us. I know this is an unusual time to be calling, but my husband needed to speak with Mr. Tarleton away from his office, so I offered to come along and make it a social visit."

Mrs. Tarleton was still staring at them, speechless, when a man said, "It's all right, Mother."

Sarah saw Wendell then, coming down the hallway. He was still adjusting the suit coat he had obviously just donned, not wanting to receive visitors in his shirtsleeves, she supposed.

Mrs. Tarleton stepped back and opened the door wider, although she was frowning now. "Come in, then."

"What's this all about?" Tarleton asked Malloy, obviously not pleased to see him.

"Maybe Mr. Norcross told you, I'm investigating Hayden's death."

"Why would you be investigating anything at all?" Tarleton asked, trying for outrage.

"Because I'm a private investigator, and I have some questions for you, now that I know more about the murder. I thought you'd prefer answering them in privacy," Malloy said.

"What kind of questions?" Tarleton asked uneasily.

"He doesn't know anything about it," his mother said, closing the door. "I don't know why you'd think he does."

"Because he's the one who helped Mr. Norcross clean up Hayden's office before the police arrived," Malloy said baldly.

Tarleton scowled and his mother blanched. "You didn't tell me that," she said to her son.

"It wasn't important, and what does it matter?"

"It matters if you saw something that could help identify the killer," Malloy said.

"But I didn't."

Malloy smiled. "Then you won't mind answering my questions."

"I suppose you won't leave until I do, so what choice do I have?" Tarleton said. "Come along. Mother, I'll take Mr. Malloy into the library, if you wouldn't mind entertaining Mrs. Malloy while he interrogates me."

Malloy cast Sarah an apologetic smile and followed Tarleton back down the hallway. Mrs. Tarleton was still frowning, obviously not happy at being left with Sarah. Af-

ter an awkward moment, she said, "This way," and led Sarah
into the parlor, which was just off the entryway. It was a
comfortable room with all new furniture and carpeting.

"This is a lovely building," Sarah said, exaggerating a bit.
"It must be very new."

"Wendell pays for the apartment," Mrs. Tarleton said
defensively, indicating with an impatient wave of her hand
that Sarah should sit down in one of the two stuffed chairs
flanking the cold fireplace. She took the other.

Sarah blinked in surprise at her odd reply, but she needed
only another moment to figure out the meaning behind it.
"Yes, I understand Mr. Tarleton has done very well at Norcross and Son."

"He earned everything he got there. Bram didn't show
him any favoritism," she insisted.

Sarah doubted that very much. Men in their twenties
were not normally made partners in investment banks. Even
Hayden Norcross had to wait until he was thirty. "I'm sure.
I've heard that Mr. Tarleton is quite good at what he does."

"Don't humor me, Mrs. Malloy. We both know your husband is here so he can somehow blame Wendell for Hayden's
death."

"I'm sorry if you got that impression, but that isn't at all
what my husband is doing. He's merely trying to find out
what really happened."

"What really happened is that Hayden finally offended
the wrong person and paid the price, but that person wasn't
Wendell. He had no reason to kill Hayden."

"I thought Hayden had gotten Wendell fired from Norcross and Son," Sarah said without the slightest trace of malice.

The color flared in Mrs. Tarleton's face. "Bram hired him back, didn't he?"

"Only after Hayden was dead. Mrs. Tarleton, I know that Hayden had tricked Wendell somehow in order to cause the scandal that got him dismissed, but I also know that Hayden only did it because he was so jealous of Wendell. Everyone knew which son Mr. Norcross favored."

Mrs. Tarleton expressed no surprise that Sarah knew this. Perhaps she assumed everyone did. "Because Wendell was the son who should have been on the sign, because he's smart and honest and hardworking and he did everything Bram told him to do."

"None of which Hayden ever did," Sarah agreed. "In fact, until Hayden got Wendell fired, Hayden had more reason for killing Wendell than the other way around."

"And why do you think he worked so hard to blacken Wendell's name? He must have thought Bram would finally love him if Wendell was out of the way."

Sarah thought she might well be right. She decided to prod at Mrs. Tarleton's weakest spot. "You've done a wonderful job raising your son, Mrs. Tarleton. You should be very proud."

"You mean I've done a wonderful job for a former chorus girl."

"I didn't know your background," Sarah said, "and I'm not here to judge you."

"Why shouldn't you? Everyone else does."

"And yet you made a home for your son and raised him to be a good man."

"Which is more than Greta Norcross can claim," she said bitterly. "Wendell could have had a real home with both his parents if she'd given Bram a divorce, but she wouldn't let him go, even though she was never a wife to Bram again after their daughter died. She didn't want him, but she wouldn't let him go either."

"I'm sure that was very difficult for you," Sarah said.

Finally, Sarah's kindness seemed to wear down Mrs. Tarleton's bitterness, and she softened just a bit. "It wasn't as bad as you might think," she allowed. "I never expected much out of life, and when Bram took an interest in me, I didn't think it would last. In fact, when Wendell . . . came along, I thought Bram would leave me, but he didn't. He has supported me—us—all these years, and he did right by Wendell, sending him to school and everything."

"And giving him a place in his own firm," Sarah added.

"Until Hayden couldn't bear it anymore. I'm telling you, Mrs. Malloy, I didn't kill Hayden, but I wish I had. He caused nothing but pain his whole life."

THE LIBRARY WAS A SMALL ROOM WITH ONLY A HANDFUL of books, and its lone window opened onto an air shaft. That made it rather stuffy in the July heat, but Tarleton closed the door anyway. Plainly, he didn't want his mother to overhear them.

The room held a desk and chair and a couple bookshelves that contained the books in question but mostly held stacks of folders and papers that looked like something Tarleton might have brought home with him from his office. Tarleton pulled out the desk chair and motioned for Frank to take the only other piece of furniture in the room, a straight-backed chair that had been sitting up against the wall. Frank pulled it out to a better angle and sat down.

"All right, what do you want?" Tarleton asked.

Was he angry or defensive? Defensive, Frank decided. "I'd just like to know what happened the morning you found Hayden's body."

Tarleton sighed with long suffering. "I didn't find him. I wasn't at the firm then, you will recall."

Frank did recall. Norcross had let him go because of Hayden's treachery.

"Who did find him?"

"His secretary. He hadn't seen Hayden come in yet and didn't really expect him until later. He happened to go into the office for something and saw him."

"What time was this?"

"I don't know exactly, but my father telephoned me around ten and asked me to come to the firm. He said it was an emergency. He couldn't say anything on the telephone, of course."

Everyone knew the operators listened in, and news like Hayden's murder could be sold to a newspaper.

"It must have been quite a shock when you found out why he sent for you."

"It certainly wasn't what I was expecting to see," Tarleton allowed shakily.

"I understand Hayden was naked."

Tarleton swallowed audibly. "Yes. That was the first thing that . . . that shocked me. His huge body, so very white, just lying there on the sofa. I guess I expected him to jump up, furious and embarrassed at being caught undressed like that, but he couldn't, could he? And then I saw his face."

Frank waited, knowing most people can't stand silence and will talk about anything to fill it. He didn't have to wait long.

"The blood had run down all over his face, but . . . It was his expression that I'll never forget. He looked so . . . so *surprised*."

"Mr. Norcross said you helped him dress Hayden."

Tarleton ran a less-than-steady hand over his face. "Yes. Father didn't want the police to see him like that. He didn't want people gossiping about him."

"Where were Hayden's clothes?"

"What?" he asked with a puzzled frown.

"Where were his clothes?" Frank repeated patiently. "Were they strewn all over the room or—"

"Oh no. You mean did he tear them off in a frenzy of lust or something? No, they were draped neatly over a chair. He obviously didn't want them to get wrinkled."

"And where was the rest of the blood?"

Tarleton blanched again. "The rest of it?"

"Yes. The bullet went through his skull and there would have been some blood and other . . . matter. Where was it?"

"Oh." Tarleton swallowed again, and this time Frank was sure he was trying not to vomit at the memory. "Under his head."

"On the sofa?"

Tarleton nodded, as if he didn't trust his voice.

"So he was just lying there peacefully, completely naked, while someone walked up to him and shot him," Frank mused.

"That was what Father thought," Tarleton volunteered eagerly. "He said that proved Hayden wasn't afraid of whoever shot him, so it must have been a female, but . . ."

"You disagree?" Frank prodded.

"Do you really think a woman could murder someone like that?" Tarleton asked, horrified. "He was shot right in the face!"

"I guess you don't think it was a woman," Frank said. "But why wouldn't he have tried to defend himself against a man?"

"He'd been smoking. Did you know . . . ?"

"That he used opium? Yes, I did. I understand he had everything laid out."

"Yes. I had no idea what it was at first, but Mr. Norcross did. It was very . . . orderly. He had placed a special tray on the table, and the things were on it. I don't know what they were all for, but I recognized the pipe. There was a small lamp, too, but it had run out of fuel and gone out."

"That's for cooking the opium. Do you think he might have been under the influence of the opium when he was killed?"

"That would certainly explain why he didn't resist or even get up to confront his attacker, whether it was a man or a woman."

Frank nodded. "Or maybe his attacker was already there in the office with him. Maybe it was the person who sold him the opium."

"But that was a woman."

"You're sure it was a woman?" Frank asked in surprise.

Tarleton winced, obviously realizing he probably shouldn't have known that. "Yes. Everyone knew. He'd let her in the back door late in the evening, when everyone was gone, but sometimes people work late, and she was seen, more than once."

"Did *you* see her?"

"No, I . . ." Tarleton shook his head. "Well, I saw her once. Just a glimpse."

"What did she look like?"

"She was Chinese."

"Are you sure? Did you see her face?"

"I . . . I don't think I did, but she was wearing this dress that . . . Well, no white woman would wear a dress like that, and her hair was dead black. What else could she be?"

"Is that why Hayden was naked? Because he had a woman in his office?"

Tarleton shrugged. "That's what I thought, and Mr. Norcross agreed. The woman delivered his opium and . . . and serviced him. That's what everyone thought had been going on for months, so that explains the opium and why he was naked, but it doesn't explain why he was shot, does it?"

"No, Mr. Tarleton, it doesn't."

Gɪɴᴏ's ᴘᴀʀᴇɴᴛs ᴡᴇʀᴇɴ'ᴛ ᴘʟᴇᴀsᴇᴅ ᴡʜᴇɴ ʜᴇ ᴀʀʀɪᴠᴇᴅ home only to convince Enzo to go back out with him again.

"He has work at the shop tomorrow," his mother protested.

"He'll be home in plenty of time," Gino assured her.

His mother was not impressed. "He needs to get some sleep in between!"

"I'll be fine, Ma," Enzo assured her.

She was still yelling at them in Italian when they drove away.

"So where are we going, little brother?" Enzo wanted to know. "And why isn't the lovely Maeve with us?"

"We're going to Chinatown, and I didn't think Maeve would enjoy going with us to an opium den."

"You're taking me to an opium den?" Enzo crowed. "Wait until Ma hears about this!"

Gino shrugged. "If you don't want to go, I can let you out."

Enzo scowled his big-brother scowl, but it had long ago lost its power to intimidate Gino. "All right," he finally agreed. "I won't tell Ma. But I'm going to tell somebody. What are we going to do in an opium den?"

"Not smoke opium," Gino assured him. "But we are going to look for a prostitute who may or may not be Chinese."

"I'm definitely not telling Ma that." They both laughed at the very thought.

Chinatown was only a short drive from Little Italy. The parked motorcar drew a lot of attention. Even though they were becoming more common on the streets, very few of them stopped in Chinatown. Gino gave several boys each a penny to watch it while they went about their business, and one of them was helpful enough to tell them where they could find an opium den.

Gino's instructions to Enzo were to pretend to be a little

drunk. In Gino's opinion, Enzo went a bit overboard, but they were convincing enough to fool the proprietors of the first three opium dens they visited. They left each in a huff when the proprietor could not provide them with a female companion of Chinese extraction. At the fourth place, the proprietor was only too happy to help, but it turned out he thought they were good candidates for a little shakedown. They had to teach a very surprised thief a lesson before moving on.

"This is a lot more fun than I thought it would be when you told me we weren't really going to hire the prostitute," Enzo said, licking the blood off the broken skin of his knuckle.

Gino couldn't help grinning. "I just hope we're not on a wild-goose chase here."

The fifth place they found was a bit fancier than the others, and the clientele reflected that. In fact, the proprietor looked down his nose at Gino and Enzo when they came in. Before Gino could speak, Enzo slapped him on the back a little harder than was really necessary and told the very dignified Chinese man, "It's my brother's birthday, and I promised him he could have a Chinese woman to go along with his hop. I heard you have one here."

The proprietor actually smiled, or maybe he just had a facial twitch. At any rate, he said, "Five dollars."

"We need to see the woman first," Gino said. "We've been tricked once tonight already."

Without a word, the proprietor stepped back to his desk and rang a small bell sitting there. A few moments later, a slender woman stepped through a curtained doorway. She was wearing a jade green garment that fell loosely from her shoulders to her feet but which was made of heavily embroidered satin and had the same kind of stand-up collar Gino had seen on the coats of Chinese men. Her raven hair was done up real fancy, and she had stuck some paper flowers in it here and there. She had her hands clasped in front of her and kept her head bowed. Her cheeks and lips were rouged.

"Will she do, brother?" Enzo asked.

"Yes," Gino said, tamping down his excitement. She might not be the right woman, he reminded himself. He fished five dollars out of his wallet and gave it to the proprietor. "Do you have a private room?"

The woman made no sign that she had even heard, but she turned and started back through the curtained doorway. Gino went after her and Enzo made to follow, but the proprietor stopped him. "Five dollars each one."

Gino smiled. Jack Robinson was paying, but he'd let Enzo stew for a bit before telling him that. When they had both paid, they followed the woman down the dimly lit hallway lined with closed doors. The place was eerily quiet, and the aroma from the many pipes that had been and were being smoked in this building was making Gino dizzy.

She stopped in front of one of the doors and went inside, leaving the door open for them to follow. Enzo shut it behind them. The room was small, furnished with only a bed with a bare mattress and a small bedside table with an opium layout.

Gino squinted at the woman, silently cursing the single gaslight. "Turn that up, will you?" he asked Enzo, gesturing toward the light. "Now, let me see your face," he said to the woman.

"I no understand," she said, still keeping her gaze fixed firmly on the floor, but when Enzo had twisted the knob to raise the gas flame Gino grabbed her chin and lifted her face.

Gino hadn't ever seen a Chinese woman up close, but even though this woman had drawn black lines around her eyes, he wasn't fooled. "You aren't Chinese, are you?"

She smiled then. Gino had seen that wheedling smile on the faces of many unfortunate women who had to seduce men for a living. "I can pretend to be."

"Is that what you tell all your customers?"

"What do you care?"

"I care because I'm here to ask you some questions."

"I never heard it called that before," she said, still using that lilting tone that prostitutes used to entice.

"Stop trying to charm me. We're not interested in your services."

"We aren't?" Enzo said with feigned disappointment.

"Shut up, Enzo. Why are you pretending to be Chinese?"

"None of your business," she snapped. "If all you want to do is talk, I'm leaving."

"I'll pay you another five dollars to answer my questions, and you'll get to keep all of it this time." He figured she got only half or less of the usual fee.

He finally had her full attention. "Let me see the money first."

He pulled out another five dollars but didn't let her have it yet. "Why are you pretending to be Chinese?"

"Why do you think? Do you have any idea how many whores there are in New York? A girl needs to stand out if she wants to make any money. Men come to Chinatown looking for a Chinese woman, but they can't find any, so I'm the next best thing."

Gino couldn't argue with her logic. "How did you end up in an opium den?"

She sighed impatiently. "A customer brought me here once. He had an idea the hop would make it more fun or something."

"And does it?" Enzo asked with interest.

She laughed at that. "I can see you ain't a hophead. The drug makes it *impossible*, but I didn't tell him that. He couldn't even remember after, so I told him he was like a stallion."

"And that's when you decided to start working here," Gino guessed.

"The white men always want a woman with them, even if they can't do anything once they smoke the pipe. It's a lot easier than walking the streets, I can tell you."

"And that's how you met Hayden Norcross, I guess."

She frowned at that. "What's Hayden got to do with this?"

"Everything," Gino said with satisfaction. "Let me tell you what I think happened. Hayden came here and hired you to make his visits more fun, but then his father found out and forbade him from coming to an opium den again."

"Who told you all this?" she demanded, which proved he was right.

"But Hayden didn't want to give up the pipe, so he hired you to bring the opium to his office."

"There's nothing wrong with that. We didn't bother anybody."

"And did you visit him last Tuesday?"

"What if I did?"

"I was just wondering."

"Sure I did. I went on Friday, too, as usual, but he never came to let me in."

Gino exchanged a glance with Enzo, who didn't seem to understand the significance of that statement. "You went to his office on Friday?"

"I go every Tuesday and Friday."

"Tonight's Tuesday. Why didn't you go tonight?"

"I don't go until later, but I was thinking about not going at all. Teach him a lesson for standing me up."

"I'm sorry to tell you, but you don't need to go at all anymore."

"Why not? You ain't gonna tell me Hayden stopped smoking hop."

"Oh, but he did. You see, he's dead."

He watched the shock register on her heavily made-up face, but then she shook it off. "His old man sent you, didn't he? He thinks if I stop coming that Hayden will quit smoking, but he's wasting his time. Hayden won't stop for anything."

"Mr. Norcross did not send me, and Hayden is really dead. Someone murdered him on Tuesday night."

"What?" She looked to Enzo and back at Gino, as if trying to judge their honesty. Whatever she saw convinced her and a new idea dawned. "Do you think I killed him?"

"You have to admit, it looks bad," Gino said mildly.

"I never! He was fine when I left him," she insisted almost hysterically. "Are you cops or something?"

"Private investigator," Gino said. "I can't arrest anyone. I just want to find out what happened."

"I didn't do it, I swear! He was fine, I tell you!"

"Calm down. No one's accusing you of anything," Gino assured her. "Maybe you should sit down."

She sank down onto the bed, which was the only place to sit, and looked up with terror-filled eyes. "Why would I kill him? He was my best customer. All I had to do was bring him the hop and take off my clothes, because he liked to look at me, and then just wait until he finished smoking and went to sleep."

"What condition was he in when you left that night?"

"Sleeping or whatever it is, like they get. He'd smoked the pipe. You have to lay down to do it, you know."

"I don't know, but go on."

"You have to hold it over the flame, so it's easier if you lay down. He was on the couch, so he could just drift off."

"What was he wearing?"

She looked up in surprise. "Oh, I see what you mean. Nothing. He'd take off his clothes, too. He said it was exciting, although I never did know what he meant by that. I never saw a hophead who looked excited."

"So you left him naked, sleeping on the sofa."

"I don't know if he was sleeping. He was peaceful, like they get. I took my money and left."

"What time was this?"

"I don't know. Midnight, maybe, or a little later."

"And did you see anyone else?"

"I saw lots of people. It's a big city."

Gino sighed. "I mean, in the office building or outside of it."

"Oh. No, I didn't see nobody. Sometimes that slimy

night watchman is creeping around. Once he tried to get me to give him a free one so he wouldn't tell anybody he saw me, but I told him to go ahead and tell. Hayden's father owns the place, don't he?"

"And you didn't see the night watchman that night?"

"No, nor nobody else either. I told you. But how did Hayden get murdered? There was nobody there."

Gino sighed again. "That's what we're trying to find out."

"Then how did he die? Did he smoke too much or what?"

"That wouldn't be a murder, would it?" Gino asked.

She blinked. "No, I guess it wouldn't."

"He was shot."

"Shot? You mean with a gun?"

"That's right."

"That proves it, then. I couldn't've done it. I don't even have a gun," she said with some satisfaction.

"The gun belonged to Hayden."

Her satisfaction faded. "Oh."

"Did you know he had a gun?"

"Me? No. How would I know that?"

"I thought he might have threatened you with it."

"Why would he? I only ever did just what he said I should. I brought him the hop and pretended to like him."

"Hayden was known to be, uh, rough with women sometimes."

"Was he? I ain't surprised. He could be nasty, but I know how to handle men. He . . . Oh!" Her blackened eyes widened with surprise. "Now that makes sense," she mused.

"What does?"

"I told you he could be nasty, and back before, when he

wasn't on the hop so much, he'd want me to pretend that I didn't like it. You know, beg him to stop and tell him he was hurting me. Are you saying he really liked to force women?"

"Yes, he did."

"Well, I never did like him much. I didn't shoot him, though, and I didn't know he had a gun. So what do you want from me?"

"Nothing." He handed her the five dollars.

She stared at it suspiciously. "Ain't you going to try to pin Hayden's murder on me?"

"I don't think so."

Her eyes narrowed. "And what do you want in exchange?"

"Nothing," Gino was glad to say. "But if you think of anything that might help us find the real killer, let me know. There'll be a reward for you." He handed her his card and then he had to give Enzo a little nudge to get him to leave.

"Is that what you do every day?" Enzo asked as they walked back to where they'd left the motorcar.

"Yes, except I don't usually do it in an opium den."

WE SHOULD HIRE A CHAUFFEUR," SARAH SAID AS THEY left the Tarletons' apartment building and walked over to the nearest avenue to find a cab.

Frank frowned at the very thought. "Gino would never forgive us."

"I know, but if we had a chauffeur, he'd be waiting for us and we wouldn't need to find a cab to take us home."

Frank had to look at her again to make sure she wasn't serious. "We'd have to buy Gino his own motorcar, then."

"Or give him a raise so he can buy his own."

"I don't think he's worth that much of a raise." Motorcars were hideously expensive.

"Don't let him hear you say that. What did you learn from Mr. Tarleton?"

"That finding Hayden's body upset him, that Bram Norcross thinks a woman might have killed Hayden because he didn't put up a fight, and that Tarleton doesn't think a woman could commit a murder like that."

"He has a rather idealistic view of women, then."

"He does, but he's young yet."

Sarah gave him a swat that made him grin. They'd reached the avenue, and he craned his neck, looking for a cab. One came along after a few minutes and they were soon heading back downtown to Bank Street.

"And what did you learn from Mrs. Tarleton, although I assume the correct title should be Miss Tarleton."

"I didn't inquire, although she said she was a chorus girl when Bram Norcross took up with her, so you're probably right. He's supported her all these years, though, so maybe he was telling the truth when he said he would have married her."

"I wonder why Greta wouldn't give him a divorce."

"Are you serious? Why would she give up her comfortable home and her place in society to enable her husband to make an honest woman out of a chorus girl? Although . . ."

"Although what?" he asked, intrigued by her change of tone.

"Mrs. Tarleton did mention that Greta stopped sharing Bram's bed after their little girl died. Or at least that's what he claimed. She seemed to think that's why he went looking for female company elsewhere."

"That could explain it, although I think lots of rich men have done the same without the slightest provocation."

"You're undoubtedly right," she said. "But why would the little girl's death have made her want to punish her husband?"

Frank needed to think that one over, but in the end, the answer was obvious. "Because she blamed him for it somehow."

"That's not the story we heard, though. Rumor had it that Hayden was responsible."

"So maybe we haven't heard the right rumor yet."

"Maybe we haven't. I'll have to put my mother to work on this one."

VIII

Frank was pleased to receive a telephone call from Jack Robinson the next morning. Jocelyn was still not ready for Sarah's services, but Jack had managed to arrange for Frank to meet with Charlie Quinn so he could learn first-hand the details of Quinn's relationship with Hayden Norcross. To Frank's surprise, Quinn had suggested the three men meet at the Citadel, which was what New Yorkers called Delmonico's restaurant on Fifth Avenue.

Frank stopped at his office for a few hours first to get Gino's report from Chinatown and bring him up to date on what little they had learned from the Tarletons.

"I guess Enzo has a good story to tell your other brothers," Frank said when he'd heard Gino's account.

"I don't know if he'll even admit it. He seemed disappointed. He didn't even get to see anybody smoking hop."

"He got to meet a prostitute, though. Surely, he can brag about that."

"Not if all he did was talk to her," Gino said with a grin.

"And you're sure this woman didn't kill Hayden?"

"If she did, she's a good actress."

"Prostitutes generally are."

Gino squirmed a bit at that. "She was really surprised he was even dead, though, and mad, too. He was her best customer."

"Well, at least we know where to find her if it turns out she did it, and don't forget, Mr. Norcross is convinced a woman killed him."

"Only because Hayden didn't put up a fight, but he probably doesn't know much about opium if he thinks that. According to the prostitute, Hayden was practically unconscious when she left him."

"That sounds right for an opium user. I wonder why Hayden started using opium in the first place."

"Too bad we can't ask him," Gino said with a sigh. "Maybe that would help find his killer."

"Maybe his father knows."

"And what are the chances his father will talk to you again so we can ask him?"

This time Frank sighed. "Probably not very good, so we'll have to keep looking."

FRANK TOOK A CAB TO THE CITADEL, WHERE THE MAÎTRE d' escorted him upstairs to one of the smaller private dining rooms, which Quinn had reserved for them. They would be able to speak in complete privacy while enjoying a delicious luncheon.

Frank was the last to arrive, and Quinn and Jack rose to welcome him.

"Charlie is trying to impress us," Jack said when they had both shaken his hand and seen him seated at the elaborately laid table.

"Yes, I am," Charlie agreed amiably. "Jack told me you're the best detective in New York, and I might need your services even more than he does."

"What have you told him?" Frank asked Jack uneasily.

"Just that I hired you to find the real killer so I won't get the blame," Jack said. He glanced at Quinn, who was grinning. "But only after he assured me he's also not the killer."

Frank decided to adopt their nonchalant attitude. "You're sure of that, are you?"

"Do you really think I killed that little chiseler?" Quinn asked with interest.

"What you told me at the funeral does give you a good reason to want him dead."

Quinn laughed at that. "If I killed everybody who tried to cheat me, there'd hardly be anybody left in New York."

"But Norcross really did cheat you," Frank reminded him. "So you will understand why some people might think you did it."

But Quinn was shaking his head. "If I'd killed him, I wouldn't do it myself and they never would've even found the body. Who would be crazy enough to shoot a man in his own office? Anybody might've seen him."

"That's a good point," Jack said.

"But somebody who didn't actually intend to kill him might do something foolish in the heat of passion," Frank said, leaning back in his chair.

Before anyone could respond, the waiter came in quietly and filled their wineglasses.

"I took the liberty of ordering for all of us," Quinn said. "I hope you don't mind."

"We'll let you know when we've seen what you picked," Jack said, and they chatted idly until the waiter withdrew.

"At the funeral, you mentioned that you weren't the only dissatisfied investor, Mr. Quinn," Frank said.

"And you think one of them might've killed Hayden?" Quinn asked with a frown.

"It's possible. He was killed at his office, so that seems to indicate it was related to his business. But why would somebody have gone to his office so late at night?"

"How late was it?" Jack asked.

"Sometime after midnight."

"Midnight, you say? That's strange," Jack said. "Even if you wanted to meet with Norcross after regular business hours, presumably when nobody was around to see you, why wait until midnight?"

"Unless it was a man used to doing business at that time of night," Quinn said with a knowing glance at Jack.

"Ah, I see what you mean," Jack said with a small smile. "Before I became respectable, midnight was a much more reasonable hour to me than it is now."

"Remind me not to get respectable," Quinn said, smiling back.

"I don't suppose you'd give me the names of the other

investors Hayden cheated, would you, Mr. Quinn?" Frank asked.

"So they can get pinched for killing Norcross?" Quinn scoffed. "Not likely."

The waiter came in then with their soup course, giving Frank time to think of a suitable reply.

I JUST WANT TO MAKE SURE I UNDERSTAND," SARAH's mother said with far more enthusiasm than Sarah knew her father would approve. "We want to find out from Greta Norcross exactly what she knows about Mr. Tarleton and his mother."

"I'm not sure we can do that, of course," Sarah explained patiently. They were in the Deckers' carriage on their way to the Norcrosses' home. "Mrs. Norcross may not want to discuss her husband's mistress and illegitimate son, and even if she does, we may not be able to figure out how to work it into the conversation."

"And Greta may not even see us at all. She'd be perfectly within her rights to turn us away since she's in mourning."

"But we know she's not really mourning Hayden all that much, so perhaps she'll be glad for a little company," Sarah said.

"We can hope," her mother replied.

They asked the carriage to wait until they were sure they'd be received. The maid took their calling cards and returned shortly to say Mrs. Norcross would see them in the parlor, which had been rearranged back into a formal sitting room after the funeral reception. They were surprised to find she was not alone.

"Mrs. Malloy, it's so nice to see you," Violet said with a bright smile. She looked so much better than she had at the funeral that Sarah couldn't help smiling back, even though Violet's presence meant they probably wouldn't be able to talk about the Tarletons.

"I'm glad to see you, too. I hope you're feeling well."

"Violet is doing remarkably well," Mrs. Norcross said.

"I'm very glad to hear it," Sarah said.

"Thank you for receiving us, Greta," Sarah's mother said when they were seated. "I wasn't sure if you'd welcome visitors or not."

Greta gave her a stiff smile. "I wouldn't have, but Violet was delighted by the opportunity to see Mrs. Malloy again."

They had been properly put in their place, but Sarah's mother wasn't about to let that faze her. "Has Bram returned to work?"

"Nothing keeps him away from the firm very long," Mrs. Norcross said. Sarah noticed she didn't seem embittered by that knowledge. Perhaps it suited her well to have her husband at his office as much as possible.

"I'm sure your mother-in-law appreciates your company," Sarah said to Violet, who was sitting beside Mrs. Norcross on a sofa. Sarah and her mother had taken chairs facing them.

To Sarah's surprise, Violet gave Mrs. Norcross a loving smile. "I hope so. Mother Norcross has always been very kind to me."

"No one could want a sweeter daughter-in-law," Mrs. Norcross said, returning the smile. "I've been trying to convince Violet that she should come and live with us now. There's no point in her staying in that big house all alone, and she'll need help when the baby comes."

It would be unusual for a widow to choose to live with her in-laws when her parents were alive and well and perfectly capable of taking her, but Sarah could understand that Violet wasn't feeling particularly charitable toward her parents after they had forced her to marry Hayden. On the other hand, her husband had been a beast, so how could she reconcile herself to living with his parents?

"Mother Norcross was just explaining that I won't have much money now that Hayden is dead," Violet said innocently.

Mrs. Norcross and Sarah's mother were both understandably shocked. Ladies rarely discussed money and then only out of necessity and with close family members. They certainly didn't discuss it with virtual strangers. Sarah saw no reason to allow this tradition to stop her from learning more, however.

"I don't suppose Hayden had time to accumulate any wealth of his own aside from his income from the family business," she said just as innocently as Violet.

"That's what Mother Norcross was explaining," Violet said. "My father did make some financial arrangements when I married, but I believe Hayden spent most of that money on the house."

"You could sell the house, then," Sarah said before either of the older women could interrupt.

Violet frowned, but before she could speak, Mrs. Norcross said very reluctantly, "There are some debts."

Of course there would be. A man like Hayden Norcross would never be financially responsible.

"But Violet need never worry," Mrs. Norcross added. "She is always welcome here with me. I would never allow anyone to hurt her or the baby."

What an odd thing to say, but then Mrs. Norcross was an odd woman. Before anyone could think of a response, the maid tapped on the door and brought in a tea tray.

"I'd already ordered tea for Violet and me," Mrs. Norcross said. "I hope you don't find it too warm on a day like this."

"That's fine," Sarah's mother said. They waited while the maid served them and left.

An awkward silence fell, so Sarah decided to try shocking Mrs. Norcross into cooperation. "Perhaps your husband told you, Mrs. Norcross, that my husband is a private investigator."

Plainly, she found this news strange. Sarah felt certain no one of her acquaintance had ever been a private investigator. "I don't believe he mentioned it. Why would he?"

"Because Malloy is investigating Hayden's murder." Sarah was sure her mother had winced at such a frank confession, but Sarah had found that shocking people often brought the truth.

Mrs. Norcross didn't wince, but she did frown. Violet was the one who spoke, however. "Why is he doing that? I thought the police were going to find the killer."

Sarah's mother jumped in, bless her. "The police aren't always very good at things like this."

"Why not?" Violet asked.

"Because people like us don't talk to the police, dear," Sarah's mother said gently.

Plainly, Violet was still confused, but Mrs. Norcross patted her hands where they were folded in her lap. "The police are rather uncouth, I'm afraid. They said some unkind things to Bram when they came to the office that morning. He was quite upset." She turned her gaze to Sarah and stared at her for an uncomfortably long moment. "I suppose that's why he hired your husband."

Sarah heard her mother's indrawn breath and gave her mother a warning glance before she could deny it. "My husband never reveals who his clients are, Mrs. Norcross," Sarah said quickly.

"Of course not. I suppose that's why they're called *private* investigators," Mrs. Norcross said acidly.

"But, Greta," Sarah's mother said, "you must be desperate to find out who killed poor Hayden."

"Of course I am," she said, sounding anything but desperate.

"I'm not sure I want to know," Violet said.

"And no one can blame you for that," Mrs. Norcross assured her. "Sadly, Hayden was not the man I'd hoped he would become, and the less we know about his life and the enemies he made, the better."

"Aren't you worried that the person who killed Hayden might kill again, though?" Sarah's mother asked with credible concern.

"Kill one of us, you mean?" Mrs. Norcross scoffed. "I can't even imagine it. Hayden's activities—at least the ones that might have led someone to kill him—did not involve his family at all, I assure you."

"Is it true a woman killed him, though?" Violet asked suddenly.

"Who told you that?" Mrs. Norcross demanded, obviously furious that someone would have said such a thing to her.

"No one *told* me. I heard someone say it at the repast, after the funeral."

"Do you remember who it was?" Sarah asked, ignoring Mrs. Norcross's glare of disapproval.

"Just some ladies, gossiping. They stopped when they realized I was listening, but they said he'd had a woman in his office that night and she must have shot him."

"That's ridiculous," Mrs. Norcross said. "Men don't entertain women in their offices, even immoral women. You mustn't listen to gossip, Violet. That is a sure way to break your heart."

"It is indeed," Sarah's mother said, apparently commiserating. "I heard some cruel gossip at the funeral, too, about little Susie."

Sarah watched in alarm as the blood drained from Mrs. Norcross's face. "I can guess what it was, too. I can't believe people are still saying such vile things." She laid a hand over her heart, as if merely remembering caused her physical pain. Perhaps it did. "They have no idea how much it hurts me to hear that."

"I'm so sorry, Greta. I should never have mentioned it," Sarah's mother said. Sarah could see she was truly sorry.

Mrs. Norcross didn't seem interested in accepting her

apology, though. She was only interested in soothing Violet, who had gone just as pale as Mrs. Norcross had a moment ago. "You mustn't think about any of this anymore, Violet. It's bad for the baby. Hayden is gone now, and you must think only of your child and pleasant things, like how happy you will be to hold the baby in your arms."

"I hadn't thought about that," Violet said with her usual honesty. "I hadn't let myself think about the baby much at all."

"I know, dear, but you mustn't worry anymore. You can come to live here, and I'll take care of everything."

"Mrs. Malloy said I could live anywhere I wanted," Violet said.

Mrs. Norcross gave Sarah a horrified glance before turning back to Violet with a forced smile. "I don't know why she would tell you that."

"She said a widow can do what she wants," Violet said.

"Violet told me she doesn't like her house," Sarah hastily explained. "I simply told her she could choose a different one now that she's a widow."

"But only if she has the means," Mrs. Norcross said, discreetly reminding them that Violet had no means at all.

"Fortunately, you don't need to decide anything today," Sarah's mother said with false cheer. "Perhaps your father or Mr. Norcross would help you with some arrangements."

"I don't think my father will," Violet said. "He'll let me come home, but he won't give me a penny. He already told me so."

"And you're so young," Sarah's mother said. "You'll probably want to remarry eventually."

From the flash of panic that twisted Violet's lovely face, Sarah felt sure she wouldn't be remarrying anytime soon. Before she could reassure Violet, however, Mrs. Norcross beat her to it.

"As Mrs. Malloy said, a widow can do as she likes, and Violet never has to remarry if she doesn't wish it. I can also assure you that Bram Norcross will not leave his only grandchild penniless. We take care of our own."

M Y GOODNESS," SARAH'S MOTHER SAID WHEN THEY WERE well away from the Norcross home, walking toward the nearest avenue to find a cab. "I realize I don't know Greta Norcross very well, but I never expected her to behave like that."

"Perhaps she's just being protective. She's lost both of her children in horrible ways. We can't blame her for wanting to keep Violet and the baby safe, can we?"

"I don't suppose we can, but she's so . . . I'm not sure I can even describe her behavior. She was so *adamant* that Violet come to live with them."

"Did you find that odd, too?"

"I certainly did. I've never liked Isabel Andriessen very much, and from what you told me, they weren't particularly kind to Violet when they found out about the baby, so I suppose Violet might not want to go back to them, but for Greta to absolutely insist on taking her . . ." She shook her head in wonder.

"What disturbed me was how Mrs. Norcross said she would *protect* them, but with Hayden dead, I'm not sure they need protection anymore."

"I didn't think of that," her mother said, "but you're right."

They had reached the avenue and Mrs. Decker signaled for a cab. When they had engaged one and were heading to the Decker house, her mother said, "I'm sorry we didn't get to discuss the Tarletons, but I couldn't think of a way to bring it up with Violet there."

"Neither could I, but maybe I can see Mrs. Tarleton again. She seemed very eager to criticize Mrs. Norcross, and she might tell me even more with a little encouragement. She doesn't seem to mind at all that we're investigating Hayden's death."

"Which reminds me, why didn't you want Greta to know that Bram isn't the one who hired Frank?"

"Because what I said is true, a private investigator doesn't reveal the name of his client."

"But you didn't have to reveal the real client's name, just admit it wasn't Bram."

Sarah shrugged. "Honestly, I thought she might be more cooperative if she believed he was working for her husband."

"I see. Do you think she was?"

"Oddly, no. She actually seemed to be less cooperative after that, and more determined than ever to protect Violet."

"That's too bad, I guess, but she'll find out soon enough that Bram didn't hire Frank."

"How can you be sure?"

"Because she'll most certainly confront Bram when he gets home, and he'll tell her."

"You're probably right." Sarah considered the situation for a moment. "I wonder who started the rumors about

Hayden having a woman in his office the night he was killed."

"You heard Violet. It was some women at the funeral."

"But they couldn't have known about it unless they heard it somewhere else. It certainly wasn't in the newspapers, and not many people at the firm knew about it. One of them must have spread the word."

"Or at least told one other person, which is usually all it takes for a story like that to get started."

Sarah sighed. "You're right. I'm just sorry Violet heard about it."

"She's hardly likely to be jealous, is she?" her mother scoffed.

"No, but she doesn't need any more tribulation in her young life. First she was raped, then accused of being promiscuous when she turned up with child, then forced to marry the man who attacked her, then mistreated by him in ways we'll never know, and now to have her husband murdered, perhaps by a prostitute."

"It's a shame she's so young and naïve. A more sophisticated woman could rise above these things and make them part of her allure."

"Mother, are you serious?" Sarah said in wonder.

"I certainly am. I've seen it before, but someone as sweet and sensitive as Violet might well sink under the weight of all this."

"In which case, Mrs. Norcross may know exactly what she's doing."

"Let's hope so, dear. Let's hope so."

· · ·

Delmonico's shrimp bisque was delicious, and the men devoted themselves to it for a few minutes. Frank decided to wait for a while and let the good food and wine relax Charlie Quinn before he broached any more questions. It was a good decision. Even Frank was feeling mellow by the time they were halfway through their tender beefsteaks, roasted potatoes, and asparagus spears.

"So, Quinn, I'm wondering if you'd mind telling me about the deal that Hayden Norcross managed to cheat you on," Frank said.

Quinn laid down his knife and fork and cursed roundly. "You sure know how to ruin a good meal, don't you, Malloy?"

"I thought you might enjoy the retelling since you know Norcross is dead," Frank said mildly.

As he'd expected, Quinn grinned. "Norcross hit me in my pocketbook, which hurts a lot, but it does hurt a bit less when I think of him with a bullet in his head."

"Then it was Norcross who brought you in at first."

"Yeah." He glanced at Jack, who was listening with avid interest. "He used to come to one of my gambling hells. He always lost, but then, everybody loses, so that wasn't unusual. Looking back, I wonder if he didn't come because he wanted to get me for a client and didn't mind losing a bit just so he could get to know me."

"Do you make a habit of befriending your customers, Charlie?" Jack asked with amusement.

"Never," Quinn said with equal amusement, "but Norcross thought he was winning me over, I guess. Then one night he told me he was looking for investors into this railroad scheme. It was three small lines merging into one big one, but they needed some cash quick to buy up the land they'd need to lay the extra track to hook them up or something."

"And you trusted him?"

"I asked around first. I'm not a fool," Quinn assured them. "The firm had a good reputation. Old man Norcross had been in business a long time, and it wasn't a lot of money, or at least not more than I was prepared to lose if it all went bad."

"Which it did," Frank said. "But how did Tarleton get involved if Norcross was the one who brought you in?"

"The way Norcross explained it, he was doing Tarleton a favor. Tarleton was new and just a kid, and Norcross was going to throw some business his way by letting him take over this deal. It was a simple one, he said, and he thought the kid could handle it."

"Did you know who Tarleton was?"

Quinn grinned. "You mean did I know he was the old man's bastard? No, not then. Norcross didn't mention it, of course, and neither did Tarleton, and I'd never met the old man, so . . ." He shrugged.

"So you never suspected Norcross might be trying to get Tarleton in trouble," Frank said.

"Not for a minute. Strangely enough, I liked Tarleton a lot better than Norcross. He's a smart boy, which is why I couldn't figure out why everything went wrong."

"How did it go wrong?"

"I'm not sure I really understand it all, to tell the truth, but the way Tarleton explained it, whoever was supposed to use the money we invested to buy the property just disappeared with it instead. They thought he went to South America or somewhere."

"I thought firms like Norcross and Son were supposed to investigate the people they were raising money for, to make sure things like that didn't happen," Frank said.

"That's where it all got so strange. Norcross had supposedly ordered reports on the companies involved, and he was to have given them to Tarleton, but somehow he never got the one bad report."

"Or so he said," Jack guessed.

Quinn shrugged again. "Or so he said, and Norcross insisted he'd given Tarleton all the reports. In fact they found them all in his files."

"But . . . ?" Frank prodded.

"But if you knew both men, you'd be inclined to believe Tarleton, although why would Norcross want to sabotage a deal in his own firm?"

"Did you ever find the answer to that question?" Frank asked.

"It took a little digging, but I finally figured out who Tarleton was, and when the old man let him go from the firm, it all made sense to me. Norcross wanted to get rid of the boy and probably embarrass his father into the bargain. I had to admit, it was pretty clever."

"And it gives Tarleton a good reason to want Hayden Norcross dead," Jack pointed out.

"Yes, it does," Frank said. "But what about the other investors? Are they all as resigned as you are over being cheated?"

Charlie Quinn smiled. "Well, maybe not all of them."

THAT EVENING, GINO CAME BY THE HOUSE AFTER DINNER to find out what Sarah had learned from Mrs. Norcross. Malloy's mother offered to put the children to bed so Maeve could sit with them while they discussed the case. Maeve was obviously a little annoyed at not being able to participate in the investigation, but she was putting on a brave face. She was, after all, officially a nanny and not a private investigator, so she wasn't going to complain, at least not out loud. The really odd thing, though, was the concerned expression on Gino's face when she sat down beside him on the sofa. Usually, he'd be teasing her.

"I could come over on Saturday, and we could take the children to the Central Park Zoo," he said to her.

Her smile wasn't quite as bright as it could have been. "They'd enjoy that."

"Or maybe Malloy and I could take them, and the two of you could go for a drive somewhere," Sarah said. She glanced at Malloy, who was vigorously rubbing a hand over his mouth to hide a grin.

"Let's see what the weather's like," Maeve said without betraying a single thing. "Now, tell us what you both found out today."

Malloy told them about his lunch with Jack Robinson and Charlie Quinn.

"Why doesn't anybody ever take *me* to Delmonico's?" Gino lamented.

"Because they don't take you seriously," Maeve replied.

"The next time a couple of gangsters want to buy me lunch, I'll insist that they invite you, too," Malloy said generously.

"Jack isn't a gangster anymore," Sarah objected.

"You're right," he said. "A gangster and an ex-gangster."

"Did you believe Quinn when he said he didn't mind losing the money, though?" Maeve asked.

"Of course not, but he's a smart man. Murdering somebody over something like that would be dangerous. He's more likely to figure out how to get his money back."

"But you said he thought at least one of the other investors might have been out for blood," Gino reminded him.

"Someone who isn't as sensible or as reasonable as Charlie Quinn."

"I hope you don't intend to ask this person if he killed Hayden Norcross," Sarah said.

"Not directly, no."

"What does that mean?"

"That means Charlie Quinn is going to see what he can find out. In the meantime, what did you and your mother find out from Mrs. Norcross?"

"We were very lucky. Violet happened to be visiting her when we arrived."

"She must be doing better," Maeve said.

"She looked very healthy, I'm happy to say."

"And did you learn anything helpful?" Maeve asked.

"I'm not sure. I did learn that Hayden died in debt, so

Violet will have to sell her house. Mrs. Norcross has offered to take her and the baby in to live with them."

"Wouldn't she want to live with her own parents?" Gino asked.

"You obviously haven't met her parents," Malloy said.

"They forced her to marry Norcross, remember?" Maeve reminded him.

"In all fairness," Sarah felt compelled to say, "they probably thought that was the only way to save Violet from a terrible scandal."

"You're too kind," Maeve decreed. "The man was a brute."

"They couldn't know that, though, and since they didn't believe Violet's story that he forced her, they were only doing what they thought was right."

"Well, I'd never forgive them if they were my parents," Maeve said.

"Fortunately, they aren't," Gino said, "but are Hayden Norcross's parents any better?"

"Violet seems very fond of Greta Norcross. She said Mrs. Norcross has always been very kind to her, and of course she's offering to give Violet and the baby a home."

"Which is the least they should do since their son was so cruel to her and left her with nothing," Maeve said.

No one could argue with that.

"Did you find out anything more about the little girl's death?" Malloy asked.

"Just that it upsets Mrs. Norcross to talk about it, and she apparently doesn't think Hayden had anything to do with it."

"It is hard to believe," Gino said. "He was just a little boy."

"But you should be aware that it's now common knowledge that Hayden was entertaining a female in his office the night he was killed," Sarah said. "Violet actually overheard some women gossiping about it at the funeral."

"I'm surprised it hasn't been in the newspapers, then," Malloy said.

"But how did they find out? I thought Mr. Norcross did everything he could to keep it a secret," Gino said.

"Something that titillating is almost impossible to keep a secret," Sarah said. "The night watchman probably said something to someone, even though he claims he didn't actually see the woman that night."

"Or maybe the other men in the firm just assumed, because Hayden entertained the woman regularly," Malloy said.

"Every Tuesday and Friday, according to her," Gino said.

Maeve gaped at him. "How do you know that?"

Gino gaped right back at her while he was obviously trying to concoct a suitable lie. "I, uh, Mr. Malloy told me."

"He did not," Maeve said, having learned at a very young age to spot a lie. "You talked to that woman. Is she really Chinese?"

"Of course not."

"But she's really a prostitute."

Gino's face was scarlet by now. "I . . . I gave her five dollars, so I assume she is."

Now Maeve was glaring. "You *what*?"

"Just as a bribe, so she'd talk to me," he hastily explained.

Maeve crossed her arms. "All right, you'd better tell me everything you talked to this woman about, every single thing."

Sarah sighed. It was going to be a long evening.

IX

SARAH WAS HAVING A TEA PARTY WITH THE CHILDREN the next morning when Maeve, who had been enjoying a few minutes of solitude while Sarah was entertaining them, came into the nursery to tell her that Violet Norcross was asking to see her.

"Did she say what it's about?" Sarah asked.

"She wouldn't tell me a thing. She just said she needed to see you right away."

"I hope it isn't a problem with the baby. If it is, she shouldn't be out."

"She doesn't look sick at all, just very serious. Go ahead. I'll take your place at the tea party."

"Mama," Catherine protested, and Brian's little fingers flew to echo Catherine's outrage.

"I'm sorry," Sarah said, signing for Brian's benefit. "I

have a visitor, but I'll be back, I promise, and I'll bring some real cookies when I return," she added to placate them. They both were pouting, but at least she had avoided a more dramatic scene.

Their maid, Hattie, had shown Violet into the parlor, and she rose anxiously the moment Sarah entered the room. She wore the same black ensemble she had worn at the funeral, probably because she hadn't had time to enlarge her mourning wardrobe yet.

"I'm sorry to bother you so early," Violet said, "but I couldn't wait to see you." No one paid morning calls in the actual morning, which was why Sarah had been surprised at the visit.

"That's all right. I hope you're feeling well."

"I'm fine." Violet waved away her concerns with one gloved hand. "It's Mr. Norcross."

"Is he ill?"

"He's dead."

"Oh dear. I'm very sorry to hear it. Did he . . . ? Was it an accident?" Sarah asked in confusion. Or perhaps the shock of Hayden's death had caused a heart attack or a stroke.

"It was a murder. Somebody shot him."

Shot him? The same way that Hayden had died. "In his office?"

"No, at his house."

This was more than shocking. Sarah needed a moment to absorb the news. Then she realized they were both still standing and she remembered Violet's delicate condition. "Please sit down. Let me get you some tea or would you prefer something cold?"

"Tea would be fine."

Sarah rang for Hattie and asked for the tea, then got Violet settled on the sofa and sat down beside her. "How did you hear about this?"

"Mother Norcross came to see me first thing this morning. It happened last night, and she didn't want me to hear about it from anyone else." Violet smiled knowingly. "She thought it might be bad for the baby."

"It's nice of her to be so concerned about your welfare," Sarah said tactfully.

Violet's smile didn't waver. "I'm hardly likely to be prostrate with grief over Mr. Norcross, am I?"

Sarah couldn't argue with that. "But it must have been shocking, especially since he was murdered the same way Hayden was."

"I know. It's so very strange."

"What did she tell you? How could he have been shot in his own house?"

"She said someone came to see him late last night. She didn't know who because she was already in bed. They have separate bedrooms, did you know?"

"No." Of course they did, if what Pamela Tarleton had told her was true.

"But she did hear them arguing, apparently, and then she heard the shot. Mother Norcross said she ran downstairs, but whoever it was had already gone."

How brave of Mrs. Norcross to run toward the sound of a gunshot, Sarah mused. "What about the servants? Didn't they see or hear anything?"

"They were in bed, too. I told you, it was late. They also

heard the shot and came running, but nobody saw who did it."

"I see. How terrible. Poor Mrs. Norcross," Sarah said, although she doubted Mrs. Norcross would be mourning her husband too deeply either.

"Yes," Violet said with very little sympathy. "Poor Mrs. Norcross." Then she folded her hands and stared at Sarah expectantly.

But Sarah had no idea what she expected. "Why did you come here to tell me this?"

"Because your husband is investigating Hayden's murder. I thought he'd want to know as soon as possible."

Sarah was certain that he would, but she couldn't help marveling that Violet had thought of that before Sarah had a chance to. What had been her reasoning? "Do you think the same person who killed Hayden also killed his father?"

Violet gave Sarah a pitying look. "A father and son are both murdered in a little over a week, both by being shot. It seems likely the two deaths are connected, doesn't it?"

"It does seem likely, and I'm sure my husband will agree with you. Thank you for bringing this to our attention, Violet. I'm just sorry you will have another death to deal with."

Hattie brought the tea tray in then, and Sarah served Violet and herself. She was happy to note that Hattie had included cookies in her delivery. Sarah could take the extras up to the children.

Violet sipped her tea in silence for a few minutes, and then she said, "Do you have any idea why somebody would want to kill Mr. Norcross?"

"Actually, I was hoping you might have a theory."

Violet smiled sadly. "He wasn't a very nice man, and he did keep a mistress for all those years, but only Mother Norcross would care about that and why would she wait all these years to take her revenge? So, I have no idea why someone would kill him."

"Do you think it could be for the same reason someone killed Hayden?"

"I can think of many reasons someone would want to kill Hayden," Violet said with a frown, "but none of them have anything to do with Mr. Norcross."

"Perhaps it had something to do with their bank, then."

"Perhaps it did. I don't know anything about their bank."

That seemed perfectly reasonable. "Although Mr. Norcross's death might change things, have you given any thought to where you are going to live? I know Mrs. Norcross wanted you to go to them, but with Mr. Norcross dead, perhaps she will make other plans herself."

"I haven't, but I'd be much more likely to live with her now that Mr. Norcross is dead, although my family was furious that I'd even consider it."

"You told them, then?"

Violet's smile was a tad mischievous. "They had invited me to dinner last night. They said they wanted to discuss my future. I had to tell them what Mother Norcross had explained about how I wouldn't have any money and I'd have to sell the house to pay Hayden's debts."

"That can't have pleased them."

"No, especially after my father had given me a generous dowry. He was livid. Both my parents were. They thought Mr. Norcross just wanted to cover up for his wastrel son. By taking me in, he wouldn't have to repay them or give me any money to support myself. Louis, bless him, was more concerned about me. He didn't trust Mr. and Mrs. Norcross to take good care of me, you see, not after their son proved to be so evil."

Sarah couldn't blame Louis, but she also couldn't help remembering what Violet had reported about Bram Norcross's late-night visitor. "Do you think Louis or your father would have confronted Mr. Norcross about the situation?"

"It's too late for that now, isn't it?" she replied, but then she frowned. "Oh, I see. You think one of them might have gone to his house last night."

"I didn't mean to suggest your father or your brother might have killed Mr. Norcross," Sarah lied.

But Violet only shook her head. "I think Louis might have gone to tell Mr. Norcross what he thought of him, but he's much too gentle to ever kill anyone, and my father . . . Well, my father is too much of a coward, I'm afraid."

It was an interesting assessment. For Violet's sake, Sarah hoped she was right.

MALLOY AND GINO CAME STRAIGHT TO THE HOUSE AFter Sarah telephoned the office to give them the news about Bram Norcross. Malloy had picked up a newspaper extra edition that had been hastily produced to report Bram Norcross's murder in his own home, but when they compared the report to the one Violet had given Sarah, they found few similarities. Hastily written newspaper stories often relied more on the reporter's imagination than actual facts. After lunch, Mother Malloy took the children out for a walk while Frank, Sarah, and Gino discussed the best way to proceed. Maeve was uncharacteristically quiet.

"No one is paying you to investigate Bram Norcross's death," Sarah reminded Malloy.

"And we don't know for sure that it's connected in any way to Hayden's," Malloy agreed.

"But how could it not be?" Gino scoffed. "It's times like this I wish we were still working for the police. Then we'd have a right to go in and question everybody at the Norcross house."

"I could do that," Maeve said.

They all looked at her in amazement.

"I could. They'd never suspect me."

Gino didn't actually roll his eyes, but he did give her a rather skeptical frown. "You don't think they'd be suspicious if a young woman showed up on their doorstep and started asking all kinds of questions?"

"Not if I had a good reason for being there. And it's not like I'll be questioning Mrs. Norcross. She already told Violet all that she knew, but servants see everything. They might've been in bed, but somebody heard something or knows something."

"But why would they tell you?"

"Because servants also like to gossip," Maeve said.

No one could argue with that. They'd often questioned the servants to great effect when investigating a murder. "But why would they talk to you?" Gino asked.

"That's just it," Maeve admitted. "I'd need a reason for being there so they'll let me in. Then they'll want to talk about the murder, which is only human nature."

"Is that all?" Gino said with a condescending grin. "Maybe you could tell them you're a newspaper reporter. They'd be only too happy to tell you everything then."

Maeve glared at him, since the last person they'd tell *everything* to was a newspaper reporter. Sarah interrupted her before she could tell him exactly what she thought about his idea, though. "Or you could be another servant."

All three of the others turned to her in surprise.

"They certainly aren't going to speak to a reporter, but Maeve said it herself, servants like to gossip, but only among themselves. Maeve could present herself as a servant looking for a job."

"A household where there's just been a murder wouldn't be hiring new servants," Malloy pointed out gently.

"No, but Maeve won't know about the murder, so they'll have to tell her all about it."

Gino wasn't convinced. "What job could she be applying for?"

"Nanny," Maeve said with great satisfaction.

"But Mrs. Norcross doesn't have any children," Gino pointed out unkindly.

Maeve gave him a pitying look. "She will if Violet moves in with her. It seems I have a friend who works for Violet, and she heard all about the plans. My current job will be ending in the fall when school starts again, so I wanted to get hired before anyone else heard about it."

"Maeve, that's brilliant," Sarah said.

"It is, isn't it, Gino?" Malloy taunted him.

"It's pretty good," Gino admitted with obvious reluctance, "but you still have to convince them to tell you everything they know."

"And Mrs. Malloy will have to watch the children this afternoon," Maeve added.

"This afternoon?" Gino echoed.

"We can't waste time," Maeve said, mimicking Gino's condescending tone. "There's a killer on the loose."

Maeve found the Norcross house easily enough. She'd refused Gino's offer to drive her there. No nanny would arrive in a chauffeured motorcar, she informed him. She'd also changed into her most modest outfit, a rather old black skirt and a simple shirtwaist. A straw boater shielded her face from the summer sun, although she made a point of choosing the shady side of the street whenever possible on her journey.

A couple of men were loitering on the sidewalk in front of the Norcross house, and Maeve decided they were probably reporters. She wasn't going to give them anything to write about. Like a good servant, she went down the alley and knocked on the back door, unobserved by the newsmen.

A plump woman in a stained apron opened the door, probably the cook. She eyed Maeve up and down suspiciously. "What can I do for you, miss?"

"I'm here about the job."

"What job?"

Maeve looked around as if checking for eavesdroppers, then leaned in closer and said softly, "The nanny job."

The cook frowned. "We ain't looking for no nanny."

"Maybe you haven't heard about it yet. I know they haven't advertised, but I wanted to be the first."

"The first what?" the cook asked in confusion.

"The first to apply. You see . . ." She glanced around again. "One of my friends works for Mrs. Norcross, and she's going to need somebody to help her with the baby."

"Mrs. Norcross don't have no baby," the cook said with confidence.

"Not the Mrs. Norcross who lives here. Mrs. *Hayden* Norcross. Her husband just died, and my friend told me she's going to come live here with her baby. It sounded like the perfect place for me, so I wanted to get here before anybody else heard about it. I have a good reference." Maeve reached into her pocket and pulled out an envelope. It really was a good reference, too. She'd written it herself.

"Who is it?" a female voice called from inside.

"Some girl who wants . . ." the cook began, and then glanced around herself, as if checking for reporters. Then she sighed in defeat. "You'd better come in. Can't be talking about this on the doorstep."

Maeve thanked her and scurried inside.

A middle-aged woman in a maid's uniform was sitting at the kitchen table, polishing silver. She looked at Maeve with unabashed curiosity. "You don't look like a reporter."

"Why would I be a reporter?" Maeve asked innocently.

"She says she's a nanny," the cook reported.

"What's she doing here, then?"

"She says Mrs. Hayden is moving in here, and she's going to have a baby."

The maid frowned with obvious skepticism. "How would you know that?"

Maeve smiled, hoping she looked eager. "I have a friend who works for Mrs. Hayden Norcross. Now that her husband is dead, she's going to close up her house and come to live here, so she'll need a nanny to help her with the baby."

"Even if that's true about her coming here, she's not very far along. She won't need a nanny for months," the maid said.

"I've got a job until school starts in the fall, so I can wait." Maeve fanned herself with her letter of reference. "It's awful hot out there."

"Give the poor girl something to drink, Ellie," the maid told the cook.

"I'd be obliged," Maeve said gratefully.

"Take a load off," the cook said, going to fetch a glass from the cupboard.

Maeve pulled out a chair and sat down with a weary sigh. "Why did you ask me if I was a reporter?" she asked the maid as the cook poured her a glass of water.

The two servants exchanged a glance. "We had some trouble here last night," the maid said.

Maeve was suitably alarmed. "What kind of trouble?"

"The master got himself killed," the cook said baldly.

"Killed?" Maeve echoed, appropriately shocked. "How did he get killed? And who killed him?"

"He was shot," the maid said, obviously annoyed that the

cook had already revealed the worst of it. "And we don't know who did it."

"How can a man get shot in his own house and nobody see who did it?"

"We was all in bed," the cook said.

"Didn't the shot wake you up?"

"It did," the maid said. "I sat bolt upright in my bed, I did. Couldn't figure what it was that woke me."

"I knew what it was, all right," the cook claimed. "I woke up everybody else."

"You must've been terrified," Maeve said.

"We was that," the maid agreed.

"I would've crawled under my bed," Maeve said.

"What good would that do?" the cook scoffed. "We all went running downstairs."

Maeve gaped in surprise. "Weren't you afraid of getting shot yourself?"

The two women exchanged another glance. "To tell the truth, I thought he'd done hisself in," the cook said.

"I think we all did," the maid agreed. "He's been awful glum since Mr. Hayden got killed."

"Somebody shot him, too, didn't they?" Maeve said, remembering.

"That's right," said the cook, "but I don't guess we thought of that last night. We all just went running downstairs, or at least the house staff did."

"What other staff do you have?"

The maid didn't bother to hide her smirk, and the cook gave her a friendly cuff on the shoulder.

"There's Kevin," the maid said.

"The groom," the cook added.

"Sleeps out in the mews."

"Most nights," the cook added with a smirk.

Now, wasn't this interesting. "Was he sleeping in the mews last night?"

"As far as we know," the maid said. "He claimed he never heard the gunshot and never even woke up."

"What about Mrs. Norcross? Did she hear it?"

"She did," the maid said. "We come down the back stairs, of course, and she was still on the front stairs, frozen-like, her wrapper only half on."

"She was scared," the cook defended her. "Who wouldn't be?"

"So she started down but stopped," Maeve said. "Probably she realized she might get shot herself."

"No danger of that. Whoever did it was long gone," the maid said.

"Went right out that door," the cook said, nodding to the back door. "Left it hanging open, too."

"How did he get in?"

"We figure Mr. Norcross let him in," the maid said. "At least that's what the coppers decided after we told 'em we always lock the doors before we go to bed."

"I don't suppose they found the gun," Maeve said.

"You'd suppose wrong, girl," the cook said. She had really warmed to her subject. "Whoever it was left the gun laying right on Mr. Norcross's desk."

"Then they just need to figure out who it belonged to, I guess," Maeve said with credible naïveté.

"It belonged to Mr. Norcross," the cook assured her.

"Mrs. Norcross said so when she saw it."

This was even more interesting. "Where was he shot?" Maeve asked.

"In his office," the maid said. "It's the closest room to the kitchen, which I guess is why the killer ran out this way."

Maeve nodded, but that's not what she wanted to know. "I mean where did he get shot? In the chest or . . . ?"

"Right here," the maid said, pointing to her forehead. "I was the only one brave enough to look once we all got downstairs."

"Mrs. Norcross didn't look. She said she couldn't bear to see him," the cook said, "although I would've thought she'd be glad to."

"For shame, Ellie," the maid scolded her, but not sincerely.

So it was true that Mr. and Mrs. Norcross didn't get along. "Did the police talk to you?"

Both women snorted with laughter. "Just to ask us did we see who done it, and when we said we didn't, they sent us about our business."

"But you have an idea who did it, don't you?" Maeve said, eyes wide.

The cook grinned smugly, but the maid just shook her head. "Kevin would never leave the back door hanging open."

"You think the groom did it?" Maeve marveled.

"She's romantic," the maid said, gesturing toward the cook, who frowned. "She thinks Kevin is sweet on the mistress and killed the master so he could have her."

"You're crazy," the cook said. "I don't think no such thing."

"Is the mistress likely to run off with a groom?" Maeve asked.

"Not at all," the maid assured her, "although you don't have to run off when he's right here all the time, now, do you?"

"Don't pay her no mind," the cook said. "She's just jealous. She wants Kevin for herself."

The maid didn't deny it. "He's a looker, all right, but I've got my heart set on a butler."

"Maybe Mrs. Norcross will make Kevin a butler now," Maeve said just to be provocative.

The maid and the cook both laughed at that.

"I said Kevin is sweet on her," the maid said. "I didn't say she's sweet on him, too."

"Do you think she knows, though?" Maeve asked.

"'Course she knows. Any woman would notice how he fusses over her."

Maeve tucked that tidbit away for future consideration. She frowned as if she were distressed. "Now I don't know if I should try for the nanny job or not."

"I'd say you'd best wait awhile," the maid advised.

"Mrs. Norcross won't be thinking about anything else until after the funeral anyway," the cook added.

"And Mrs. Hayden might not want to bring a baby into a house where there's been a murder," Maeve added ominously.

"Can't neither of them get away from murder, can they?" the cook said. "But you're right. Better to wait and see what happens."

MAEVE FOUND GINO AND MR. MALLOY AT THEIR OF-fice. She sighed as she walked through the door and saw her desk sitting empty, her typewriter covered. She hated that typewriter, but she still missed it.

Gino came out to see who their visitor was, and she was gratified by how his face lit up at the sight of her. She was pretty sure her own face lit up as well.

"You're back," was all he had time to say before Mr. Malloy came out of his office as well.

"Did you find out anything?"

"A little."

Gino went off to get her some water and Mr. Malloy escorted her into his office. When Gino returned and Maeve had refreshed herself somewhat, she told them about her visit with the Norcrosses' maid and cook.

"Do they really think this Kevin fellow killed Mr. Norcross because he's in love with Mrs. Norcross?" Gino scoffed.

"I think they were just joking about that, but somebody should talk to him all the same. He sleeps in the mews, so he might've seen something, regardless of what he told the police."

"I can do that," Gino said.

"Good, since I'm going to visit the other unhappy investor who had a reason to kill Hayden Norcross," Mr. Malloy said. "Charlie Quinn telephoned a little while ago and told me he'd arranged it."

"Who is it?" Maeve asked when Gino and Mr. Malloy grinned at each other.

"Remember how Enzo and I went to an opium den the other night?" Gino said.

Maeve scowled at him. She didn't even have to pretend she was still annoyed. "A lot of opium dens, if I remember, and all to find a prostitute who . . . Wait a minute. She's not the investor, is she?" Maeve asked in renewed outrage.

"Not likely," Gino said, still grinning.

"No," Mr. Malloy said, "it's her boss, the Chinese man who owns the opium den."

Since Maeve had warned him about the reporters, Gino managed to slip down the alley behind the Norcross house unnoticed. He found the building behind the house where the horses and carriage were kept and where the groom apparently had his rooms. The pleasant odor of horses and nothing else alerted him to the fact that Kevin kept the stables clean and the animals well tended. The carriage was spotless, but Kevin was still giving it a buffing.

"Good afternoon," Gino said with more enthusiasm than was strictly necessary.

Kevin was a handsome young man in his thirties, tall and blond and impressive in his navy blue uniform. He'd opened the top buttons of the jacket in deference to the heat, giving him a rather rakish air. If Mrs. Norcross returned his affections, Gino guessed he could see why. When Kevin turned to acknowledge Gino's greeting, he didn't look very friendly, though.

"I got nothing to say to any reporters."

Gino's smile widened. "Good thing I'm not a reporter, then. I'm investigating Mr. Norcross's death." Not exactly the truth, but not exactly a lie either.

"I told them other coppers, I didn't hear anything and I didn't see anything."

Gino glanced around, silently judging the distance between the stables and the house. "A sound sleeper, are you?"

"I didn't hear *nothing*," Kevin insisted. He was still buffing the carriage, not giving Gino the courtesy of his undivided attention.

"Then maybe you saw who came to visit earlier."

That at least stopped his buffing. He turned to face Gino. "It was dark."

"Not that dark. It's summertime. It stays light pretty late."

"Not back here, and his visitor didn't come until around ten o'clock."

"You did see him, then."

"I didn't say that. The coppers told me."

"But you heard him."

Kevin sighed. "A visitor would've gone to the front door, and I can't hear that from back here."

"Would Mr. Norcross have let somebody in at that time of night?"

"How should I know?"

"You've worked for these people for a while, haven't you? Was Mr. Norcross in the habit of entertaining visitors late at night?"

"No, he wasn't. Even young Mr. Norcross didn't have people coming to the house at all hours. His mother wouldn't have stood for it."

"Why do you think Mr. Norcross let this visitor in?"

"I don't know. It's not my place to guess either."

"No, I don't suppose it is. But we know the killer ran out the back door." Gino looked around again. "He probably came right by here." He glanced up to where two dormer windows jutted out from the roof. "Is that where you live?"

Kevin was getting irritated. "How many times do I have to tell you? I was asleep. I didn't hear nothing."

"Do you remember the night Mr. Hayden Norcross died?"

Kevin stiffened at the sudden change of subject. "I guess I do."

"Tuesday a week ago, wasn't it?" Gino mused.

"If you say so."

"It's your job to take Mr. and Mrs. Norcross in the carriage, isn't it?"

"I drive them, yes."

"Do you usually drive Mr. Norcross to and from his office?"

"Not unless the weather is bad. Most times he takes a cab or the El."

"Did you drive him to his office the night Mr. Hayden was killed?"

Kevin gaped at Gino for a long moment. "Did I drive Mr. Norcross to his office that night?"

"That's right."

Kevin pursed his lips, as if he was considering his words with great care. "No. I did not drive Mr. Norcross to his office that night, or anyplace else, for that matter."

Gino nodded. "Did he go out anywhere that night on his own?"

"I don't know. He didn't consult me about his appointments. But he went out most nights, so he was probably out that night, too."

How interesting. Did Norcross visit his mistress that often or did he have other interests? "Are the Norcrosses good people to work for?" Gino asked, hoping to catch Kevin off guard with the sudden change of subject.

"What kind of a question is that?"

"I mean, do you get along with them? Do they treat you well?"

"What difference does that make?"

Gino shrugged. "Not much, I guess, but the women who work in the kitchen think you're in love with Mrs. Norcross."

As Gino had expected, this made Kevin furious. The color rose in his face, and he threw down the cloth he'd been using to buff the carriage. "Nosy old biddies!"

"Did you ever meet a female who wasn't?" Gino said, knowing a statement like that would get him in deep trouble with all the women who mattered to him, but he figured it was for a good cause. Besides, they'd never know.

"That's an awful thing to say." Kevin must also know some strong-minded women.

Gino changed tactics. "I guess you have to spend a lot of time with Mrs. Norcross."

"Of course I do," he said defensively. "I take her shopping and I have to carry her packages."

"She's still attractive, too. For her age, I mean."

Plainly, Kevin did not like being reminded of her age. "She's a lady. She's never said a harsh word to me."

"She's lucky to have such a loyal servant."

"We don't call ourselves servants," he informed Gino acidly. "And Mrs. Norcross never treats us like that."

"Sorry. I didn't mean to offend. So I guess you do like working here."

"Mr. Norcross wasn't like his wife, though, and he treated her like dirt."

"What do you mean?"

Kevin glared at Gino for a long moment, as if trying to decide whether to answer him. "He had a woman. A mistress, they call it, but that just makes her sound like she's not a whore when that's exactly what she was."

"And another son, too."

"Mr. Tarleton, yes."

"It wasn't a secret, then."

Kevin gave him a pitying look. "Did you ever see the two of them together? Norcross and Tarleton, I mean? Everybody knew."

"It must have been difficult for Mrs. Norcross. The gossip, that is."

Kevin winced. "She never said anything to me about it."

Mrs. Norcross would hardly be likely to complain about such a thing to her groom, though. "But knowing your husband had another family can't have been pleasant."

Kevin smiled a little at that, a sly grin that told Gino he knew more than he was saying. "Maybe she was glad that he spent most of his time with them. I know I was."

X

CHINATOWN ALWAYS MADE FRANK A LITTLE UNCOM-fortable, which was strange considering it was probably the least troublesome of all the neighborhoods in New York. Not that the Chinese were more law-abiding than other New Yorkers, but they did keep violence to a minimum. That meant the police didn't need to travel in groups for their own safety when they went to Chinatown, as they occasionally did in other parts of the city. Maybe it was that very lack of violence—which the Chinese avoided in order to keep from giving the police a reason to invade their territory—that made Frank uneasy. He knew how to handle violence. What he didn't know was what went on behind closed doors in Chinatown.

For some reason, Frank had expected the opium den to be closed or at least doing very little business at this hour of the afternoon, but people were coming and going freely. He actually had to wait in line in the small entry area to speak with the man who was greeting the arriving customers. The customers weren't exactly what he had expected. They mostly seemed to be female and at least half of them were well dressed and veiled. Frank hadn't exactly doubted the information Sarah had gotten from Cora Lee, but he hadn't quite let himself believe it either.

The Chinese man greeting them was too young to be the same one Gino and Enzo had encountered on Tuesday night. He wore a fancy jacket with elaborate embroidery over a pair of loose pants and satin slippers. He stiffened visibly as he took in Frank from head to toe, probably believing him to be a cop, since he wasn't wearing an expensive suit today.

"I'm Frank Malloy," he said. "I have an appointment with Mr. Young."

The young man didn't relax but he did nod his reluctant acknowledgment and said, "Follow me."

He took Frank through a different door than the one the customers had entered. This door led to a short hallway and up a flight of stairs. The sweet scent of opium faded as they climbed the stairs. The young man stopped outside one of three doors that opened onto the upstairs corridor and knocked. Then he opened it without waiting for a reply.

"Mr. Malloy is here," he said, and stepped back so Frank could enter.

If Frank had been expecting something exotically oriental like the downstairs, he was disappointed. In fact, the office was strangely similar to his own, plainly furnished with a desk and a few wooden chairs for visitors. A window opened onto the rear alley, but little air circulated. Frank could no longer smell the opium. Or maybe he was just used to it by now.

The man behind the desk was also Chinese, although Charlie Quinn had told Frank his name was John Young. The *John* might be an attempt to Americanize his name, but his last name was probably *Yung*. Frank had jumped to conclusions. Mr. Yung said something to Frank's guide in Chinese, and the boy left, closing the door softly behind him.

"Thank you for seeing me, Mr. Yung," Frank said.

"Charlie does not often ask me for favors," Yung said in excellent English. "Please sit down, Mr. Malloy."

Frank chose one of the two straight-backed chairs facing Yung's desk. They were not made for comfort, which probably meant Yung didn't encourage his visitors to linger. "I don't know what Mr. Quinn told you."

"He said you are investigating Hayden Norcross's death."

"I'm sure you were surprised Mr. Quinn asked you to help me, since you both have good reason to be glad Hayden is dead."

"Death was too easy for Mr. Norcross," Yung said with a small smile. "I would have chosen a different fate for him."

Frank nodded his understanding. "I haven't met anyone who is mourning his loss, and I'm not particularly interested in avenging his death either, but my client is concerned he might be accused of the murder, so he'd like the real killer identified."

"I can understand his concern. As you say, I, too, have a good reason to hate Norcross, and I am also Chinese."

He didn't have to explain to Frank that if the police were

just looking to close the case, Yung would be the most logical person to scapegoat because of his race. That would explain his willingness to assist Frank in finding the real killer.

"What I've learned so far about the night that Hayden Norcross was killed is that he entertained a woman in his office."

"Yes, Iris." Yung frowned. "Did you send those two wops to question her?"

Frank almost smiled at the insult. Gino would be interested to know that the Chinese were just as prejudiced against the Italians as everyone else. "One of them is my partner, yes. I'm sorry if they were disruptive."

"Not at all, but Iris did not like it."

"She was rewarded for her trouble," Frank said.

Yung nodded his understanding.

"I have learned that Hayden Norcross used to visit opium dens," Frank continued. "Until someone told his father about it."

"Yes, he used to come here. This is where he met Iris. When his father told him he could not be seen in an opium den any longer, he hired Iris to deliver it to him."

"Did she go alone?"

"I am not a fool, Mr. Malloy. I always send a guard with her. Iris is valuable and Norcross paid for more than her services."

How interesting. "Could I speak to this guard? He might have seen something the night Norcross was killed."

"He says he did not. When Mr. Quinn told me you wanted to speak with me, I asked him what happened that night. Nothing different from all the other nights. Iris goes into the building with opium and comes out with money. No murderer is waiting in the shadows with a gun. No one is shot and no one is killed."

So much for a witness, but Frank wanted to know more about the guard. "Hayden Norcross had a bad reputation with women. Is it possible that Norcross got rough with Iris and the guard had to stop him?"

Yung smiled slightly. "By shooting him, you mean? But Norcross did not *get rough* with Iris, Mr. Malloy. Why do you think Norcross smoked the pipe? As you say, he was full of anger, and sometimes he could not control himself. His father had threatened to disown him. Is that the right word, *disown?*"

"Yes, it is." Poor Bram Norcross must have spent his life threatening to disown his wayward son.

"Someone told Hayden that the pipe would make him not so angry, so he came here to try it."

"Did it work?" Frank thought of Jocelyn and Violet. Opium hadn't kept Norcross from raping them.

"I do not know, but he was calm while he was smoking. And then he had to keep smoking it. Once you start, it is difficult to stop," he added almost apologetically.

"Which is good for your business, I'm sure," Frank said, not bothering to keep the disapproval from his voice. Yung didn't seem to notice or perhaps he just didn't care what Frank thought of him. Frank decided to change the subject. "I heard that you were one of the men Norcross cheated in that railroad deal. Charlie Quinn thought you might be a little angrier at Norcross than he was."

"I was very angry."

"How did you get involved in the first place?"

Frank thought he saw the flash of fury in Yung's dark eyes, but he controlled the rest of his features very well. "I thought it was an honor when he asked if I would like to invest with his bank."

Of course he did. Norcross and Son did business with only the elite citizens of New York. Yung must have been flattered to be invited. "It wasn't an honor, though."

"Men like him—in fact, most white men—think they can cheat us without consequence because we are different."

"And because the police aren't interested in protecting you," Frank offered.

"Only when I pay them," Yung said, not bothering to hide his bitterness.

Naturally, he would have to pay the police not to raid his place, even though selling opium was perfectly legal. Anyone could buy it at the drugstore. But other things went on here, too, things that weren't legal, so Yung would pay just like men of every color who owned brothels or gambling dens. Sadly, he probably paid even more for this protection because he was Chinese. "But they are still willing to falsely accuse you if it suits them," Frank said.

Yung nodded his agreement. "I am not sorry Hayden Norcross is dead, but I do not know who killed him or why. Even if I knew, I do not think it will help me if the police decide to accuse me."

Frank was afraid he was right. He sighed and tried to think of anything else he could learn from Yung. Only one question occurred to him. "Who told Norcross that opium would calm him down?"

Yung smiled at that, the first genuine emotion Frank had seen on his face. "I cannot know because he did not tell me."

"But you have a good idea, don't you?"

"Yes. It is someone I have known for many years. His mother."

GRETA NORCROSS SMOKES OPIUM?" SARAH COULD HARDLY believe it. Malloy had come straight home after visiting the opium den to tell her the news. They were in their private parlor upstairs, where the children could not overhear them.

"So it seems. She's done it for many years, too, at least according to Yung."

"I don't suppose I should be too surprised," Sarah mused. "I've known for a long time that otherwise perfectly respectable women frequent the opium dens."

"I remember one in particular." They'd solved that woman's husband's murder back when Malloy had been a police detective.

"Yes. It's a terrible habit, though, and very difficult to break."

"Which is probably why Greta Norcross is still smoking."

"How would she have started in the first place, though? And why?"

"She did lose a child," Malloy reminded her.

"Yes, I can imagine the pain of that was terrible, but that was well over twenty years ago."

"Maybe she started then and couldn't stop."

"I suppose that could have happened. She might have

started with laudanum and decided she needed something stronger. But she must have regretted her reliance on opium for so many years. How could she not have? So why would she have sent her own son down the same path?"

"You're thinking like a loving mother, Sarah, but is that the way Greta felt about Hayden?"

Sarah frowned. "Oh. I see what you mean."

"And maybe it was like Yung said, she thought it would calm him down, make him less dangerous."

"How long did he say Hayden was using the opium?"

"He said he didn't remember exactly when Hayden started going to his place, but Iris has been delivering it to him for about six months now."

"Longer than six months, then. He raped Jocelyn about nine months ago, but he raped Violet only about four months ago, so whatever Mrs. Norcross had hoped to accomplish with the opium obviously failed miserably."

"So it would appear."

Sarah sighed and laid her head on Malloy's shoulder. He wrapped his arm around her and pulled her close to his side. "Is there any chance that Mr. Yung or even Mr. Quinn really did kill Hayden?"

"I suppose they could be lying, but I don't think Yung did it because no matter how much he might want to, he wouldn't want to risk drawing the police's attention by killing such a prominent citizen. It's hard enough being an immigrant in this city, and when you add being Chinese into the bargain . . ."

He didn't need to explain the amount of prejudice Mr. Yung would have endured or how foolish it would have been for him to murder a wealthy white man. "I don't suppose he had any reason to kill Bram Norcross either."

"No, and it seems unlikely Bram Norcross would have admitted a Chinese man into his house under any circumstances."

"That does seem unlikely, but Charlie Quinn isn't an immigrant," Sarah pointed out.

"No, but Jack seemed convinced he didn't do it, and I trust his judgment. Besides, Charlie is a gangster. Bram wouldn't have admitted him to his house."

"So the killer had to be someone Bram Norcross wouldn't have been frightened of," Sarah said. "And if that's true, it would also explain why Hayden didn't seem to be frightened of him either."

"Strangely, that's the reason Bram thought Hayden must have been killed by a female."

"If only we had a good female suspect. There's the woman who brought him the opium," Sarah said. "What was her name?"

"Iris."

"Hayden might have attacked her and she killed him in self-defense."

"I suggested that to Yung, but he didn't think it was likely. He even sent a guard with Iris, and I thought maybe the guard had killed Hayden to protect her, but the guard apparently didn't even go inside with her."

"If she killed Hayden, she probably wouldn't have told her guard or Mr. Yung, so they wouldn't know anything about it."

"But Hayden didn't have any marks on him to indicate

he'd been in a struggle, and he was peacefully relaxing on his sofa when he died."

Sarah frowned. "Self-defense doesn't sound very likely, does it?"

He shrugged. "No, and I think we already decided his mother wouldn't have shot him. What about his wife, though?"

"Violet? She certainly had good reason to, but could she have done it? She would have had to leave her house late at night and travel to Wall Street alone, get into the building somehow, and find Hayden's gun—which means she also had to know it was there in the first place—while he was lying on the sofa in a drugged stupor."

Malloy sighed. "Then she would have had to coolly shoot him in the head, which is a difficult thing to do even in the heat of passion. Does Violet strike you as the type of woman who could do that?" He wasn't being sarcastic. He genuinely wanted her opinion.

"I don't think many people could do it, but if she was desperate enough . . ."

"Would she have been desperate enough?"

"Facing a lifetime of living with a man who beat her and tormented her and knowing her own family wouldn't help her or even believe her . . ." But Sarah shook her head. "I keep remembering how terrified she was that first time I saw her. She hadn't been out of bed for days."

"It had been days since Hayden was killed, though. Maybe she took to her bed after she killed him because she couldn't live with the guilt."

"Why would she have killed *Bram* Norcross?"

"I don't know, but Bram certainly would have let her in the house."

"Who else would he have let in the house?" Sarah asked. "That's what we're trying to figure out, remember."

"And who wouldn't Hayden have been alarmed to see in his office?"

"Maybe that isn't as important," Sarah said. "If he was groggy from the drug, he might not have realized he was in danger no matter who came in."

"Good point, but it's still something to consider. We also need to ask ourselves who could have had the nerve to shoot two grown men right in the face."

"I hadn't thought of it that way, but you're right. It would take a tremendous amount of nerve."

Malloy grinned. "I wonder how sure Bram would have been that a woman killed Hayden if he'd thought of that."

"Are you saying that a woman wouldn't have the nerve to do it?" Sarah teased him.

He grinned. "If she was angry enough, but what could make a woman that angry?"

"I assure you that many wives have wanted to put a bullet through their husbands' heads at least once in their lives."

Poor Malloy looked horrified. "Really?"

"Well, not *all* wives," she allowed. "But some."

"But they don't actually do it," Malloy quickly responded. "Or very few of them do, so let's think about who else might have wanted to kill Hayden and his father."

"And that person was also someone whom Bram Norcross wouldn't have hesitated to invite in late at night."

"He probably would have let Wendell Tarleton in."

Sarah rolled her eyes. "The good son? I grant you Wendell might have wanted Hayden dead, but surely he wouldn't have killed his father."

"Wendell might have been bitter because the old man fired him for Hayden's mistake."

"Enough to kill him?"

"Who knows? And I suppose you'll say Mrs. Tarleton wouldn't have killed her protector, although she's another female who wouldn't have scared either man."

"All right, I suppose we must consider both of the Tarletons. What about Violet's family?"

Malloy frowned. "I thought Violet's family didn't care how Hayden treated her."

"Her parents did insist that she marry him, but her brother was horrified at the way Hayden treated her."

"Louis seems like a fine lad, but we can't discount him because of that."

"In fact, his good heart makes him even more likely to be outraged at the way Hayden abused Violet."

"I can see that, but why would he kill Bram?"

Sarah frowned again. "I can't think of a reason, unless . . ."

"Unless what?"

"Unless Bram figured out Louis had killed Hayden."

"Ah, Mrs. Malloy, I'm going to have to put you on the payroll."

"About time, too. But I'm not sure that's such a brilliant observation because it could be the reason Bram was killed no matter who the murderer is."

"It does help us narrow down the suspects to people who just wanted Hayden dead, though."

"Unless I'm wrong, and the killer had another reason for killing both father and son."

Malloy gave her a phony scowl. "I'm taking back my offer to put you on the payroll."

"So you expect me to continue working for free?"

"Consider it an act of charity."

"And who is it you want me to question this time?"

"Who do you think would know if Louis was out on the nights the Norcrosses were killed?"

Sarah groaned. "His mother."

"And I'm sure your mother will go with you."

Sarah sighed. "Just don't mention it to my father. What will you do?"

"I'll pay Louis a visit. He works in his father's firm, doesn't he?"

THE ANDRIESSEN FAMILY WAS ONE OF THE OLDEST IN THE city, and they had somehow managed to keep a lot of their money along with their social status, which wasn't always the case with the old families. The next morning, Frank had no trouble finding the office building from which Mr. Andriessen managed the many properties his father and grandfather had acquired, starting when New York City had been little more than a collection of farms and saloons.

A young man sitting at a desk just outside the elevator greeted Frank and frowned when he learned Frank didn't have an appointment with Louis.

"I need to speak with him about his sister, Mrs. Norcross," Frank explained, figuring that was the one thing that would convince Louis to see him. It wasn't even a lie.

The young man left Frank waiting while he threaded his way through the rows of desks behind him, where a dozen men worked at their accounts. Then he disappeared into a private office at the rear of the room. When he returned, Frank was gratified to learn Louis had agreed to see him. The young man took him back.

Louis's office was comfortably but not opulently furnished. The window overlooked the street, however, so a small breath of air was stirring and they were high enough up that you couldn't even smell the horse droppings.

Louis greeted him with a suspicious scowl when Frank introduced himself, but he invited Frank to sit in one of the client chairs.

"What do you know about my sister?" Louis asked.

"I believe you have met my wife, Sarah Malloy."

Louis's expression went from belligerent to frightened in an instant. "Is Violet ill? Is something wrong?"

"No, not at all," Frank hastily assured him. "As far as I know, your sister is just fine. My wife may have mentioned to you that I'm a private investigator, though."

That news did not please him. Louis was back to belligerent again. "No, I don't believe she did."

Frank ignored his attitude. "I've been hired to investigate Hayden Norcross's death."

"I thought the police were doing that."

"My client has little confidence that the police will succeed."

"Who hired you, then?"

"I never reveal the identity of my clients, but I thought you would be interested in helping identify the killer."

"Why should I be?"

"Because Hayden was your brother-in-law."

"And you think I should feel some sort of family loyalty to him because of that? Surely Mrs. Malloy has told you how Norcross mistreated Violet."

"As a matter of fact, she did."

"Then you will understand that I don't care a fig that Hayden is dead."

"Then maybe you should, because you are one of the people who had a good reason to want him dead."

Plainly, Louis hadn't considered this. "But . . . No one would think I killed him."

"Why not?"

"Because . . . I didn't even know he was mistreating Violet until after he was dead."

"Can you prove that?"

"I don't have to prove it."

"You do if the police arrest you."

"They aren't going to arrest me because I didn't do anything." He sounded a bit less confident with every passing minute.

"Of course, if you have an alibi for the night Hayden was killed, nobody will bother you."

"An alibi? What's that?"

"It means that you can prove you were someplace else so you couldn't have killed Hayden. Do you remember where you were that night after, say, ten o'clock?"

"I . . . Home in bed."

"Are you sure?"

The color rose in his face, but he nodded. "Yes. My parents can vouch for me."

"Do they sleep in the same room with you?"

"What? Of course not," he said, outraged.

"Then how can they be sure you were in your bed?"

"I . . . Because they can. And the servants, they'll know."

"Would they know if you had decided to sneak out that night?"

"I didn't sneak out that night or any other night!" he nearly shouted.

Frank raised a hand to calm him. "It's all right. I'm not the police. I can't arrest you for anything, but your alibi isn't very convincing. What about Wednesday night? Where were you then?"

"Wednesday? You mean this past Wednesday?"

"Yes, the night Bram Norcross was murdered."

"You can't think I had anything to do with that. I might have hated Hayden, but I had nothing against Mr. Norcross."

"Didn't you?"

"Of course not. I can see why someone might have wanted to kill Hayden, but Mr. Norcross never hurt anyone."

Frank nodded, although he had no idea if this was true or not. "And I suppose you were in bed asleep on Tuesday night as well, and your parents and the servants will confirm it."

"I . . ." Louis glanced out the window and up at the ceiling and down at his desk before finally meeting Frank's eye again. "I went for a walk that evening."

"A walk?" Frank didn't bother to hide his skepticism.

"Yes, I . . . I had an argument with my father that evening and I went out to clear my head."

"How long did that take?"

"I don't know. I didn't pay attention to the time. I was . . . upset."

"And what did you and your father argue about?"

"I'm sure that's none of your business, and all of this speculation is ridiculous. I haven't done anything and no one can say I did. Now, if you'll excuse me, I have work to do, Mr. Malloy."

Frank briefly considered asking another question, but there was little chance Louis would answer it, and he might very well cause a scene and get Frank thrown out. With a sigh of resignation, he rose from the chair. "Thank you for your assistance, Mr. Andriessen. If you think of anything that might help me identify Hayden's killer, I'd appreciate it if you'd let me know." Frank laid one of his business cards on Louis's desk.

Louis gave him and his business card a murderous glare. "I just happened to think, nobody would care who murdered Hayden Norcross except his father. Is that who your client was, Mr. Malloy? Because if so, he's dead, as you just mentioned. I can't believe he still cares, and he certainly isn't going to pay you."

Frank merely smiled benignly. "It's been a pleasure, Mr. Andriessen."

THE OPIUM USE EXPLAINS SO MUCH ABOUT GRETA," Sarah's mother said as her carriage carried them to the Andriessen home that afternoon.

"What do you mean?"

"She's always been . . . Well, Bram always claimed she was ill. She never entertained, and only occasionally would she attend anything. He gave the impression it was female troubles, so no one ever questioned it, of course. One doesn't like to mention unpleasant things like that."

"No, one doesn't," Sarah agreed. "That was clever of him, if she really is an opium user. I'm surprised no one ever found out, though. I know how your friends love to gossip."

Her mother gave her a disapproving glare that Sarah ignored. Then she sighed in dismay. "I don't suppose anyone ever cared enough about Greta to even gossip about her. She was just . . . not there."

"How sad."

"It is. I'm feeling very guilty now for never having felt even the slightest urge to find out any more about her. Suppose she had been suffering at the hands of a violent husband, the way poor Violet was?"

"She must have been suffering when her little girl died."

"Oh, she was. I just remembered she was very different before that happened. She was a part of our set and we did know her then. I remember calling on her after the funeral. She was devastated, and of course she was in mourning so she stopped socializing, but then she never started again."

"And no one ever noticed?"

"As I said, Bram made excuses for her and . . ." Her mother winced. "I'm afraid it was just simpler not to think about her."

Sarah could see how it could happen, especially when Greta Norcross made it easy because she had her own secrets to hide. "Now I'm concerned because Mrs. Norcross wants Violet to come and live with her."

"I could certainly understand why she would, but Violet should know that Greta uses opium before she makes her decision."

Sarah sighed. "She absolutely should, and I suppose I'm the one who will have to tell her."

"And in the meantime, what is it you want to find out from Isabel?"

"If she knows where Louis was the nights Hayden and Mr. Norcross were killed."

"I can't imagine that she'll appreciate being asked a question like that," her mother said.

"No, which is why we'll have to be very subtle."

"How do you ask a question like that subtly?" her mother marveled.

"I'm not sure yet," Sarah confessed.

It wasn't Isabel Andriessen's "at home" day, but she decided to receive them that afternoon when the maid had presented their calling cards. The Andriessens lived in the house near Gramercy Park where Thomas had been born. The furnishings hadn't been updated since his parents had moved in over fifty years earlier, but the place was far from shabby. The family—or Isabel at least—seemed to have taken great pride in the heritage of the place and replaced the draperies and upholstery and carpets as needed while maintaining its antique style. She received them in the formal parlor.

"I've sent for some lemonade," she said, not bothering to greet them. "Unless you prefer something hot."

Since the day was quite warm, Sarah's mother assured Isabel that lemonade was fine.

"I suppose you're here about Hayden's death, or is it Bram's death this time?" Mrs. Andriessen asked, plainly unhappy about whatever reason they were here.

"I've been concerned about Violet," Sarah said. "I told her to send for me if she needed me, but she hasn't. I hope that means she's doing well."

"Oh yes, let's talk about poor Violet, who is now penniless. Did she tell you? Hayden died in debt, apparently."

"How awful," Sarah's mother said with apparent sincerity. "I suppose she'll have to come home to you now."

Mrs. Andriessen pressed her thin lips so tightly together that they disappeared completely. A moment passed before she could speak. "I would, of course, like nothing better than to have my daughter home again, but Thomas feels very strongly that it is . . . or rather *was* Bram Norcross's responsibility to provide for her and the child since it was Hayden's fault they're left with nothing."

"Hasn't Mrs. Norcross offered Violet a home with her?" Sarah said, hoping she sounded merely curious.

This, for some reason, made Mrs. Andriessen even angrier. "She has indeed. She thinks she can look after Violet and the baby better than I can, I suppose."

"Perhaps she's just trying to make up for Hayden's behavior," Sarah said, earning a wince from her mother. Sometimes she really did speak too plainly.

"I'm sure Greta is appalled at how poorly Hayden treated Violet," her mother said. "But I wonder if she's still as eager to have them now that Bram is . . . gone," she added.

"I have no idea," Mrs. Andriessen said. "Violet hasn't told me a thing about her plans except that the funeral is tomorrow. Two funerals in a week. Can you imagine?"

"It's truly awful," Sarah's mother said. "Poor Greta, it must be horrible for her, especially with her health being so poor."

"Oh yes, her health," Mrs. Andriessen said impatiently. "I told Violet that Greta is probably just looking for someone to nurse her. I can't imagine another reason Greta would be so anxious to have her."

"Perhaps she's still mourning her own daughter, and now she's lost her son, too," Sarah said. "A new baby in the house can be a joyous thing."

"I've never thought so," Mrs. Andriessen said sourly.

"Well, if Violet goes to Greta, at least Hayden's family will support her," her mother said. "Which is only right, after all."

"What is *right* is for Violet to come home to us. I'm sure that's what everyone expects, but we can't also be expected to support her and the child, not after we gave Violet such a generous marriage settlement. Bram should have returned that money to us when Hayden died so we could use it for Violet and the child. That's what Thomas told Bram when he went to see him and—"

Mrs. Andriessen's eyes widened in alarm and she quickly clapped her fingers over her mouth, as if she wanted to catch her words and put them back.

Sarah's mother frowned in confusion, but Sarah had no trouble at all figuring out when Thomas Andriessen might have made his demand. "Did your husband go to see Mr. Norcross on the night he died?"

XI

I . . . I DON'T REMEMBER," MRS. ANDRIESSEN LIED. HER cheeks were scarlet. Too bad Maeve wasn't here. She was somewhat of a connoisseur of bad liars, and she would have enjoyed critiquing Mrs. Andriessen's poor technique.

"That was quite brave of him, I'm sure," Sarah's mother said, pretending not to notice how distressed Mrs. Andriessen was. "And you're correct, Violet should have her marriage portion returned to her, at the very least."

"Did Louis go with your husband to speak to Mr. Norcross?" Sarah asked, pretending she didn't realize how forward that question was.

Now Mrs. Andriessen looked terrified. "Of course not. Why would he?"

"I know he feels very protective of Violet. What does he think about Mrs. Norcross's offer to Violet?"

"He . . . Well, he feels Violet should have her own home." Mrs. Andriessen was overcoming her dismay, probably thinking she'd distracted Sarah and her mother from wondering if her husband had seen Norcross the night he died.

"Does he?" Sarah's mother said with obvious interest. "How interesting. And how modern of him."

Mrs. Andriessen didn't seem to find it either interesting or modern. "Nonsense. Violet is still very young. She wouldn't have the slightest idea of how to manage her own life, much less a child's."

"And yet she was married and presumably running her own household," Sarah said.

"She wasn't even married two months. Who knows how well she was doing? And besides, she has no income of her own now."

"But if Thomas could have convinced Bram to return the marriage portion . . ." Sarah's mother pointed out.

"But he wouldn't even consider it," Mrs. Andriessen informed them.

"That must have made Mr. Andriessen very angry," Sarah said.

Mrs. Andriessen opened her mouth, probably to agree, but thought better of it this time. She drew a calming breath and said, "He was quite unhappy, as you might expect, and after the Norcrosses had practically blackmailed us to get Hayden to marry poor Violet."

How odd. The version Sarah had heard was the other way around.

"I'm sure they wanted to avoid a scandal just as much as

you did," Sarah's mother said. How did she manage to sound so sympathetic?

"Are you sure?" Mrs. Andriessen said. "Men don't suffer from scandals the way women do, do they?"

She was so right about that. "But Mr. Andriessen was able to persuade them, wasn't he?"

"He was then, but now, with Hayden dead . . ." Mrs. Andriessen shook her head.

"How odd that Mr. Norcross refused to help," Sarah said. "Mrs. Norcross was so sure her husband wouldn't leave his only grandchild destitute."

"Did she tell you that?" Mrs. Andriessen asked, outraged.

"She did indeed."

"She misjudged him, then. He told Thomas he wanted nothing to do with Violet's whelp. That's what he called the baby, a whelp."

Sarah's mother was determined to help. "Perhaps he was thinking more about Hayden's part in all this, and not Violet's."

"Violet had no part in it at all. Hayden forced her." Mrs. Andriessen turned to Sarah. "Surely she told you that."

Sarah blinked in surprise. "Yes, she did, but she also told me you didn't believe her."

Mrs. Andriessen waved away such nonsense with a flick of her hand. "What does it matter if we believed her or not? The fact was that Violet didn't stop him, and she was therefore with child. Marrying him was her only choice."

"Perhaps not her only choice," Sarah's mother said softly, and Sarah knew she must be remembering her other daughter, the one who had died because Sarah's parents had tried to force another choice on her.

"It was the only one that would ensure her future," Mrs. Andriessen insisted.

Sarah couldn't help shaking her head. "But marriage to the man who raped her . . ."

"Don't be melodramatic," Mrs. Andriessen said. "Every woman must submit to her husband whether she wants to or not. So what if it happened once before they were married?"

Neither Sarah nor her mother had a response to that.

Sarah needed a moment to gather her wits and remember why she was here. That was the important thing. "Perhaps Mrs. Norcross will be more amenable to returning Violet's dowry now."

"That hardly seems likely if she's determined to force Violet to live with her. She wants that baby for some reason, although I can't think why. She's even older than I am, and babies are difficult even when you're a young woman."

"It doesn't sound as if Mr. Norcross wanted Violet to live with them, though," her mother said.

"I seriously doubt it. I suppose he made that clear when Mr. Andriessen went to see him Wednesday night," Sarah said.

Mrs. Andriessen sighed in exasperation. "Crystal clear. Thomas said that Bram flatly refused to return the money but that we'd have to take Violet in ourselves."

Sarah's mother gasped a little. Sarah wanted to think it was in admiration of her cleverness, but Mrs. Andriessen apparently thought it was in reaction to the heartlessness of Bram Norcross.

"It's difficult to believe, I know," Mrs. Andriessen said. "I suppose it's obvious why Hayden turned out to be such a cad."

"Yes," her mother said weakly. "I suppose it is."

I couldn't believe it," Sarah's mother said in wonder as their carriage pulled away from the Andriessen house. "She never even realized it."

"I know. I was fairly sure after what she'd said that Mr. Andriessen must have been the late visitor Mr. Norcross had the night he died, and now she's confirmed it."

"But how could he have killed Bram?" Her mother looked positively horrified. "They've known each other all their lives."

"People do crazy things in the heat of passion. And now we know he was there and he was angry at Mr. Norcross."

"And they quarreled, the way men do when money is concerned."

"I had the impression that the Andriessens were wealthy, though. Why would Mr. Andriessen have been so upset about Violet's dowry?"

"They do like to give the impression that they're wealthy, and it may well be true," her mother said, "but Thomas is also a bit of a miser."

"A miser?" Sarah echoed with amusement.

"He would have begrudged every penny he paid Hayden Norcross to marry his daughter, whether it was a hardship for him to pay it or not."

"Which is probably why Mrs. Andriessen called it blackmail."

"They probably saw it that way, while the Norcrosses would also have felt ill-used by being threatened with social shunning."

Sarah shook her head in amazement. "Violet is so lucky to have escaped that marriage."

"I suppose she is," her mother said sadly. "But her choices now are to live with a reclusive mother-in-law who uses opium or parents who thought they were saving her by marrying her to her rapist, so she is only a little better off."

"I wonder . . ." Sarah mused.

"What do you wonder?"

"I wonder who gets Bram Norcross's money now that he's dead."

"I have no idea."

"If Mrs. Norcross does, then she may provide for Violet, but if Hayden was his heir . . ."

"Hayden is dead, so he can't inherit anything, can he?" her mother said.

"I believe that if Hayden is the heir, or one of the heirs, then his share would go to his estate."

"What does that mean?"

"It means that Violet or her child would inherit it."

"How nice for Violet."

"Yes, but we still don't know who the real heir is."

"That, my dear, is a very interesting question. I think I will ask your father to find out."

FRANK COULDN'T HELP SMILING WHEN HE LOOKED UP from his desk to see Sarah standing in his office doorway.

"I had Mother drop me here. I knew you'd want to know what we found out from Mrs. Andriessen."

"Come in, sit down." He'd already jumped up and hurried to hold a chair for her. "Do you want something to drink? You look like you could use it."

"I'll get her some water," Gino said. He'd heard them and come over from his office. They got her settled and refreshed.

"How did your visit with Louis go?" she asked when Frank and Gino were both seated and leaning forward eagerly to hear her report.

"All right, I guess," Frank allowed. "He claims he was at home in bed the night Hayden was killed, but he admits he argued with his father on Wednesday night. He said he went for a long walk afterward to cool down."

"Did he say what he and his father argued about?" Sarah asked.

"No, but I gathered it was about Violet. What else could it be?"

"You're right. Mr. Andriessen wanted Mr. Norcross to return Violet's dowry, and he also wanted Violet to come home to live with them so he could control her money. Louis, on the other hand, thought Violet should get the money so she could have her own home."

"Did Mrs. Andriessen tell you that?" he asked, amazed.

"She certainly did. Well, not the part about controlling Violet's money, but it was obviously the only reason they wanted Violet back. She also admitted that Mr. Andriessen went to see Mr. Norcross the night he died, to make his demands."

"She told you that?" Frank marveled.

"She didn't realize it, but yes, she did."

"So Andriessen was already pretty angry before he even got to Norcross's house," Gino said.

"And Mrs. Andriessen also told us that Mr. Norcross refused to return the money but he fully intended to return Violet, so Mr. Andriessen would have been even angrier about that," Sarah said.

Frank sat back in his chair and considered. "That could certainly explain how Norcross got shot."

"Yes, it could," Gino said. "Andriessen was so furious he lost control and shot him."

"But the gun belonged to Norcross. How did Andriessen get it?" Frank asked.

They all considered that for a moment. "Maybe Norcross was feeling nervous and pulled it out of his desk in case Andriessen got violent," Gino said.

"And then what?" Frank asked. "He handed it to Andriessen?"

"Maybe they fought over it," Sarah said.

"But the maid told Maeve that he was sitting peacefully in his chair with a bullet hole in his forehead. How did that happen if they fought over the gun?"

"I think we need to talk to Mr. Andriessen," Gino said. "See what he has to say for himself."

Sarah nodded. "If he killed Mr. Norcross, I'm sure he's being consumed by guilt. My mother said they'd known each other all their lives."

"And if he didn't kill Norcross, he must be terrified somebody will find out he was there that night and blame him anyway," Frank said. "Either way, he'll be easily frightened into telling us what happened." He pulled out his watch. "I think I have time to catch him before he leaves his office today. I wouldn't want him to get home and find out from his wife that Sarah had already been asking questions."

"No, then he'd be on his guard," Gino agreed. "I can go with you."

"I think I need to see him alone, man-to-man. He's more likely to confide in one person than in two, I think."

Gino sighed in disappointment.

"But you and Maeve can come to Mr. Norcross's funeral tomorrow, if you like," Sarah said with false enthusiasm.

Gino winced. "That sounds like great fun, but I promised Maeve we could take the children to the zoo."

"Then you must not break your word," Frank said with a knowing grin.

"Oh, and one other thing," Sarah recalled. "Mother and I are wondering who will inherit Bram Norcross's money. We might be missing someone who had a good reason to want both Hayden and his father out of the way."

Gino and Frank exchanged a sheepish glance. "We didn't even think of that," Frank admitted.

"And money is always a good reason for killing someone," Gino said with a grin.

"Mother is going to ask Father to find out, if he can," Sarah added.

"I'm going to have to put your whole family on the payroll," Frank grumbled. Then he checked his watch again. "And I have a businessman to interrogate."

. . .

THIS VISIT TO THE ANDRIESSENS' OFFICE WENT A LITTLE smoother, although the young man at the front desk was still a bit reluctant to bother Mr. Andriessen if Frank didn't have an appointment.

Fortunately, Andriessen agreed to see him, although his greeting was rather tepid and his handshake moist. But maybe it was just the weather.

"What can I do for you, Mr. Malloy? I thought perhaps Louis would have answered all your questions this morning."

"He told you about my earlier visit, then."

"Yes. He was not pleased. He said Bram Norcross had hired you to find out who killed Hayden. With Bram dead, Louis couldn't understand why you are still bothering people about it, and I'm afraid I can't either."

"My client is still very much alive, Mr. Andriessen, and still very interested in finding out who killed Hayden." Andriessen's eyes narrowed, and Frank noticed they were red-rimmed and bloodshot. He didn't seem to be drunk, so perhaps he was having trouble sleeping. "I understand you had a rather heated argument with Bram Norcross on Wednesday night."

The color drained from his face, and his bloodshot eyes widened in apparent terror. "Who told you that?"

"Does it matter? We both know it's true. The question is, just how heated did the argument get?"

"I didn't kill him, if that's what you're insinuating," he said with hastily gathered outrage.

"Then you won't mind telling me what did happen."

"Why? So you can implicate me?"

"I'm not interested in implicating anyone. I only want to find out what really happened."

Plainly, Andriessen did not believe him. "I don't have to tell you anything."

"No, you don't, but then I'll have to assume you're guilty, and I'll feel obligated to tell that to the police."

The police would be more interested in a bribe than in arresting a man like Andriessen, but maybe Andriessen didn't know that. From the way the color rose back into his pale face, he obviously didn't. Frank breathed a silent sigh of relief. "I was there, but I didn't kill him. He was alive when I left."

"Why don't you tell me what happened?"

"Because it's none of your business."

"No, it isn't, but I know you went there to demand that Norcross return your daughter's dowry."

"Who told you that?" he demanded again, still feigning outrage.

Frank ignored the question. "You demanded the money, but Norcross refused to give you a cent and told you that Violet was now your responsibility."

Andriessen frowned, but he said, "That's not exactly how it went."

"How did it go, then?"

"I'm afraid I was already a little upset when I got there."

"Because of your quarrel with Louis," Frank guessed. "He told me about it," he added to placate Andriessen.

"Yes, well, I wasn't very tactful, I'm afraid, and Bram took offense. He said I'd given that money to Hayden, and it wasn't his fault if Hayden squandered it."

"He had a point," Frank said.

Andriessen scowled. "I reminded him that Violet's child would be his only grandchild, but he seemed unmoved by that, too."

"Maybe he was afraid it would turn out like Hayden," Frank said, earning another scowl.

"We argued some more, but he refused to change his mind, so I left."

"Why did you go out the back door?"

Andriessen frowned in confusion. "I didn't. I went out the front door. I even slammed it, because the servants were all in bed. Bram had let me in himself, and there was nobody to see me out."

Frank frowned back at him. "What time was this?"

"I don't know. Maybe around ten thirty. I didn't actually check my watch," he added sarcastically.

"And you're sure you went out the front door?"

"Of course. Do I look like a scullery maid? Why would I leave through the kitchen?"

Frank couldn't think of a single reason. "Did you know Norcross kept a pistol in his desk?"

"No, I did not. I'm not even sure that he did. Why would he?"

"I don't know, but his wife identified it as his and the killer used it to shoot him."

"That's ridiculous. Bram liked to hunt—the whole family did—but he kept his guns at his country house, and I've never seen him with a pistol."

"Probably because he never had a reason to use it."

"Are you suggesting that he shot himself?"

"Not at all. Someone apparently shot him but with his own pistol."

Andriessen shrugged and rubbed both hands over his face. "This is a nightmare. Ever since we realized there was a child . . . And now you're accusing me of killing Bram."

"And Hayden, too, don't forget," Frank said with a small smile.

Andriessen saw no humor in that. "I wish I really had killed Hayden. That boy caused nothing but trouble. Someone should have shot him years ago."

He was probably right. "When you left the Norcross house that night, you didn't happen to see anyone else?"

"On the street, you mean? I don't know. Maybe a few people, but it was late, so not many."

"But no one who seemed to be waiting around for you to leave?"

"Why would somebody be doing that?"

"Because if you didn't do it, somebody else killed Bram Norcross, and not too long after you left."

Andriessen winced. "I didn't see anything like that, and it wasn't me. I swear it. Bram was one of my oldest friends, even if he was a stubborn son of a . . . Well, I shouldn't speak ill of the dead. But he was alive when I left him."

Even though he didn't want to, Frank believed him.

GINO AND MAEVE WERE ENJOYING EACH OTHER'S COM-pany, even if they were more than well chaperoned by the

Malloy children. Brian and Catherine loved all the animals at the Central Park Zoo and kept darting back and forth between the cages, uncertain which creatures were the most exciting. Gino found Maeve to be the most exciting creature and kept patting her hand where it rested in the crook of his arm.

"I feel so sorry for those poor animals," Maeve said, watching flies buzzing around the head of a sleeping lion.

"They have a pretty easy life here," Gino said.

"Maybe, but how would you like being locked in a cage all day, every day, and having people come and stare at you?"

"I don't know the sign for bear," Catherine called out in dismay.

"I don't either," Maeve called back. "We'll look it up when we get home."

Catherine and Brian were as much objects of curiosity to the strolling crowds as the caged animals were as they chattered back and forth in American Sign Language. Happily, they didn't seem to notice.

"I suppose you're right," Gino said, having never given the zoo animals any thought. "It can't be much fun living in a cage when you're supposed to live in the jungle."

The children had run off to the next cage, and Gino and Maeve followed at a more leisurely pace. "Mrs. Malloy told me about your conversation with the groom. Do you think he's really sweet on Mrs. Norcross?"

"I can't imagine it. She's old enough to be his mother."

"Men marry women young enough to be their daughters all the time."

"Yes, but—"

"Do you think those women don't love their husbands?" Maeve challenged.

Another topic Gino had never given much thought to. "I don't know. Maybe some of them do."

"Then why couldn't a man love a woman who's older?"

"It's possible, I suppose. Kevin isn't exactly a boy himself."

"There you have it. She's probably nice to him, too, especially if he drives her to the opium dens. She'd have to trust him, and the best way to win a person's loyalty is to make the person like you."

"Is that what your grandfather taught you?" he teased. Maeve came from a long line of con artists.

"One of the more important lessons, yes," she said without a trace of embarrassment. "But Mrs. Malloy said you don't think he told you the truth."

"Not the whole truth, at least. He said he didn't hear a thing the night Norcross was killed, but how could that be true? The gunshot woke Mrs. Norcross, who was upstairs, and also the servants, who were sleeping two floors up."

"I thought the groom didn't sleep in the house, though."

"No, he's got a room over the stables, but it's not that far away. He surely heard the shot, even if he was asleep. He also should have heard the killer running away because the shot would've woken him up and we know the killer went out the back door."

"Maybe he's a very sound sleeper," she said with a grin. He loved it when she grinned at him like that.

"Or else he's a liar. Maybe you should go see him. You'd figure him out in a second."

The children were running off to another cage so they

had to hurry along to catch up. Even still, she managed to frown at Gino. "I know you're just being nice to me so I'll kiss you again."

He feigned shock. "Maybe I'm just madly in love with you."

"Of course you are, but you were never nice until I kissed you."

He grinned in delight. "Should I stop being nice?"

"Not if you really want another kiss."

He schooled the delight off his face. "Then I'll keep being nice. In fact, I'm so nice, I'm going to invite you to have Sunday dinner with my family."

To his renewed delight, she stared back at him in abject horror. "At your house? With your whole family?"

"Yes, even Rinaldo and Teo," he said, naming his married brother and his sister-in-law. "They come for Sunday dinner almost every week."

"Did you ask your mother if I could come?"

"It was her idea."

Now she looked terrified. "Why?"

"She wants to thank you for rescuing me." Gino would never admit how wounded his pride would always be that he had needed that rescue, but he would also never complain because it had finally forced Maeve to admit her feelings for him.

"But she hates me."

"What makes you think she hates you?"

"Because I'm not Italian and I'm not Catholic."

"You forgot to mention that you're Irish."

"I'm not Irish."

He looked meaningfully at where her red hair curled out from beneath her hat.

"I'm American," she insisted.

"But if you're Irish, you could also be Catholic."

"What does that mean?"

"You might've been baptized when you were born."

"Is that all it takes to be Catholic?"

"That's how it starts."

Maeve groaned. "I knew kissing you was a mistake."

"Maeve, can we go to the monkey house now?" Catherine called.

"Yes, and then we'll get some ice cream."

Catherine squealed with pleasure and signed the news to Brian, who gave a whoop as the two tore off toward the monkey house.

Gino patted her hand again as they turned to follow the children.

"Maybe you're wrong about that groom," she said.

Gino had to think whom she was talking about. "Kevin, you mean?"

"Yes. Maybe he didn't hear anything because there was nothing to hear."

Sᴀʀᴀʜ's ᴘᴀʀᴇɴᴛs sᴛᴏᴘᴘᴇᴅ ʙʏ ᴛʜᴇ ʜᴏᴜsᴇ ᴛᴏ ᴛᴀᴋᴇ ᴛʜᴇᴍ along to Bram Norcross's funeral in their carriage.

"Your father has some interesting news," her mother informed them when they were on their way again.

"Is this really the time to discuss something like that?" her father protested.

"When you are a private investigator, any time is the right time to discuss clues," her mother informed him.

"You are not a private investigator and neither am I," he replied. "And what do you know about *clues*?"

"More than you do, obviously, if you're going to refuse to share them," she replied tartly.

Malloy had a little coughing fit to cover his laughter, and Sarah pulled out a handkerchief to hide her smile.

"Are you all right, Frank?" her mother asked politely.

He nodded, still not quite able to speak and rubbing the tears from his eyes with a finger and thumb.

"Shall *I* tell them what you found out, then?" her mother asked her father.

He didn't actually roll his eyes, but he might as well have. "Rumor has it that Bram Norcross left half his wealth to Wendell Tarleton."

"Good heavens," Sarah said, and even Malloy looked surprised.

"That's pretty unusual, isn't it?" Malloy asked.

"Let's say it's a very generous bequest for an illegitimate child," her father said. "Particularly when he had a legitimate heir already."

"And what about the other half of his estate?" Sarah asked.

"Split between Greta and Hayden. Greta gets the house, of course."

Sarah glanced at Malloy, who, she could see, was thinking this put Wendell Tarleton back into the picture, although it was possible he had no idea he was to inherit half of his father's fortune.

"But what happens with Hayden dead?" Malloy asked.

"Hayden's estate will inherit, which means the money will go to Violet and her child," her father explained.

"So Violet won't be penniless after all," her mother declared a bit triumphantly.

"Which is nice for Violet, but a bit humiliating for Greta," Sarah said, thinking how awful it would be to learn her husband had provided more for his mistress's son than for her. But then she must have known of Bram Norcross's devotion to his other family.

"Do you suppose she knew about the will?" Sarah's mother asked. "Greta, I mean."

"Whether she did or not, it doesn't give her a motive for killing her husband," Malloy said. "In fact, just the opposite."

"And since we didn't think she killed him in the first place, it probably doesn't matter," Sarah said.

"How does Wendell really feel about his father, though?" her mother asked of no one in particular.

"What do you mean?" Malloy asked.

"I mean, it's obvious that Bram felt a responsibility for Wendell and probably a great deal of affection. He educated him, after all, and brought him into the firm."

"But he fired him when a deal went bad," Malloy said, "even though Hayden was the one who set it all up."

"So Wendell must have been very angry or at least very hurt," her mother said. "Anyone would be, particularly when he was already the illegitimate son and then he was falsely accused and punished for Hayden's mistake."

"But Bram did take him back into the firm after Hayden died," her father said.

"Which probably made it worse," Sarah said. "Mr. Norcross only backed Wendell when his *real* son was dead."

"Does this mean we've solved the case?" her mother asked, her eyes a little too bright.

"Elizabeth," her husband chided, "we're on our way to a funeral."

"I do remember that, Felix."

"Unfortunately, I don't think we've solved anything," Malloy said gently. "But we have a bit more to think about now. I was already going to talk to Wendell again, so this gives me one more thing to discuss with him."

Bram Norcross's funeral was even better attended than Hayden's had been, and they had to wait for a while as their carriage moved through the traffic until they were close enough to the church to get out.

Malloy told Sarah's parents to go ahead and find a seat closer to the front, because he and Sarah would sit in the back where they could see who came and how people behaved.

"You don't really think the real killer is going to confess during the service, do you?" Sarah teased him.

"Wouldn't that be convenient? But no, I just want to see if anybody looks a little too happy."

Nobody looked happy as they filed in and found their seats, particularly the heavily veiled woman who was actually sobbing as she stumbled into the church. The young man with her was doing far more than politely guiding her. Sarah was afraid he might actually be holding her up. He very quickly led her into the empty pew directly in front of Sarah and Malloy. It was only when they were seated that Sarah realized the young man was Wendell Tarleton. The woman beneath the veil must be his mother, which meant that Bram Norcross's mistress had come to publicly mourn him.

XII

Sarah glanced at Malloy and saw he had recognized them, too. Mrs. Tarleton's grief was noisy and probably genuine. Her shoulders were actually shaking as she wept.

"Mother, please, people are staring," Tarleton whispered. He happened to turn his head just a bit and caught sight of the Malloys. He frowned in dismay and slipped an arm protectively around his mother's shoulders.

Mrs. Tarleton drew a shaky breath in a futile effort to regain her composure, but she had already advanced to the hiccuping stage of weeping and seemed unable to calm herself. Fortunately, the organ began to play, making the sounds of her distress less noticeable, although that didn't stop the rest of the mourners from staring and whispering behind their hands. What a delicious piece of gossip. It would undoubtedly be recounted in every gossip column in every newspaper in the city.

Sarah wasn't sure whom she pitied more, Mrs. Norcross for the embarrassment or Mrs. Tarleton for her loss.

Then Mrs. Norcross emerged from the same door at the front of the sanctuary that the family had used at Hayden's funeral, and Sarah decided she didn't pity Mrs. Norcross at all. While she didn't look happy, which would have been totally inappropriate, she did look oddly triumphant. There was no other word to describe her expression. Even more disconcerting was the fact that Violet was with her. Violet also didn't look as if she were grieving much, but her lovely face at least reflected nothing besides concern for her mother-in-law.

The two women sat down in the front pew, and the service began. This time, two of Mr. Norcross's partners eulogized the deceased's good qualities and uncommon business sense. This seemed to upset Mrs. Tarleton all over again, although she managed to weep more quietly than she had when she had first arrived. Even Wendell had to use his handkerchief a time or two.

After what seemed an eternity, the service ended. The congregation rose for the final hymn, although Mrs. Tarleton remained seated, still dabbing at her tears.

They remained standing as the pallbearers carried the coffin out of the church. Did Wendell look wistful? As the dead man's son, he should rightfully have been one of them, but Mrs. Norcross would hardly have chosen him.

Mrs. Norcross and Violet followed, escorted by the minister in the absence of male relatives. Sarah held her breath as they approached. Would Mrs. Norcross know who the

Tarletons were? She had probably never seen Mrs. Tarleton, and besides she was wearing the heavy veil, but did Mrs. Norcross know Wendell?

Apparently, she did, because she actually stopped right in the middle of the aisle. The minister very nearly bumped into her, but she didn't seem to notice. She just stared at Wendell and his mother for a long moment.

"Mother Norcross?" Violet said with obvious concern. Plainly, she didn't know who these people were or their significance to Greta Norcross.

For one horrible moment, Sarah thought Mrs. Norcross might speak. Would she berate this woman for invading her husband's funeral? For daring to show her face and flaunt her shameful existence for all to see?

But she didn't speak. She simply shook her head a bit, as if to clear it, and then moved on, following the coffin.

Sarah let out the breath she had been holding, and when Malloy would have gone after them, she stopped him and indicated he should sit down with her to wait for the crowd to disperse, just as Mrs. Tarleton was doing.

Wendell remained standing, nodding to the people who acknowledged him, although no one stopped to speak, and certainly no one expressed condolences to him for the loss of his father. While most everyone in the church probably knew his history, no one would dare mention it at Bram Norcross's funeral, even if many of them did try to catch a glimpse of his mother as they walked by.

When Sarah's parents passed, her mother gave her a questioning look, but Sarah motioned for them to go ahead.

At long last the church was empty except for the Tarletons and the Malloys. Wendell gave them an impatient look, but Sarah ignored him.

"Mrs. Tarleton? Are you all right? We have a carriage and we would be glad to drop you somewhere," Sarah promised rashly.

Mrs. Tarleton's head came up in surprise, and she half turned in her seat to see who had addressed her. "I might have known you'd be here," she said unsteadily.

Sarah chose not to take offense because then she'd never find out anything useful. "You were very brave to come out today, and I think perhaps you and your son are the only two people truly mourning Mr. Norcross."

Mrs. Tarleton turned farther in her seat and lifted her veil so she could see Sarah more clearly. When she did, she could tell Sarah was completely sincere.

"You are right, Mrs. Malloy. I know his wife wasn't sorry to see him dead. Did you see her? She finally has her revenge."

"Revenge?" Sarah echoed.

"Mother, please," Wendell tried, his expression pained. "We should go."

"Yes, revenge," his mother said as if he hadn't spoken. "She never forgave him for protecting Hayden all those years. That's why she wouldn't divorce him, you know. Not because she was jealous of me, but because he would have left her alone with Hayden."

"Mother, no one cares about this," Wendell tried.

"She was afraid of him," Mrs. Tarleton said with satisfaction.

"Afraid of Mr. Norcross?" Sarah asked in surprise.

"No, of course not. She was afraid of Hayden. After he murdered the little girl. She—"

"Mother, stop it," Wendell said more firmly. "Mrs. Malloy doesn't care anything about all this. Come along now. We need to get you home."

He was wrong, of course. Mrs. Malloy cared very much about all of this.

"Can I help you find a cab?" Malloy offered as Wendell practically yanked his mother to her feet.

"We don't need your help," Wendell said. "Put your veil down, Mother. You don't want people staring."

She lowered her veil and managed to gather her dignity. "He would have married me, but she wouldn't let him go because she was afraid of being left alone with Hayden," she told Sarah before allowing her son to escort her out of the church.

So was the rumor about Susie really true? Because if it was, Mrs. Norcross would have had good reason to be afraid of Hayden. Sarah and Malloy followed them, being careful not to catch up with them. Most of the mourners were waiting on the church steps for their carriages to be brought around, but the Tarletons hurried down the steps and vanished into the crowd.

Sarah had no trouble finding her parents, who had stayed close to the door so they could waylay them. "That was amazing," her mother said when the four of them had closed into a small circle so they could speak without being overheard. "I don't think I've ever seen a man's mistress attend his funeral. Felix, you must never allow that to happen to me."

Her father never even blinked. "If I ever take a mistress, I will make that a firm condition."

Sarah was very much afraid Malloy would have to start coughing again so she was careful not to even glance at him. "Mother, Mrs. Tarleton said something very strange."

"I'm not surprised," her mother said, but before Sarah could say more they heard their name called. Their carriage was ready, so they made their way down the steps and climbed into it.

"I do so hate graveside services," her mother said. "But maybe the mistress will make another appearance."

"I don't think she will," Sarah said.

"She was pretty upset," Malloy added.

"Everyone could hear her sobbing when she came in," her mother said. "I suppose she wanted to make sure Greta knew she was there."

"I think she was genuinely grieving," Sarah said. "She did stay with him for over twenty years."

"Over *twenty-five* years," her mother said. "He took up with her right after little Susie died."

"And that's the strange thing that Mrs. Tarleton said just now in the church. She said that Hayden had *murdered* his sister."

"Murdered?" her mother echoed. "That's an odd word to use. I know he was supposed to have pushed her down the stairs but—"

"She also said that Mrs. Norcross was terrified of Hayden after that."

"And that Mrs. Norcross wouldn't give him a divorce

because he would have left her alone with Hayden," Malloy added.

"She seemed to think Mr. Norcross was protecting Hayden somehow, too," Sarah said. "It's all very confusing."

"It's not difficult to figure out, though," Sarah's father said. "If Greta really thought Hayden had *murdered* his sister, she might well have been afraid of him."

"But he was only a little boy," her mother protested.

"Hayden was a large child, as I recall," her father said. "And how old would he have been then?"

"Only about ten," her mother said.

"I've arrested children that young," Malloy said. "They can be pretty dangerous."

Her father gave her mother a nod that fell just short of triumphant. "And no one said her fears would have to be rational."

"Oh, I see," her mother said. "If she was afraid her son might murder her in her sleep, whether her fears were justified or not, she would naturally not want her husband to leave her alone with the boy and go off to live with another woman."

Plainly, her father thought this explanation had been unnecessarily explicit, but he soldiered on. "I would imagine that Bram did find her fears to be irrational, so naturally, he would have defended the boy."

"A boy who had murdered his sister?" her mother asked with a touch of outrage.

"We have no proof that the boy did any such thing," her father argued. "And Hayden was his son, after all."

"And boys will be boys," her mother said, rolling her eyes.

"But we're hardly talking about a youthful indiscretion," Sarah reminded them.

"So I'm going to see if I can learn anything else about little Susie's death," her mother said. "I suppose you'll be questioning Wendell Tarleton again, Frank."

"But not at the repast, even if he shows his face, which I doubt he will," Malloy said. "I also don't think any of our other suspects will even talk to me now, especially not at Bram Norcross's house."

"Maybe you can look around, though," Sarah suggested. "You haven't had a chance to see the room where the murder took place, have you?"

"No, so that might be helpful."

"Who will you talk to, Sarah?" her mother asked.

"I guess I'll have to see who is there."

"And I will mind my own business," her father said.

Her mother gave him a pitying look and patted his hand. "That sounds terribly boring, dear."

THIS TIME FRANK AND SARAH DID MAKE A POINT OF GIV-ing Mrs. Norcross their condolences. Violet was standing with her in the parlor, dutifully fulfilling her obligation as the daughter-in-law and the only surviving member of Mrs. Norcross's family.

"Violet looks well," Sarah whispered to Frank as they waited their turn in the receiving line.

"So does Greta Norcross," Frank said. She actually looked better than good, if the truth was told. Frank couldn't help wondering if she'd had to smoke an opium pipe this morning to prepare for this trying day. Funerals were exhausting, even if you didn't care a fig about the dead person.

Mr. and Mrs. Decker were ahead of them in the line, and they said all the right things, of course. Mrs. Norcross responded with just the correct amount of gratitude and Violet was her sweet self, thanking them for coming. Then Mrs. Norcross saw Frank and Sarah and her expression hardened into icy formality.

"Mrs. Malloy," she said. "And this must be your husband, the private investigator." She made the words *private investigator* sound somehow illicit, but Sarah never flinched, he was happy to note.

"Yes," Sarah said. "We're so very sorry."

"Are you?" It sounded like a challenge. "But perhaps you are. With Bram dead, there is no one to pay you to continue investigating Hayden's death, Mr. Malloy."

Frank blinked in surprise. Did she honestly believe her husband had hired him? Apparently, she did. He could deny it, of course, but why bother? "It must be very difficult holding two funerals so close together," he said instead.

"It is devastating. I hope you never have to experience it," Mrs. Norcross said, although she looked far from devastated. "You know my daughter-in-law, of course."

"Mrs. Malloy, it's so nice to see you," Violet said, taking Sarah's hand.

"How are you feeling?" Sarah asked.

"I'm very well, thank you, and I've decided to come live with Mother Norcross," she said with just a trace of defensiveness. "I can't leave her here alone now, can I?"

That sounded like something Mrs. Norcross might have

said to convince Violet, and Frank thought perhaps Violet's question—"can I?"—sounded like a sincere request for an opinion. Sarah could hardly give her true opinion in front of Greta Norcross, though. Instead she said, "I'm sure you'll make the right decision."

Did Violet look disappointed? Frank was pretty sure Sarah would find an opportunity to speak with her privately, though. Indeed, when they had stepped away to allow the next mourners in line to speak with the Norcross ladies, Sarah said, "You go ahead and look around. I'm going to try to catch Violet alone after she's done greeting people."

"Good. Did you notice, Mrs. Norcross thinks it was her husband who hired me."

"Yes, she mentioned that the day Mother and I went to visit her. I didn't bother to correct her since I shouldn't even know who your client is, and I assumed she'd confront her husband about it if she really cared. He would certainly have set her straight."

"Except he didn't."

She had no answer for that, so Frank wandered off, glancing at the mourners gathered in small groups to see if he knew anyone. He did see Louis Andriessen and then his father, but both men made a concerted effort to avoid making eye contact, so Frank figured they wouldn't welcome his approach. Charlie Quinn had no reason to attend this funeral, so he would not be available either. With nothing to stop him, he wandered down the hallway until he found Bram Norcross's study.

The door was closed, of course, probably to discourage

people from gawking at the scene of Norcross's murder, but Frank wasn't interested in gawking. He slipped into the room and shut the door behind him. Frank had seen many rooms like this, variously labeled as a study, an office, or a library, but they all were pretty much the same, a room where a man could retire, alone or with friends, to escape the rest of his family and enjoy some peace and quiet.

The room did have a desk, but it wasn't sitting in the middle of the floor and facing the door, as Frank had pictured. Instead, it was a rolltop desk placed against the left-hand wall. Hadn't Maeve said Norcross was found sitting at his desk with a bullet hole in his forehead? How could that have happened if he was working at this desk? He would have had to turn in his chair to face his killer.

The desk had no chair, and Frank didn't see one that would go with the desk anywhere else in the room. If Norcross had indeed been sitting at his desk, his blood and other parts of his head would have ruined the chair. That probably explained its absence.

Frank studied the rest of the room. Two comfortable-looking leather chairs sat in front of the cold fireplace with a table between them. This would be a perfect place for two friends to sit and chat while they enjoyed a drink and a smoke. A credenza on one side of the fireplace held several decanters of liquor. Bookcases filled the rest of the wall space, and the window, opposite the door, looked out on the tiny yard between this house and the one next door.

Frank tried to imagine the events of Bram Norcross's last night on earth. His old friend Thomas Andriessen had come to see him. He'd knocked on the front door, and

Bram had answered it, since the servants were in bed.
Would Norcross have sat at his desk after his visitor arrived,
leaving Andriessen to stand and berate him?

But no. Andriessen might have been angry when he arrived, after his argument with Louis, but Norcross wouldn't
have been angry yet. He would have welcomed his friend,
probably even tried to calm him down so they could discuss
their situation rationally. They would have sat in the comfortable chairs. Norcross would have poured them each a
drink. Eventually, they would have argued and both become angry, and Andriessen would have stormed out.

Andriessen wouldn't have gone out the back door either,
just like he had said. Men like Andriessen never went into
a kitchen, not even their own kitchens. He would have
come and gone through the front door, the way men of his
station in life always did, even if he had to open the door
himself to leave.

And then what? Norcross might have followed, making
sure the door was locked behind his visitor. Then he would
have returned to his study. Norcross might have been working at his desk when Andriessen arrived, so he went back to
his desk. He was sitting there when his killer came in.

Frank looked around again and pictured the scene in his
mind.

Now, wasn't that interesting?

SARAH MANAGED TO DRIFT AROUND THE VARIOUS ROOMS
without being trapped into a conversation so she would be
free to seek out Violet when Violet had finally finished

greeting the mourners. Sarah was careful to stay out of sight until Mrs. Norcross had left Violet's side. Mrs. Norcross said something to Violet and then made her way up the grand staircase, probably to visit the bathroom.

Sarah waited until Mrs. Norcross was gone before approaching Violet. Oddly, Violet didn't even seem to notice. She was still staring after Mrs. Norcross, who had vanished down the second-floor hallway. Violet was so transfixed, she seemed completely unaware of Sarah's presence.

"Violet?" Sarah said softly so as not to startle her.

Violet started anyway, and then she actually shuddered. When she finally turned to Sarah, her eyes were wide with terror and she hardly seemed to recognize Sarah.

"Is something wrong?" Sarah asked.

Violet drew a shaky breath. "No, I just . . ." Her gaze went back to the stairs, or at least that was what Sarah thought at first. The stairs swept up to the second floor and then to the third. The foyer reached all the way up to the third story, and the corridors on each floor were open to the foyer below. When Sarah followed Violet's gaze, however, she could see Violet was actually looking at the railing that ran along the third-floor corridor above. "That's where he threw her down."

"Who? What are you talking about?"

"Hayden," Violet said, her face chalk white. "He threw his little sister over the railing."

Sarah gasped, but she slipped a comforting arm around her. "Come along. You need to sit down." Sarah led her back into the parlor, to the same corner where she had spoken quietly with Mrs. Norcross at Hayden's funeral.

Sarah got her safely seated and pulled up a chair beside her. "Who told you such a horrible thing?" she asked when she was sure no one was listening.

"Hayden did," Violet said, her eyes still filled with terror. "He bragged about it. She annoyed him, he said. She followed him around, and he got tired of her, so he threw her over the railing and her head broke open like a—"

"Stop," Sarah cried in an urgent whisper. "You don't have to think about it anymore."

Violet didn't seem to hear. She was staring at something far away, something Sarah couldn't see. "He said I annoyed him, too. He said if I didn't stop, he'd throw me over the railing, and no one would care, just like they didn't care about his sister."

"Violet," Sarah said sharply, taking the girl's hands in hers and squeezing them. They were like ice. "Violet, look at me."

She did, finally, and this time she seemed to actually see Sarah.

"Hayden is dead," Sarah said firmly. "He can never hurt you again."

Violet drew an unsteady breath. "I know. It's foolish to still be frightened, but when I saw the staircase just now, it brought it all rushing back. He played so many tricks on me that I can't seem to believe he's really gone."

"Do you think it will be difficult living here, then?" Sarah asked as diplomatically as she could.

"I . . . Mother Norcross said I will get over it. As you say, Hayden is dead and can't hurt anyone now."

"You don't have to decide anything today, do you? I

mean, surely you can take a week or two to think about it. So much has happened and in your condition . . ."

Violet smiled sadly. "Yes, so much has happened. Sometimes I think I'll shatter into a million pieces, but Mother Norcross has been very kind. She said she'll take care of me and the baby, and I'll never have to worry about anything ever again."

How wonderful that must sound to a girl who had been through all that Violet had endured these past months. She certainly hadn't heard those assurances from her own mother.

"There are some things you need to know about Mrs. Norcross before you decide," Sarah said.

"There you are, Violet," a strident voice said, and they looked up to see Violet's mother bearing down on them. Her mouth was smiling, but her eyes were glaring at Sarah. Plainly, she did not appreciate Sarah monopolizing her daughter. "You must come and get something to eat. We can't have you fainting, can we?"

Sarah tried a placating smile in return. "Violet was feeling a bit shaky after greeting all the guests, so I thought she should sit down for a while."

"That was very thoughtful of you, I'm sure, but I'm here now, and I'll make sure she's looked after. Come along, Violet."

"Thank you, Mrs. Malloy," Violet managed before her mother hustled her away.

Sarah cursed Mrs. Andriessen silently. Between Mrs. Andriessen and Mrs. Norcross, Sarah would never get close to Violet again today. She'd have to call on her at her home so they could speak privately and Sarah could warn her about Mrs. Norcross's opium use. Violet might still feel obligated to move here, but at least she would know the truth.

And now Sarah had to tell Malloy what she had learned about Hayden Norcross, even if it did give poor Violet a motive for killing him.

I DIDN'T LEARN A SINGLE NEW THING," SARAH'S MOTHER reported when they were on their way home in the Deckers' carriage.

Frank thought she sounded far more disappointed than was proper. "I hope you had better luck, Sarah."

Sarah gave him a sidelong glance that told him the answer was yes, but she said, "I learned that Violet has decided to live with Mrs. Norcross."

"How odd, but then she may not know she inherited some money from Bram," her mother said.

"I believe the lawyers notified the family members," her father said, "but Violet may not have read the letter. Young ladies are typically not in the habit of attending to things like that, and she doesn't have a man looking out for her interests at the moment."

Frank figured Sarah would be annoyed by that, even though her father was right. "Did she say anything to you about the inheritance?"

"No, but we didn't have very long together before her mother came barreling down on us and swept Violet away. I'm going to have to visit her, I guess, and hope I catch her home alone."

"What about you, Frank?" Mr. Decker asked. "Did you learn anything?"

"No one would talk to me because they all know I'm investigating now, but I did get a look at Norcross's office."

"I can't believe Greta didn't have that room locked," Mrs. Decker said with a delicate shiver. "How ghoulish to leave it open where anyone might walk in."

"They'd cleaned up the blood, if that's what you're worried about," he assured her with a small smile, although he had a feeling Mrs. Decker wouldn't mind seeing a little blood.

"Did you learn anything?" Sarah asked him.

"I have a better understanding of how the murder happened," he said, trying to be vague.

"And how did it happen?" Mrs. Decker asked with interest.

"Elizabeth, really," her husband chided her. She ignored him.

"I was mostly interested in how the killer got into the house and back out again," Frank said, hoping that sounded boring enough that she would lose interest.

He had underestimated her. "And how did he get in and out again?"

"Mr. Andriessen said Norcross let him in through the front door."

"Did Thomas kill him?" Mr. Decker exclaimed in understandable surprise.

"We don't think so, Father," Sarah assured him.

"But he did admit he visited Norcross that night. They

argued over who was going to support Violet and her baby," Frank said.

"And poor Bram ended up doing it anyway," her mother remarked.

No one had any reply to that.

"If Thomas didn't do it, how did the real killer get into the house?" Mr. Decker finally asked.

Frank sighed. "That's something we may never know unless the killer tells us."

THE CHILDREN HAD BEEN WAITING TO TELL THEIR PARents all about their trip to the zoo with Gino and Maeve, so Sarah and Malloy were immediately distracted by Catherine describing their adventures while Brian signed furiously.

"We had to look up the signs for some of the animals when we got home," Catherine said, outraged. "I don't think that school of Brian's teaches him enough words."

"Maybe they don't think he'll be encountering many bears in New York City," Malloy said quite solemnly.

"Or lions either," Sarah added.

Catherine stared back at them in amazement. "But we did!"

They had to agree, and they all had to learn the signs for the various animals right away.

Because of this, they had no opportunity to discuss their findings from the funeral until after they'd finished supper. Mother Malloy offered to take the children up for their baths so Maeve could sit in on the discussion. Gino had, of course, stayed for supper so he could hear their report as well.

"How horrible," Maeve said when Sarah had told them how Hayden Norcross had threatened Violet.

"She must have been terrified of him," Malloy said.

"I knew she was, of course, but I thought it was only because he'd beaten her," Sarah said. "You should have seen her face when she was standing in the hallway. Even knowing Hayden was dead, the sight of that staircase horrified her."

"I can't believe she'd agree to live there, then," Maeve said.

"She may not believe she has any choice. We don't think she knows about the inheritance yet, so I'm going to have to call on her and tell her about it and about Mrs. Norcross using opium."

"Hopefully, that will give her the courage to refuse Mrs. Norcross's offer," Maeve said.

"Unfortunately, I'm afraid her fear of Hayden gives her a good reason for wanting him dead, but I still can't imagine her having the courage to shoot him right in the face," Sarah said.

"And why would she kill Mr. Norcross?" Gino asked. "That doesn't make any sense at all."

"No, it doesn't," Malloy said ominously.

They all turned to him expectantly. "I knew you'd figured something out," Sarah said.

"I did, but I didn't want to say anything in front of your parents."

"In front of my mother, you mean." She turned to Maeve and Gino, who were sitting beside each other on the love seat. "My mother is a bit too enthusiastic about solving this case."

"We should hire her at the agency," Gino told Malloy with a twinkle. "Think of all the people she could talk to that we can't."

Malloy gave him the glare that had intimidated a thousand hardened criminals, but it just made Gino laugh.

"So tell us," Maeve said impatiently. "What did you find out?"

"Nothing really, because nobody would talk to me at the repast, but I did explore the room where Norcross was killed, and I realized something very important. Maeve, tell me again what the servants said about how Norcross was found."

Maeve frowned as she tried to recall. "They said the sound of the gunshot woke them up, and they went running downstairs. One of the maids looked in the room and saw Mr. Norcross sitting at his desk. He'd been shot in the forehead."

"Where was Mrs. Norcross?"

"She was on the front stairs. The servants came down the back stairs, of course."

"What was she doing on the front stairs?"

Maeve frowned again. "She'd apparently come down after hearing the shot, just like they did. I think they said she was just standing there, as if she was too terrified to go any farther."

"Was the front door locked?"

Maeve considered. "They didn't mention that, and I didn't think to ask, because they said the back door was not only unlocked but open, like someone had run out and not taken the time to pull the door closed behind them."

"Presumably the killer," Gino said.

"That's what they thought," Maeve said, nodding.

"And what did the groom tell you, Gino?"

"He said he didn't hear anything, but I didn't believe him." He exchanged a glance with Maeve. "He must've at least heard the shot."

"And you said the killer had to have run right under his window."

"Yes, but he claimed he didn't hear that either."

"What are you thinking?" Sarah asked Malloy.

"We know Andriessen went to see Norcross that night. He claimed that Norcross let him in the front door and that they argued. I didn't think to ask him where they met, but that probably doesn't matter if Andriessen didn't kill him. Then he claimed he let himself out by the front door because he's not a scullery maid and why would he use the back door?"

"That's true," Sarah said. "I can't imagine my father using the kitchen door unless the house was on fire, and even then . . ."

"But the killer used the back door," Maeve said knowingly. "Why would he do that?"

"Maybe," Malloy said, "because it was closer to his home."

XIII

I KNEW IT!" MAEVE CRIED, GIVING GINO A LOOK THAT clearly said, *I told you so!* "Didn't I say that the groom didn't hear anything because there wasn't anything to hear?"

"Because he is the killer, so he couldn't hear himself running away," Gino said just as triumphantly as Maeve had.

"Let's not get ahead of ourselves," Malloy cautioned, "but I really am starting to think the killer was already in the house or at least didn't need to knock on the door to get inside."

"What makes you so sure?" Sarah asked, thinking she'd also figured it out but wanting to hear his reasoning.

"I had pictured Norcross sitting at his desk, facing the door, when the killer comes in and shoots him, or maybe the killer was sitting in a chair on the other side of the desk, talking to Norcross, but the desk sits against the wall. Norcross would have had to turn in his chair in order for the killer to shoot him straight on."

"Wouldn't that be a normal reaction to someone coming into the room, though?" Sarah asked. "He would have turned to see who it was, at least."

"Yes, except he had to answer the door when Andriessen called, because the servants were in bed, so why didn't he have to answer the door when the killer called?"

"Because the killer came in the back door," Maeve said, "and he probably even has a key."

"And he surprised Mr. Norcross, who was sitting at his desk," Gino said.

"Why would the groom kill Norcross, though?" Malloy asked, sitting back to enjoy their analysis.

"Because he's in love with Mrs. Norcross," Maeve said. "The servants made that pretty clear to me."

"But murdering your rival only makes sense if it wins you the woman you love," Sarah reminded them.

"You're right, Mrs. Norcross is never going to marry a groom," Maeve said, "so maybe he had another reason. Maybe he was sick of seeing Mr. Norcross abuse his wife."

"Do we think he abused her?" Sarah asked. "Besides having a mistress, we haven't heard anything about abuse. And why would the groom have killed Hayden?"

"Maybe Mrs. Norcross asked him to," Maeve said.

"Why would she do that?" Malloy asked.

"Because Violet told her that Hayden had threatened her life," Gino said.

Nobody disagreed with him.

"I think we need to ask a few more questions," Malloy said.

"But who should we be asking?" Maeve asked with a frown.

Malloy turned to Sarah, who said, "The Tarletons."

Everyone gaped at her. "Why the Tarletons?" Malloy asked.

Sarah sighed in exasperation. "Because they know a lot of family secrets, and they're probably the only ones who will actually tell them to us."

"Why do you think so?" Maeve asked.

"Because Mrs. Tarleton said some strange things at the funeral that Violet later confirmed. I didn't have an opportunity to ask Mrs. Tarleton any questions, but I think she might tell us more if we give her an opportunity."

"But she didn't tell us more because Wendell cut her off and made her leave," Malloy reminded her. "He still might not let her tell us."

"But Wendell knows things he's not telling, too. They are our only chance of finding out, so that's where we're going tomorrow."

"It's Sunday, so we'll have to wait until after church," Malloy said.

Maeve groaned and Gino grinned in delight.

"What?" Sarah demanded. "What's going on?"

"I'm afraid *we* can't question anyone tomorrow," Gino said. "Maeve is coming to Sunday dinner with my family tomorrow."

"That's . . . interesting," Sarah said, exchanging a glance

with Malloy, who was obviously thinking this marked a new phase in Gino and Maeve's relationship.

"Mrs. Donatelli just wants to thank me for rescuing Gino," Maeve hastily explained.

"Is that all?" Sarah asked, unconvinced.

"Of course that's all," Maeve said.

"Will Teo and Rinaldo be there?" Sarah asked.

"Everyone will be there," Gino reported gleefully, making Maeve groan again.

Sarah couldn't seem to stop smiling. "Please send them my regards. At least you'll have a friend in Teo."

"And all my brothers love her," Gino said, grinning.

Maeve was not grinning at all. "That will be a great comfort when your mother poisons me."

Poor Maeve," Sarah said the next afternoon as they made their way down Bank Street to find a cab.

Frank shook his head. "I couldn't believe she went to Mass with my mother and Brian this morning. Was she praying for her immortal soul or something?"

Sarah laughed, as he had intended her to do. "Gino's family is Catholic. I think she was trying it out."

"Is she going to convert?" he asked in amazement.

"Malloy, they aren't even engaged yet," Sarah chastened him. "But Maeve confided in me that she might actually have been baptized Catholic. She doesn't really know."

Frank shook his head. He hadn't been to church since his first wife had died in childbirth, so it was hard for him to remember how important religion was to many people. "You didn't convert when we got married."

"Because I'm a rebellious heathen, but I did get married in the church, so your mother wouldn't always believe we were living in sin."

"And I will forever be grateful to you for that, but Maeve doesn't have to worry about what my mother thinks."

"She does have to worry about what Gino's mother thinks, though. Italian mothers are just as difficult as Irish mothers."

"That's hard to believe, but I'll take your word for it. Now, what will we do if the Tarletons won't talk to us?"

"I think Mrs. Tarleton is dying to talk to someone. I know she was nearly hysterical at the funeral yesterday, but she wanted me to understand that she really cared for Mr. Norcross and he really cared for her. I think she'll welcome a sympathetic ear."

Frank sighed. "I don't think Wendell is looking for any kind of an ear. He's going to keep us from talking to his mother at all if he can."

"Then you'll have to mention that we know he inherited half of Mr. Norcross's fortune, which gives him an excellent motive for killing his father."

"Do you think that will frighten him enough to make him cooperate?"

"It will give him something to think about, at least, and of course he had no love for Hayden after what he did to get Wendell fired from the firm, so he had an excellent reason for killing him, too."

"Do you suppose he's got a key to the Norcross house?" Frank teased. "Because that's the only thing missing to convince me he killed them both."

"Let's be sure to ask him," Sarah said with a grin.

Wendell Tarleton answered their knock in his shirtsleeves. In about two seconds his expression went from mildly puzzled over who might be calling on a Sunday afternoon to furious at seeing the Malloys. "What do you want?"

"We'd like to speak to you and your mother about Bram Norcross's death," Sarah said. They had decided she should do the talking since she was far less threatening than Frank. He bit his tongue while they waited for Wendell's reply.

Wendell seemed unmoved. "My mother isn't feeling well."

"I'm very sorry to hear that," Sarah said with genuine concern. "I'm a nurse. I would be happy to examine her to make sure it's nothing serious." Frank never ceased to be amazed at how clever she was.

Wendell's chagrin was almost comical. "I . . . I don't think that will be necessary."

"But if she's ill . . ." Sarah said with a worried frown.

"Who is it, Wendell?" his mother called.

Sarah gazed up at Wendell expectantly, and although he hesitated and actually winced, he begrudgingly said, "Mr. and Mrs. Malloy."

"We've come to offer our condolences, Mrs. Tarleton," Sarah called.

Mrs. Tarleton appeared from around a corner, her face drawn but smiling. "How very nice of you. For heaven's sake, Wendell, let them in."

Wendell sighed in defeat but stepped aside to allow them to enter.

"Please come in," Mrs. Tarleton said. She was still dressed for church, so she couldn't be so very unwell. She showed them into the parlor, the room where Sarah had met with her before. Newspapers were scattered around, and Mrs. Tarleton snatched them up into a haphazard stack in an attempt at restoring order. "We were just reading the reports of Bram's funeral."

Which would have included mention of Mrs. Tarleton's attendance, at least in the gossip columns, Frank was sure.

Mrs. Tarleton invited them to sit down on the sofa and instructed Wendell to order some refreshments sent up from the restaurant downstairs. Sarah didn't protest, so probably this was her way of ensuring they could have a nice long visit with the Tarletons. Wendell plainly hated doing so, but he went out to the hallway to telephone downstairs.

"We're so very sorry about Mr. Norcross," Sarah said, echoing what she had said at the church that had inspired Mrs. Tarleton's outburst.

"It's been very difficult," Mrs. Tarleton said. "I believe you are the only ones who recognized that we are grieving, too."

"And you can't even mourn him openly," Sarah said.

"You can stop pretending that you care about us," Wendell said, coming back into the parlor. "Just tell us what you want to know and get out."

"Wendell!" his mother cried, outraged. "How dare you speak to our guests like that?"

"They aren't here to offer you sympathy, Mother. They're just trying to figure out who they can blame my father's murder on."

"But Mr. Malloy is investigating Hayden's death, not Bram's," she said.

"That's true, Mrs. Tarleton," Frank said gently, "but it seems logical to assume that the same person killed them both."

"And you want to blame it on me, don't you?" Wendell said, not even bothering to hide his bitterness. "Just like everyone always tries to blame the bastard boy."

His mother cried out as if he'd struck her, and laid a hand over her heart. Sarah was on her feet and beside her instantly. "Are you in pain?"

Tears flooded Mrs. Tarleton's eyes as she stared at her son in disbelief. "We never use that word," she said, her voice a mere whisper.

To his credit, Wendell looked stricken. "I'm so sorry, Mother. Forgive me, please." But he turned to Frank with renewed fury. "But that's why you're here, isn't it? Did she send you? His widow? She's always hated us."

"No one sent us, Mr. Tarleton," Frank said as calmly as he could. "In fact, we don't believe you killed either Hayden or your father, but we wanted to warn you that the terms of Mr. Norcross's will appear to give you a very good reason to have done so."

The color rose in Wendell's face, and he sat down in the

chair beside his mother's. "I had no idea he would name me in his will."

"We thought that might be true," Frank said as Sarah came back and sat down beside him, satisfied that Mrs. Tarleton wasn't going to swoon. "It's difficult to prove you didn't know something, though. I don't suppose you have an alibi for the night Mr. Norcross died."

"He was home all night," his mother said. "I can vouch for him."

Frank smiled sympathetically. "I'm afraid the police wouldn't consider the word of a loving mother as proof of anything."

"But you said you thought the same person killed both Hayden and my father," Wendell said.

"And you had an excellent reason for killing Hayden," Frank reminded him. "After he lied and got you fired from your father's firm. In fact, that's also another good reason you might have been angry at your father."

"But he didn't want to let me go," Wendell said, leaning forward in his chair as if anxious to make Frank understand. "He had no choice, you see. He couldn't fire Hayden, so . . ."

"You mean because Hayden was his legitimate son?" Frank said provocatively.

"No," Wendell snapped, angry again. "Because he'd just negotiated with Thomas Andriessen for Hayden to marry Violet. She was . . ." He looked away, embarrassed.

"Violet was with child," Mrs. Tarleton said solemnly. "Her father was desperate for Hayden to marry her, so Bram threatened to fire Hayden from the firm and cut him out of his will if he didn't."

"Why was Mr. Norcross so willing to force Hayden to marry Violet?" Sarah asked, even though she and Frank thought they already knew the answer.

"Because Mr. Andriessen had promised to ruin Norcross and Son if he didn't," Wendell said. "The Andriessens don't have as much money as people think, but they still wield a lot of influence. If Mr. Andriessen started whispering bad things about our firm, people would start withdrawing their funds and investing with someone else."

"Bram had just gotten Hayden to agree to marry Violet," Mrs. Tarleton continued, "which would save Violet's reputation and also save the firm from ruin, so he couldn't turn around and immediately fire Hayden for the nasty trick he'd pulled on Wendell."

Frank could see it now, how it made sense. "Because Hayden would take his revenge by refusing to marry Violet and then Andriessen would do his worst."

"Father explained it all to me," Wendell said, still angry but not as bitter.

"He was devastated at having to hurt Wendell," Mrs. Tarleton said. "But he had no choice."

"He had to be seen to remove the person responsible for the mistakes," Wendell said. "Otherwise, no one would trust him again."

"And it couldn't be Hayden," Mrs. Tarleton said. "Bram promised that Wendell wouldn't suffer, though."

"After a few months, he was going to find me a place in another investment bank," Wendell said.

"But then Hayden conveniently died so he was able to hire you back again," Frank said. "You can see how bad that might look."

From their expressions, both mother and son could see it very plainly.

"But I didn't kill Hayden," Wendell said. "I swear it."

"We don't think you did either," Sarah said gently. "But we need your help to figure out who did."

"How can we possibly help? We don't have any idea who might have done it," Wendell said.

Sarah ignored him and turned to Mrs. Tarleton. "At the church yesterday, you were saying something about Mrs. Norcross being afraid of Hayden because he had murdered his little sister."

She raised an unsteady hand to her forehead. "Did I? I . . . I shouldn't have said something like that."

"But it's very important, Mrs. Tarleton. Why would Mrs. Norcross have been afraid of a ten-year-old child?"

"He . . . Hayden was a horrible child," Mrs. Tarleton said. "It pained Bram to admit it, but he couldn't pretend it wasn't true."

"Do you know what really happened with the little girl?" Sarah asked gently.

Mrs. Tarleton shuddered. "Hayden had hated her since the day she was born. Poor child adored her big brother, though. The meaner he was to her, the more she craved his attention. I didn't know Bram then, of course, but he told me all about it later."

"Of course," Sarah said, nodding her encouragement.

"Hayden was always hitting her or pinching her, anything to make her cry, so Mrs. Norcross told the nurse she was never to leave the child alone with Hayden."

"But the nurse failed."

"You know how children are," Mrs. Tarleton said, her eyes bleak. "Little Susie got away from her one day, and Hayden . . ." She shuddered again.

"Mother, you don't have to tell them anything," Wendell said in dismay.

"If it will help clear your name, I'll tell them everything," she said fiercely. She turned back to Sarah. "No one saw what happened, of course. Hayden said the little girl had climbed over the railing and fallen all by herself, but she was much too small to have done that. He had to have lifted her up and over the rail. The fall killed her instantly."

Sarah nodded. She'd already heard the story from Violet Norcross. "And Mrs. Norcross was afraid of Hayden after that?"

"I think everyone was. All the servants quit, but Bram and his wife couldn't quit, could they?"

"No, they couldn't. Did they believe Hayden's story, though?"

"*She* didn't. Mrs. Norcross, I mean. Bram tried to, or so he told me. He wanted to, at least, because what else can you do? You can't have a ten-year-old child arrested for murder, not when it's your own son. The boy couldn't have known what he was doing was wrong."

Frank could have argued with her about that, but he bit his tongue again. Sarah was doing beautifully.

"And yet they let him live with them another twenty-five years," Sarah marveled.

Mrs. Tarleton smiled bitterly. "They had no choice. Bram had to keep an eye on him, to make sure he didn't get into any more trouble. That suited Hayden fine, since he didn't have the expense of his own lodgings, and his father really couldn't keep that close a watch on what he did when he was away from home."

"But you said Mrs. Norcross was afraid of him. Wouldn't she have wanted him gone?" Sarah asked with a puzzled frown.

"She probably did, but Bram didn't care what she thought. She'd left his bed and hardly even spoke to him after Susie died. He told her that if she wanted to be free of Hayden, she could divorce him, but she was afraid he'd make her take Hayden with her, so she never would. Instead she started carrying a gun."

Sarah's jaw dropped, and even Frank was stunned. "A gun?" he said.

Mrs. Tarleton smiled with satisfaction. "You would never imagine such a thing, would you? A fine lady like her. But her family enjoyed hunting and so did Bram, and she had learned to shoot when she was a girl. I never saw the gun myself, of course, but Bram told me it was a little pistol. She carried it with her at all times so she could shoot her son if he ever tried to kill her, too."

It took a full minute for Sarah to respond. Frank hoped she was remembering that both Hayden and Bram had been shot with a pistol.

"Did Mr. Norcross carry a pistol, too?"

She did remember!

Mrs. Tarleton frowned. "Bram? Of course not? Why would he?"

"Father wasn't afraid of Hayden," Wendell said.

Or he would never have admitted it if he was.

"Did he keep a pistol in his desk at home, though?" Sarah asked.

"How would we know that?" Wendell scoffed.

"I thought perhaps he might have mentioned it."

"I can't imagine why he would need one," Mrs. Tarleton said.

Sarah smiled sweetly. "Perhaps for Hayden."

But Wendell was shaking his head. "Hayden was wicked, but he only ever hurt those who were weaker than he."

"Like his sister and his wife," Sarah said.

"And Wendell," Mrs. Tarleton said sadly.

"But he was too much of a coward to lay a hand on me," Wendell said. "He had to trick me instead."

"He must have been a tortured soul, though," Sarah said. "He smoked opium, you know."

"Lately, yes," Wendell said. "He used to just drink himself into a stupor."

"But drinking gave him no peace, or so he complained to his father," Mrs. Tarleton said.

And perhaps to his mother, too, because she had finally taken him to the opium den. Had that been an attempt to tame him at last?

"Father was furious when he discovered Hayden was going to Chinatown," Wendell said. "But Hayden was much calmer, at least until Father made him marry Violet Andriessen."

"And smoking the pipe didn't make him hate you any less," Frank observed.

"It didn't make *me* hate *him* any less either," Wendell said bitterly, "but I still didn't kill him."

MAEVE WAS SURE SHE WOULDN'T BE ABLE TO EAT A SINgle bite of the dinner Mrs. Donatelli had made that day. Her stomach was full of butterflies that seemed intent on beating their way out.

"You have to eat a lot," Gino reminded her as they reached the ramshackle house in Little Italy. "If you don't, my mother will be insulted."

Maeve actually groaned, making Gino grin.

His younger brothers had been playing kick the can in the street, and they descended on them with shouts of greeting. They were teasing Gino in Italian because they knew she wouldn't understand.

"What are they saying?" she demanded.

"Nothing," Gino lied, although his face was scarlet.

Enzo had been waiting on the front porch, and he welcomed Maeve with much more charm than the younger boys had shown, taking her hand in both of his and telling her how beautiful she looked and how honored they were to have her as a guest and a lot of other claptrap that they both knew he didn't mean but would make Gino crazy.

Gino got even redder and said something to Enzo in Italian that didn't sound very friendly. Enzo didn't seem to notice and escorted her into the house, completely ignoring Gino.

"Maeve!" a familiar female voice called, and to Maeve's great relief, she saw Teo coming to greet her. Maeve had met Teodora, who was married to Gino's oldest brother, Rinaldo, a few weeks ago when they had been working on a case in Italian Harlem. Maeve was so happy to see a friendly face that she didn't even mind when Teo kissed her on both cheeks.

"Don't worry," Teo whispered. "We will make our announcement today and then everyone will forget about you."

Maeve smiled her first real smile of the day and all the butterflies in her stomach went immediately to sleep. It was a good thing, too, because Mrs. Donatelli seemed intent on stuffing her until she exploded.

"Too skinny," she huffed when she saw what a small portion Maeve had taken of her spaghetti. She piled more onto Maeve's plate. "You eat." If she didn't speak English, how did she happen to know those words?

When they had finished the meal and were picking at their desserts, Gino's father stood up and made a short speech in Italian, which Maeve realized was about her, because he and everyone else were all looking at her.

At least they were all smiling.

"He says you are a brave girl and very smart for saving me and for not crashing the motorcar," Gino translated with a smirk.

Teo, Rinaldo, Enzo, and the other brothers who spoke English laughed uproariously at Gino's translation.

"He didn't say anything about crashing the motorcar," Maeve guessed, giving him a scowl. She was a very good driver.

"But he did say you are smart and brave," Teo confirmed.

Maeve felt the heat in her cheeks as everyone raised a glass to her.

"*Mangia, mangia*," Mrs. Donatelli ordered, pointing to the pastry in front of Maeve. Maeve needed no translation for that.

To her great relief, Teo gave Rinaldo a nudge, and he stood up when his father sat down and made his own announcement. He spoke in Italian, so his parents would understand, but Maeve already knew what he was going to say, because Teo had shared her secret with Maeve weeks ago. A moment of stunned silence greeted the news of the conception of the first Donatelli grandchild, and then the room erupted into cheers and laughter, and Gino's mother burst into tears. Everybody had to hug Teo, except the younger boys, who took the opportunity to escape unnoticed and returned to their play.

"Thank you," Maeve whispered to Teo when she took her turn.

Teo only laughed.

As soon as they were out on the street in front of the Tarletons' apartment building, Sarah turned to Malloy and said, "Mrs. Norcross carried a pistol, and Bram and Hayden were both shot with a pistol."

"I noticed you had made the connection," Malloy said.

She glanced around. The sidewalk was crowded, so they could easily be overheard. "Let's get home."

They managed to find a cab and returned home to find

Mrs. Malloy had taken the children to the park. Maeve and Gino had not returned yet either, so for once Sarah and Frank had the house to themselves.

After getting something cool to drink, they retired to their private parlor that adjoined their bedroom upstairs.

"It's so quiet," Malloy said with a frown as they sat down on the love seat.

"I know. Enjoy it while it lasts. All right, now we know that Mrs. Norcross had learned to shoot."

"I remember that somebody said the whole family hunted."

"I know, but I thought they meant all the men, but I suppose she could have learned to shoot, too. They do have a country house, or at least they did at one time."

"Where Norcross kept his guns," Malloy remembered.

"So what do we think happened?"

Malloy shrugged. "I don't know what you think, but I'm thinking Mrs. Norcross could have killed them both. We just have to figure out how she could have done it."

"I'm not sure of the how, but I'm positive of the why. She was afraid Hayden was going to kill Violet and the baby."

"And according to Violet, he had actually threatened to kill her the way he'd killed his sister."

Sarah nodded. "Mrs. Norcross knew her son was capable of murder, and she probably knew he had been abusing Violet. If Violet actually told her about the threats . . ."

"Yes, I can see she might have been furious and also terrified that Violet and her innocent child would be killed."

"So let's see if we can figure out how she did it. We decided Violet couldn't be the killer because how would she—a female alone late at night in the city—have gotten to the office and back safely?"

"But Mrs. Norcross has a coach and a driver."

Sarah smiled knowingly. "A driver who is rumored to be in love with her."

"And if he is, or if he's just a devoted servant, he could have driven her there and back. But yesterday, we were thinking devoted Kevin was actually the killer."

"He still might be, except for the problem with the pistol," Sarah said.

"Yes, it might have been Hayden's, as the police thought, but how would Kevin have known Hayden had it? How would he have even gotten into the office building in the first place? And how would he have known Hayden would be there, groggy from smoking his opium?"

"And why would he have suddenly decided to murder Hayden in the first place?" Sarah asked.

"We did consider the possibility that Mrs. Norcross asked him to," Malloy said. "If he's besotted with her, he might have done it to please her."

"So either she did it herself or asked Kevin to do it. Either way, she's guilty of killing Hayden," Sarah said.

"So either Mrs. Norcross got Kevin to drive her to Hayden's office and back again or Kevin went by himself."

"And maybe he took Mrs. Norcross's pistol or she took it herself."

"Which would explain where it came from. How did they get into the office?"

"I'm sure Mr. Norcross has keys. They would have just borrowed them."

"You are so sensible, Mrs. Malloy," he said.

She rolled her eyes. "But why kill Bram? With Hayden dead, Mrs. Norcross didn't have to worry about Hayden hurting Violet and the baby, and surely she wasn't worried Mr. Norcross would harm them."

Malloy considered the problem for a long moment. "Could he have figured out that she did it? Or at least that she was responsible?"

Sarah's blood turned to ice in her veins. "Oh no, this is all my fault!"

"What is?" Malloy said, obviously not convinced.

"I did it! I said . . . Well, I don't remember exactly what I said, but I let Mrs. Norcross know that her husband thought a woman had killed Hayden!"

"Why did you do that?"

"I don't know! I can't remember. It came up when Mother and I were visiting her, I think."

"I thought Bram Norcross blamed the phony Chinese prostitute, though."

"Did he say that? Or did he just say he thought a woman had done it?" Sarah challenged.

Malloy had no answer for that.

"I knew it!" Sarah groaned, covering her face with her hands. "It's my fault that Bram Norcross is dead."

"It's the fault of the person who shot him that he's dead," Malloy reminded her mercilessly.

"But if I hadn't told her—"

He sighed. "We don't know what happened, Sarah. Maybe Bram really did suspect her and accused her to her face. That would have made it his fault entirely. She would have had no choice but to kill him if she thought he would tell the police."

"But would he have?" Sarah asked. "He could have used that as leverage to finally get his divorce."

"Good point. But no one wants another person to have that kind of a hold over them, do they? She would have always been afraid he would accuse her."

"And once again we have to wonder if she shot Bram herself or if Kevin did it for her."

"Either way, it explains why Kevin didn't hear the killer running away."

Sarah nodded. "Because Kevin wouldn't have heard himself running away and Mrs. Norcross didn't run away at all."

"How very clever of her," Malloy said.

"But how do we figure out which one of them did it?"

"Maybe we can get one of them to confess. I think the first thing I should do is go down to Police Headquarters and find out which detectives are working on the case."

"I suspect none of them are," Sarah said. "You haven't even had anyone warn you off."

"I know, which makes me think Norcross was uncooperative because he didn't want his wife implicated. Think of the scandal. So he wouldn't have offered a reward, and he may have even told the cops outright not to bother."

"But why wouldn't they investigate *his* death?" Sarah asked.

Malloy smiled. "Because Mrs. Norcross made it clear she wasn't interested in finding his killer either."

"Then why do you need to talk to the police at all?"

"Because we probably want them to arrest whoever killed the Norcross men, and they'll be much more cooperative if I let them take all the glory for solving the case. Besides, I want to find out if they know anything I don't."

"And I need to warn Violet not to move in with Mrs. Norcross. I don't think she'd be in any danger, but who knows what Mrs. Norcross might do if she thought we had figured it all out."

"That's a good idea, but whatever you do, stay away from Mrs. Norcross."

Sarah smiled. "I intend to. Now, we should take advantage of having the house all to ourselves and take a nap."

"I'm not tired," Malloy said in surprise.

Sarah grinned. "Neither am I."

XIV

WHEN SARAH CAME DOWNSTAIRS AT MIDMORNING ON Monday, after changing into street clothes for her mission to save Violet Andriessen, she found her mother-in-law and her neighbor Mrs. Ellsworth enjoying a cup of coffee in the breakfast room. She greeted Mrs. Ellsworth warmly, having not seen much of her lately.

They exchanged pleasantries and asked after their respective families. Then Mrs. Ellsworth said with a touch of disappointment, "I see you're going out."

"I have an errand, but I don't have an appointment, so I'm not really in a hurry. Did you want to speak to me about something?" Sarah pulled out a chair and sat down at the table with them, silently telling Mrs. Ellsworth she was available. Mrs. Ellsworth had once actually saved her life, so delaying her visit to Violet Andriessen for a little while was a small thing.

"You'll think I'm a foolish old woman who is meddling where she has no business," Mrs. Ellsworth said.

Mother Malloy gave a snort of laughter. "But that's what you are, Edna."

Mrs. Ellsworth pretended to take offense. "Even so, I don't like people to think it."

Sarah laughed at their antics. Remarkably, the two had become good friends since Mrs. Malloy had come to live with her and Malloy, and Sarah was glad of it. "Well, *I* don't think it, Mrs. Ellsworth. I think you're a loving mother who is concerned for her family. Is it Theda?" Mrs. Ellsworth's son, Nelson, had married Theda last fall, and Mrs. Ellsworth had been desperate for some sign that a grandchild was expected. So far, she had been disappointed.

"Of course it's Theda," Mrs. Malloy said, earning a scowl from her friend.

"As I've explained to you before, it sometimes takes a year or even longer for a first baby to get started," Sarah said patiently.

"But Theda had this dream . . ."

Uh-oh. Mrs. Ellsworth was notoriously superstitious. Sarah should have expected her to start seeing signs sooner or later. She'd seen signs that Sarah and Malloy were going to marry years before it had ever even been possible. "A dream?" Sarah said cautiously.

"Yes. She told me about it because it was so strange."

Of course it was. "What did she dream?"

"She dreamed that she lost a pair of diamond earrings."

Sarah hoped her expression wasn't as dumbfounded as her brain was. "Diamond earrings?"

"Theda doesn't even own any diamond earrings," Mother Malloy added.

"It doesn't matter if she does or not," Mrs. Ellsworth continued, undaunted. "The point is, she dreamed she lost something very valuable. It is a common dream of pregnant women."

Sarah had never been pregnant, so she couldn't say from personal experience, but she'd also never had a patient who mentioned such a dream. "That's promising, I guess," she said tentatively.

Mrs. Ellsworth wasn't discouraged. "This is why I think Theda might be expecting but not know it yet."

"It's certainly possible," Sarah readily agreed, since any married woman might at any time be expecting and not know it yet.

"I know it's presumptuous, but could you pay her a visit? Not as a midwife, of course, but just as a friend? You could ask her some questions and . . ."

"I certainly could," Sarah said, relieved that Mrs. Ellsworth's request was so easily fulfilled. "As I said, I have an errand, but it shouldn't take me long. I can probably stop by this afternoon."

"I'd be very grateful," Mrs. Ellsworth said.

"Nothing to be grateful for," Sarah assured her with a smile. "I'd like to know myself."

"Are you going to see somebody about a case this morning?" Mother Malloy asked.

"Yes, I am. A young woman who is in the family way, as a matter of fact."

Mother Malloy sighed. "Can you take Maeve with you?"

"Maeve? And leave you to manage the children on your own?"

"I'd rather manage ten children than look at Maeve's long face another day. That girl has been miserable ever since school was out and she had to stop going into the office so she could watch the children."

"I'll be happy to take her, if she'd like to go," Sarah said, thinking this was a problem they'd have to deal with pretty soon.

"And let her drive you in that motorcar. That will cheer her up."

IT DID CHEER HER UP. MAEVE HAD MADE A PERFUNCTORY protest when Sarah invited her, reminding Sarah that her first responsibility was to care for Brian and Catherine, but she was amazingly easy to convince that Mrs. Malloy would be happy to watch them for a few hours if Sarah needed her.

Maeve did drive more sedately than Gino, so Sarah could relax as they drove up to Violet Andriessen's house.

"Gino's mother hates me," Maeve informed her. They had questioned her thoroughly last night about her visit with the Donatelli family, but she had not previously revealed this fact.

"I'm sure she doesn't hate you," Sarah insisted.

"She thinks I'm skinny."

Sarah decided not to address that. "Malloy's mother hated me, if you'll remember."

Maeve frowned, and Sarah wasn't sure if it was in reaction to what she said or to the man who had darted out in front of them, narrowly missing getting run over. "Idiot," she mumbled. Sarah still wasn't sure to whom Maeve referred.

"But I understood that Mrs. Malloy was only worried about what would happen to her if Malloy and I got married."

"Then she should've been nice to you," Maeve said logically.

"I'm not sure that is ever Mother Malloy's first reaction to anyone except her grandchildren."

Maeve laughed at that. "You're probably right. But Gino is a grown man and his mother must know he's going to leave home sooner or later."

"Mothers always feel responsible for their children, even when they're adults, and I think mothers are especially concerned about their sons making a bad choice of a wife because they don't always make that decision with their head."

Maeve's eyes grew round but she didn't reply to that. "I could become a Catholic, I guess."

"You should only do it if you want to. Has Gino proposed?"

"*What?*" Maeve nearly shouted. The motorcar swerved a bit until Maeve got it back under control. "No, he hasn't. Whatever gave you that idea? We're just . . . We're not . . ."

"I see," Sarah said wisely. "You're courting."

"I wouldn't call it *courting* exactly," Maeve said uneasily.

"Something very like it, though."

Maeve glared at Sarah for too long.

"Watch where you're going," Sarah advised her.

She jerked her head back in time to stop for a woman with a baby buggy.

"Mother Malloy thought driving the motor would cheer you up," Sarah said.

"It's not working. What are you going to say to Violet Andriessen?"

"I'm not exactly sure. I have to convince her not to move into the Norcross house, but I don't dare mention that we think Mrs. Norcross might be the killer."

"Because sweet little Violet might tell her," Maeve guessed.

"I think we could count on it, and that could put her in danger. Even if I can get her to delay the move for a few weeks, that will probably be enough time to clear it all up, though. And I have a feeling that Violet doesn't know she has inherited some money of her own from Mr. Norcross. That might encourage her to make different arrangements."

When they reached Violet's house, Maeve pulled the motorcar to the curb and shut off the engine.

"That's odd," Sarah said, peering at the house.

"What is?"

"The mourning wreath isn't on the door."

"Maybe somebody stole it." Maeve always expected the worst from her fellow man.

"Or maybe Violet decided she wasn't going to mourn Hayden anymore." Sarah climbed out of the motorcar. "You should come in with me. It's too hot to sit out here in the sun."

Both women removed their dusters and the lengths of

netting that held their hats firmly in place as they drove. Then Sarah climbed the front steps and rapped the knocker.

Maeve came up behind her, and they waited a little longer than usual before someone opened the front door. The maid had removed her regular cap and had a cloth wound around her head to protect her hair, the way a woman did when she was doing heavy cleaning. "Can I help you?"

"I'd like to see Mrs. Norcross," Sarah said, holding out her calling card.

The maid looked at it but made no move to take it. "She's not here."

That was a rather odd response, but Sarah kept her smile firmly in place. "Do you know when she'll be back?"

"She won't never be back."

"What do you mean?"

The maid gave a long-suffering sigh. "She's moved out. Took a trunk and all her luggage. We're closing up the house."

Sarah's heart sank. "Has she gone to her mother-in-law?"

"She don't tell us her business, but that's who come for her yesterday in a carriage."

Of course it was. Greta Norcross would waste no time. If the Andriessens heard about Violet's inheritance, they'd probably want her back with them, so she had to beat them to Violet.

Sarah thanked the maid, and she and Maeve headed back to the motorcar.

"What are you going to do now?" Maeve asked.

"Malloy told me not to go near Mrs. Norcross, but I think I should at least see Violet and make sure she knows about her inheritance. She probably won't change her mind about living with Mrs. Norcross immediately, but if I can plant that seed, she might reconsider it, at least."

"I wonder if Mrs. Norcross still carries a pistol," Maeve mused when she had cranked the engine to life and climbed into the driver's seat.

"Let's hope not."

FRANK HAD TO WAIT AROUND AT POLICE HEADQUARTERS for a while before Detective Sergeant O'Connor made his appearance. He'd had to endure a bit of razzing from his former colleagues, who insisted on calling him Millionaire Malloy. Sadly, it wasn't exactly good-natured fun, since their jealousy was all too evident. Since Frank hadn't earned, much less deserved, his newfound wealth, he felt like he probably also deserved to suffer a bit.

O'Connor stopped dead in his tracks when he saw Frank waiting for him in the lobby, sitting on one of the benches where felons waited before being taken to the cells. "You're like a bad penny."

Frank managed what he hoped was a friendly smile. "I'm here to do you a favor."

O'Connor's glare was skeptical, and rightly so. He had once arrested Frank and charged him with a murder he hadn't committed, so Frank had no reason to do him any favors at all. "What kind of favor?"

"I heard you were working on the Norcross murders."

O'Connor gave a bark of derisive laughter. "Nobody's working on them. Didn't they tell you?"

"Because the family isn't interested in finding out, but I think that's because Mrs. Norcross is the killer."

"The wife? Wait, which Mrs. Norcross? Aren't there two wives?"

"The mother. She killed her son and then her husband."

But O'Connor was already shaking his head. "Mothers don't shoot their sons, Malloy, especially society women like her."

"Why don't you listen to what I've found out so far before you run me off? You might not get a reward for solving this case, but you'll get lots of attention. The newspapers will even print your name."

"I suppose somebody hired you to solve it, though," O'Connor said.

"Yes, but they won't mind if the police get the credit, and neither will I."

O'Connor sighed. "All right, then. Tell me what you know, and then I'll decide if you've got anything."

They went upstairs to the detectives' room. O'Connor found his cluttered desk, and Frank pulled up a chair beside it. Frank told him everything he knew and why he thought either Mrs. Norcross or Kevin had committed the murders.

O'Connor still wasn't impressed. "Why did you come to me if you still aren't sure?"

"To see if you knew anything I didn't that could help me figure it out. Like the gun, for instance. What was it like?"

"There were two guns," O'Connor said. "I, uh, kept the first one. It was a pretty little thing, like a lady might carry, if ladies carried pistols."

Apparently, they sometimes did. "Like I told you, Bram

Norcross cleaned up Hayden's office before he sent for the police, so he might've moved things around, too, but where did you find the pistol?"

"It was laying on the desk. I thought that was funny, come to think of it. I mean, if it was the killer's gun, he would've taken it with him, but it was just laying there, like the killer shot the guy and put the gun down and calmly walked away."

"Then what made you think it was Hayden's gun?"

"Because his old man told me it was. He said Hayden kept it for protection, although I never saw any of those Wall Street bankers shooting guns down there, so I don't know why he'd need it."

"That makes sense. If it was Mrs. Norcross's gun that she carried for protection from Hayden, she wouldn't need it anymore after she'd killed him with it."

O'Connor didn't look completely convinced but he said, "How does the groom fit into it, then?"

"We think he might've done the actual murders at Mrs. Norcross's direction."

Plainly, O'Connor's imagination didn't stretch to such a conclusion. "Maybe. There's no telling what people will do for love, eh?"

"And Mrs. Norcross had the idea that her husband suspected her of killing Hayden."

O'Connor nodded his head. "That might make her nervous."

"But what about the other gun, the one that killed the father?"

"A pistol, not fancy, though. It was laying on the desk,

too, and nobody had moved anything in that room, I can tell you for sure. I couldn't even get the servants to go in and look around to tell me if anything was missing, and the wife was swooning or something."

"Or pretending to. The killer had some presence of mind, though. He or she shot Norcross, laid down the pistol, went to the kitchen, opened the back door, and ran out—or someplace—before the servants got downstairs."

"And the groom was sound asleep in his bed when we went to look for him, or so he claimed."

"Maybe he was, if he isn't the killer and the shot didn't wake him," Frank said.

"And the pistol belonged to Norcross. We know that."

"How do you know it?"

"Because . . ." O'Connor hesitated, then swore.

"Because Mrs. Norcross told you it did?" Frank guessed.

"Yeah. So the old man said the pistol that killed his son belonged to the son, even though no red-blooded man would own a prissy thing like that. Then the wife said the gun that killed her husband belonged to him . . ."

"And maybe it did, but she'd certainly know where it was kept. Norcross might've lied about the pistol to protect his wife or at least protect his good name, since having his wife murder his son in cold blood wouldn't be good for business. Mrs. Norcross was obviously lying to protect herself. Did anybody else know if Norcross kept a pistol in his desk?"

"Nobody." O'Connor swore again. "All right, it does look bad for the wife. Why couldn't it have been the Chinese prostitute?"

"She's not really Chinese."

O'Connor just glared at him. "So you expect me to arrest this Mrs. Norcross?"

"Not yet. I'd like to talk to the groom first, see what he has to say for himself when he knows we've figured it all out." Frank smiled. "Then I'll let you arrest whichever one it is."

THE DRIVE FROM VIOLET'S HOUSE TO MRS. NORCROSS'S house was short. The mourning wreath was still on the door, which was a good sign, at least. Sarah and Maeve climbed the front steps and clanked the door knocker.

A maid, looking a bit put out, came to the door. She was still adjusting her cap. "Mrs. Norcross isn't receiving."

"I'm a midwife," Sarah said. "I've come to check on Mrs. Hayden Norcross. I understand I can find her here now."

The maid frowned. "She's not here."

Sarah sighed. This was becoming annoying. "When will she return?"

"A few weeks is what I was told."

Sarah and Maeve exchanged a surprised glance. "A few *weeks*?" Sarah echoed.

"They went on a trip, Mrs. Hayden and Mrs. Bram. Mrs. Bram said they needed some rest after all they'd been through."

This was unusual but not surprising. Anyone would need rest after two funerals so close together. "It's very important that I speak to Mrs. Hayden. She has a delicate medical condition." Pregnancy was certainly a delicate medical condition. "Do you know where they went?"

The maid shrugged. "She didn't say, but maybe to the country house?"

"Do you know where it is?" Sarah was starting to feel very uneasy.

"In the country someplace. I don't rightly know."

"How did they travel?"

The maid gave a put-upon sigh. "In the carriage. Our driver had a time getting all the luggage loaded."

Poor Kevin. Would they have traveled by carriage all the way to a country house or had Kevin simply taken them to the train station? Or were they going someplace else entirely? This was all very odd, although Sarah could easily imagine Greta Norcross wanting to escape the city.

"Oh, there's the carriage now," the maid said. "You could ask the driver where they went."

Sarah and Maeve turned to see a carriage rolling down the street, the driver slumped in his seat and making no effort to hurry the horses along. He must be headed for the mews behind the house. "Is that your regular driver?" Sarah asked.

"Oh yes, Kevin is his name. He'll want to see to the animals first, but he could probably tell you where they went."

"Could we come in and speak to him in the house?" Sarah asked, thinking Malloy would be furious if she followed Kevin out to the stables. If he really was the killer, that could be awfully dangerous.

"I suppose." The maid gave Maeve a suspicious look, though.

"Miss Smith is my assistant," Sarah said. Without waiting to be invited, Sarah marched inside, forcing the maid to step back if she didn't want to be trampled. Maeve followed with an apologetic nod.

"Better wait until he has the horses unharnessed before you call him inside," Maeve said with more authority than anyone had granted her. "And don't tell him we're here to ask him questions. Just ask him to come inside for a minute."

The maid frowned. "Is something wrong?"

"We're afraid the ladies might be in some danger," Maeve explained. "We went to Mrs. Hayden's house to warn her, but they told us she was living here now, and you don't even know where they've gone, so . . ."

That had the desired effect. The maid's eyes were the size of saucers. "I'll just ask him to come in." She hurried away without even showing them into the parlor.

"She could have offered us something to drink," Maeve complained.

Sarah just shook her head. "Where did you learn how to do that?"

Maeve grinned. "Are you serious?"

They waited a good half hour before the maid brought Kevin in. He was a pleasant-looking man, probably in his late thirties. He hadn't bothered to change out of his dusty uniform, since he wouldn't have known why he'd been summoned to the house. His expression was grave and a bit confused.

"I'm Mrs. Malloy, and this is my assistant, Miss Smith. I'm a midwife, and Mrs. Hayden Norcross is my patient. I went to check on her this morning, but found she had moved here, and now I'm told she and Mrs. Bram Norcross have gone somewhere else entirely. If you could tell me where, I would be most grateful."

"Mrs. Bram went somewhere," he said.

Sarah's unease flickered to life again. "Where did she go?"

"On a trip."

"I know they did. The maid told me. I just need to know where they've gone."

Kevin's eyes grew bleak and his lips thinned to a bloodless line. He drew several breaths before he said, "She went to Europe."

Sarah blinked in surprise, and Maeve's breath caught. *"Europe?"*

Plainly, this news did not please Kevin any more than it pleased Sarah and Maeve. "Europe."

"But where did you take them *today*?" Maeve asked.

"To the docks, to a ship, but I just got back."

"Took whom?" Sarah asked.

"Mrs. Norcross. The girl, Hayden's wife, she wasn't with her."

Oh dear heaven! Had Greta Norcross killed Violet and left her here? Sarah turned to Maeve, who had obviously had the same thought.

Maeve nodded her understanding. "I'll get the servants to search the house."

"Why would you search the house?" Kevin asked as Maeve hurried out of the room.

"Because Mrs. Hayden might still be here," Sarah said

with what she hoped was a reassuring smile. "Did you happen to notice the name of the ship Mrs. Norcross was taking?"

"*Enterprise*," he said, and now she realized he was angry. Mrs. Norcross had left and Kevin was angry. If he really was in love with her, of course he would be.

"Did you expect her to take you with her?" Sarah asked gently.

Color flooded his face and he actually took a step back. "Why . . . why would she do a thing like that?"

Sarah smiled with all the sympathy she could muster. "Everyone knows how you feel about her, Kevin, and she must be very fond of you, too. It's none of my business, of course, but I know it must be difficult for you to lose her like this."

"I haven't lost her," he said, angry again. "She's . . . she's probably going to send for me."

"I suppose she's very grateful to you."

"Grateful?" he echoed suspiciously.

"After all you did for her, shooting her husband and Hayden—"

Now the color drained from his face. "I never shot nobody! Who told you I did?"

Sarah didn't approve of lying, of course, but sometimes it was necessary. "Mrs. Norcross did. She said you were hopelessly in love with her, and you killed Hayden because he'd threatened his wife and child, and then you killed Mr. Norcross for her, too."

Kevin was shaking his head before she'd even finished. "I never! And she loves me, too. She told me. She even let me . . ." He caught himself and took a calming breath, obviously intent on being a gentleman.

"But you drove her to Hayden's office the night he died, didn't you?"

"She said she had to talk to him in private. She had to make him see sense. He'd threatened to kill his wife like he'd killed his sister, and she had to stop him."

"Stop him by killing him?"

"He threatened her, too. She was always afraid of him. That's why she carried the pistol with her. She didn't want to shoot him, but she had no choice. He would have killed her."

But Sarah shook her head. "Did you know he smoked opium? He wasn't threatening his mother that night. He was in a drugged stupor. She just walked up to him and shot him in the head."

"She wouldn't do that!"

"And what about Mr. Norcross?"

"Mr. Andriessen killed him," Kevin said, his fury turned on Sarah now. "She told me."

"Then why was the back door open?"

"Because he ran out that way."

"But he didn't run out that way, because you didn't hear him, did you?"

"I . . ."

"Did the gunshot wake you up?"

He was trying to make sense of it now, too. "Something woke me up. I guess it was the shot."

"Did you look out the window?"

"Yes, but—"

"But you didn't see anything, did you?"

He just glared at her.

"Let me tell you what Mrs. Norcross said. She said you came into the house that night and shot Mr. Norcross, because you were secretly in love with her and had some strange notion that she would run away with you if her husband was dead. Then you ran out the back door, leaving it hanging open. You went back to your room and pretended to be asleep when the police came."

His fury had melted into despair. "She'd never . . . I don't understand."

"Is that what happened, Kevin? Did you kill Mr. Norcross?"

"No! I never killed nobody!"

He looked as if he might collapse, so Sarah gently took his arm and led him to a chair.

"I shouldn't sit in here," he mumbled.

"I won't tell anyone. Now tell me, Kevin, did you see Mrs. Hayden this morning?"

"No."

"Not at all?"

"No, why should I? I just went in and got the luggage. She had so much of it . . ."

Sarah remembered the maid remarking on the same thing. Violet had left the house with a lot of luggage, too. "Did she have a trunk?"

She had to ask him twice because he was lost in his own misery.

"Yes. It was heavy. I had to get George from next door to help me with it."

Oh no! Sarah's heart was hammering as she rushed out into the hallway and shouted for Maeve.

Maeve came running down the stairs. "We can't find any trace of her, but the maid says her luggage is gone."

"Have they seen her?"

"They saw her yesterday when she first arrived, but not this morning. They assumed they just missed her and that she'd gone with Mrs. Norcross. They were busy."

"Kevin says he didn't do either of the murders, and I'm afraid he's telling the truth."

"I am!" he called from the parlor.

"Mrs. Norcross is going to Europe. He took her to a ship this morning, but he says he never saw Violet either."

Maeve was impressed in spite of herself. "That's a good plan if she killed both of the men, but where is Violet?"

"I'm very much afraid she is stuffed into a trunk and on her way to Europe."

Maeve laid both hands over her heart. "Do you think she's alive?"

"Please God, she is. Mrs. Norcross may have decided she had to flee before anyone figured out what she had done, but she'd done it all to save Violet and the baby, so she could take care of them. I hope she still wants to do that."

"Stuffing someone in a trunk isn't exactly a good way to take care of them," Maeve said.

"I didn't say she was rational."

"What can we do?"

"If there's any chance we can get to the ship before it sails, we can rescue Violet."

"Lucky thing we brought the motor," Maeve said with a grin.

Sarah tried telephoning Malloy, but no one answered at the office. Sarah left a message for him at home to meet her at the docks, but who knew when he would get it? By the time she was finished, Maeve had the motor running and ready to go.

Kevin stopped her as she was racing out the door. "You won't tell her I told you, will you?"

"No, Kevin," Sarah said, lying again. Poor Kevin.

"Do you know how to get to the docks?" Sarah asked Maeve.

"Of course I do. I just hope we're not too late."

If Maeve was usually a careful driver, she also knew how to maneuver in what Malloy would have considered a completely reckless manner. Sarah had to hold her hat with both hands even with the netting wrapped around it.

"What will we do if the ship is still there?"

"We'll go on it and find Mrs. Norcross."

"But they won't let us on. We don't have tickets."

"Lots of people get on with their friends who are sailing, to see them off. They even have parties. Then they blow the ship's horn to warn the friends to get off so the ship can sail. I only hope we have enough time."

By the time they reached the waterfront, Sarah was whispering prayers for poor Violet. Surely, Mrs. Norcross wouldn't have taken a dead body with her to Europe, which meant Violet was most likely still alive, but if she'd been locked in a trunk for a very long time . . .

Maeve drove the motor as far as she could before they

had to abandon it and run the rest of the way to the dock. They didn't even take time to remove their dusters. By some miracle, the *Enterprise* was still sitting in its berth, although they had to fight their way up the gangplank against a tide of exiting revelers.

A steward waited at the top and greeted them with a smile. "You ladies almost missed the boat," he said, chuckling at his pun. "Do you need help with your luggage?" He craned his neck, probably expecting to see a porter behind them.

"We aren't passengers," Sarah said.

"Then you'll have to leave," the steward said. "The captain has already sounded the warning. We'll be sailing very soon."

"You can't!" Sarah cried.

"Oh, but we can."

Sarah wanted to smack the smirk off his face. Left with no choice, she had to come up with another lie. "But I must find my sister. She's sailing on this ship, but our mother is dying and . . ." And what? Sarah's mind went blank.

"She had a terrible accident this morning," Maeve continued as if they'd planned it, "just after Mrs. Norcross left for her trip. She was run over by one of those horrible motorcars. The doctor said she has only hours to live, and her dying wish is to see her other daughter."

At least the steward wasn't smirking anymore. "Well, if you hurry, but we can't hold the ship for her. She'll have to catch another one. And her luggage—"

"Just tell us what cabin she is in," Sarah said, noticing he had a clipboard with a list.

After what seemed an eternity, he found the first-class cabin number and gave it to them, and they hurried off.

"Someone should make sure the ship doesn't sail with us still on it," Maeve said.

"Can you do that? If we find Violet, she may need medical attention, and we'll need the police for Mrs. Norcross. I'll find the cabin and you find the captain."

"What shall I tell him?" Maeve said.

Sarah gave her a helpless shrug. "Tell him whatever will make him hold the ship."

XV

MAEVE HAD NEVER BEEN ON AN OCEAN LINER BEFORE, SO she had no idea where she might find the captain. Common sense said he'd be steering the ship, though, which meant he'd be someplace up high near the front so he could see. She was heading in that direction when she saw a man in an impressive-looking uniform standing around and acting very important.

"Are you the captain?" she asked, figuring he'd be flattered to be thought so, even if he wasn't.

He looked her over disdainfully. "Shouldn't you be in second class?"

"I need to see the captain at once. It's a matter of life and death."

"The captain is very busy right now. We'll be leaving port in just a few minutes."

"Which is why I have to find the captain. You can't leave because Princess Violet of Moritania has been kidnapped and is being taken away on this boat against her will." Was Moritania a real country? Maeve couldn't remember, but this fellow probably didn't know either. "She and her husband, the prince, are visiting America, but some people in her country want to overthrow the government and she's expecting the heir to the throne, so they've taken her. She's on board this boat and we have to find her and rescue her."

"It's a ship, not a boat," the man said condescendingly.

"I don't care if it's a canoe, we can't let it sail with Princess Violet still on it. If she's kidnapped on an American ship, it might even cause a war with Moritania."

"The United States would never fight a war with a European country," he said with authority. "And what has any of this to do with you?" Because Maeve was obviously not royalty of any country.

"I'm Princess Violet's maid. I'm the only one who saw them taking her. Please, just let me speak to the captain. We can't let them get away."

APPARENTLY, NONE OF THE PASSENGERS WERE IN THEIR staterooms. The hallways and decks were clogged with people greeting old friends or making new ones and celebrating the beginning of a pleasant voyage. Sarah practically had to fight her way through them. After a long and frustrating struggle, she finally reached the right cabin. It was on an upper deck in first class and was obviously a suite. Had Mrs. Norcross planned a comfortable crossing with Violet? Did she imagine the girl would become a compliant companion once they were at sea?

Sarah debated how best to get into the cabin. First, she tried the doorknob, but the door was securely locked. Then she knocked and called, "Maid service."

"I don't need anything," a voice called back.

Chills ran down Sarah's spine. Greta Norcross was in there, but where was Violet? Sarah glanced up and down the corridor and saw a real maid carrying a tray of food.

"Miss, please," Sarah called, approaching the young woman. "I've already managed to lock myself out of my cabin. Could you let me back in?"

Plainly, the maid didn't want to be bothered, but she'd also been trained to give the passengers—especially the first-class passengers—anything they needed. Balancing the tray, she pulled out a ring of keys and returned with Sarah to the door.

"This one?" she asked.

"Yes, thank you so much."

The girl slipped a key into the lock and turned it, then pushed the door open for Sarah, who rushed in before Greta could even react. The room was larger than Sarah had expected, and Greta stood at the opposite end. She was rummaging in a bag and when she looked up, she held a pistol pointed right at Sarah.

Do you have any idea how many people you are inconveniencing, young lady?" the captain said. He was a rather large man—like the huge Irish cops they called whales—and so very officious and arrogant in his elaborate uniform that he made the officer who had accompanied her to find the captain look like a poser.

"I have a fair idea, sir, but I wouldn't be asking if Princess Violet's life wasn't in danger."

"I don't understand how a young woman could have been smuggled aboard my ship without anyone noticing," the captain argued.

"We think they put her in a trunk."

Plainly, the captain found this shocking. "A trunk? How inhuman."

"And her with child," Maeve agreed, trying look as distressed as if Princess Violet really was her mistress. "Please, there's no telling what these people will do. They're desperate."

"What country did you say it was?"

"Moldavia, sir." Was that it? She couldn't remember. Why didn't this fellow just get on with it? "They're very uncivilized. I'm sure if you can help with this matter, President McKinley will be very grateful. No one wants America to go to war with a European country." She glanced at the first officer, who nodded sagely.

"I don't suppose it can hurt to check. I'll hold the ship for a short while, but be quick. Evans, go with her."

"Just me, sir?" Evans said with a hint of alarm. "If it's a group of revolutionaries—"

"It's only one woman, I think," Maeve said. "She's just guarding her at the moment, although she is probably armed," she added, not wanting it to sound too easy.

"Arm yourself, Evans," the captain said, and Evans did so, pulling a pistol out of a locked cabinet.

"Could you send for the police, too?" Maeve asked while Evans was strapping on a holster.

The captain glared at her, because she really was being a nuisance.

Maeve tried a helpless smile. "They'll want to arrest these people and get them off your boat."

"It's a ship," the captain grumbled.

"Off your *ship*," she corrected herself, "as quickly as possible, so you can be on your way."

The captain started barking orders, and Evans grabbed her elbow and steered her toward the door. Maeve needed no further encouragement.

THE MAID SCREAMED AND DROPPED HER TRAY AND THE subsequent crash made Greta Norcross jump, but she didn't drop her pistol.

"Close the door and lock it," Greta told Sarah, slowly coming toward her.

Sarah closed the door and pretended to turn the lock. "Where's Violet?"

"She's safe," Greta said. She looked oddly calm.

But Sarah had been scanning the room. She didn't see Violet, but she did see the trunk over where Greta had been standing. "Is she still in there?" Sarah asked, horrified.

"I don't know what you're talking about," Greta insisted. She was holding the pistol remarkably steady, but Sarah shouldn't have been surprised. The woman had shot two men in the face, one of them her own son.

"She could suffocate," Sarah said. "At least let me raise the lid."

"Stay back. Violet is going with me."

"And what will you do if she dies in there?"

"She isn't going to die."

"Or maybe you already killed her. Did she figure it out, what you did? Are you planning to throw her body overboard or something?"

Greta looked shocked. "I would never harm her."

"And yet you've locked her in a trunk."

"Just for a little while."

Sarah had been speaking loudly, in hopes that Violet would hear her and know she'd come to rescue her, but she heard nothing from the trunk, no shouting or even thumping. Not a single sound. Dread settled like a cold lump in her stomach. Still she kept her gaze on Greta. "Has she been in the trunk all morning? Or did you put her in last night?"

"She's *safe*," Greta insisted.

"Kevin told me what happened," Sarah said.

Greta blinked in surprise. "Who?" she tried.

"You know very well who. Kevin told me how he drove you to the office that night. You told him Hayden tried to attack you, so you had to shoot him, but we know that isn't true, don't we?"

"I don't know any such thing," she said, but her confidence had slipped a bit.

"Because Hayden was smoking opium and was in a stupor when he was killed. Did he recognize you, Mrs. Norcross? Did he realize you'd come to murder him?"

"He was going to kill Violet and the baby," she nearly shouted. "I had to protect them."

"How did you know he'd be in the office and helpless from the opium?"

She smiled bitterly. "I knew what he did there and when he did it and with whom he did it. He and Bram argued about it constantly."

"And yet you were the one who introduced him to the opium."

Her face twisted with anger. "I only wish I had done it sooner. He had gotten uncontrollable, so I told him about a place where he could really enjoy himself. It helped, but not enough. He was still too dangerous to Violet."

"But why kill your husband? He wasn't going to harm anyone."

"Because he knew! I'd left my pistol behind. It was a mistake, but it was . . . I didn't expect it to affect me like that. Shooting him, I mean. I was . . . It was terrible! I laid down the gun and forgot to take it with me."

"And your husband recognized it, but he lied. He said it belonged to Hayden. He was going to protect you."

She laughed at that, an ugly, bitter cackle. "He wasn't protecting me. He was trying to avoid a scandal, and he also was going to blackmail me into a divorce."

"If he wanted to avoid a scandal, then you didn't need to kill him. He would have kept your secret."

"Would he? Once he got what he wanted, he'd turn on

me. That's why he hired your husband, to get proof so he could punish me."

"But he didn't hire my husband. He wasn't looking for proof. He was probably as glad as you were that Hayden was dead and wouldn't be able to hurt anyone else again."

Then Sarah heard it, a faint groan coming from the trunk. Violet was alive!

Sarah started for the trunk, but Greta blocked her way, pointing the pistol at her chest. "Stop!"

"You can shoot me if you like, but if you do, this cabin will be swarming with people in about thirty seconds and you'll go to prison and never see Violet or the baby again."

While Greta absorbed this threat, Sarah grabbed her arm and pushed it aside, so when the gun went off, the shot shattered the window. Without waiting to see what Greta would do next, Sarah rushed to the trunk. The lid was un-latched, at least, and Sarah threw it open.

Violet lay on her side with her knees pulled to her chest, her skirts tucked neatly around her. With terror-filled eyes she was blinking up at Sarah.

"Are you all right?" Sarah asked.

Her only answer was another groan. Was she drugged? Quite probably. How else could Greta have prevented her from calling out for help as the trunk was transported from her house to the ship?

"What did you give her?" Sarah demanded, reaching down to help Violet, who wasn't even trying to sit up. She turned to find Greta just staring at them. She still held the pistol, but her arm hung at her side, so it was pointed to-ward the floor. Sarah hoped the bullet that had broken the window hadn't hit anyone outside, but she couldn't let Greta fire again.

She reached for the pistol.

WAS THAT A GUNSHOT?" EVANS CRIED AS HE LED MAEVE through the maze of corridors.

Terror paralyzed Maeve's throat, so she couldn't even answer. The passengers who had been socializing in the corridor had fallen silent and were looking around with puzzled expressions.

"We think we heard a shot," one of the gentlemen told Evans, who didn't even glance at him.

Evans reached the cabin door and stopped. A maid was cleaning up some broken dishes, but she scurried out of the way as he approached. He had already pulled his pistol from its holster. He glanced at Maeve. "Stand back, young lady."

Maeve ignored him and threw open the cabin door.

"She's armed," Evans cried, leveling his pistol at the woman standing at the far end of the room. "Put down your weapon."

The woman held her left hand up in a sign of surrender and carefully laid the pistol on the floor at her feet.

"She's not the kidnapper!" Maeve shouted. "She's with me. Where is . . . ?" And then she saw Mrs. Norcross, lying on the floor, all trussed up in the yards of veiling Mrs. Malloy used to keep her hat on in the motor. "She's the kidnapper," Maeve informed Evans, pointing at Mrs. Norcross, and hurried to Mrs. Malloy, who had already turned toward the trunk.

"Help me get her out," Mrs. Malloy said. Oh dear, Violet really was in the trunk.

"Is she all right?" Maeve asked, thinking Violet looked far from all right. Her eyes were open, but she wasn't even trying to help them get her out.

"She's been drugged, I think."

They managed to get Violet upright, and she took a deep breath, which cheered Maeve a great deal.

"Is Princess Violet all right?" Evans asked, still holding his pistol but still not quite sure if he should be pointing it at anyone.

"*Princess* Violet?" Mrs. Malloy asked Maeve, obviously bewildered.

"You told me to tell them whatever I needed to."

I CAN'T BELIEVE YOU WENT AFTER GRETA NORCROSS alone," Frank said, still trying to decide if he was angry at her for putting herself in danger or just relieved that she had come to no harm. How could he break her of this habit of chasing after criminals?

"I wasn't alone. Maeve was with me," Sarah replied. They were snuggled on the love seat in their private parlor. Sarah and Maeve had spent the better part of the day with the police, trying to make them understand that no foreign countries were involved in Violet's abduction and it was a simple case of a very odd woman taking matters into her own hands by murdering her husband and son.

By the time Frank had gotten Sarah's message and arrived at the docks, thcy had finally arrested Mrs. Norcross for kidnapping and taken her away. Violet's parents had come to claim her and were suitably solicitous of their daughter, at last. Fortunately, she seemed to have recovered from the dose of laudanum Mrs. Norcross had given her. Sarah would visit her soon and explain that she could, if she liked, be completely independent of her parents now.

Gino had been briefed on all that had happened and sent along home. Maeve had gone to bed early, and now Frank and Sarah were finally alone.

"How much protection do you think Maeve would be?" he asked in exasperation.

"She brought a ship's officer with a gun. He would have come in very handy if I had needed him."

Frank gave a long-suffering sigh. "You're lucky the *captain* didn't shoot you after he found out Maeve's tale was all a lie."

"I think he was a little angry, but once he realizes what a great story it will give him to tell, he'll forgive us, I'm sure."

Frank wasn't sure, but it probably didn't matter. "Are you tired?"

"Strangely, no. I haven't felt this energized in a long time."

Frank was just about to suggest an activity that would certainly relax her when someone knocked on the door. Their maid, Hattie, stuck her head in. "There's a telephone call for you, from Mr. Robinson."

Malloy turned to Sarah. "He must have heard what happened somehow and is calling for a report. I wasn't going to bother him until tomorrow."

He started to get up, but Hattie said, "No, he's calling for Mrs. Malloy. It's the baby, he said."

"At last," Sarah cried, jumping to her feet and hurrying out.

MALLOY INSISTED ON DRIVING HER IN THE MOTOR BEcause it was getting late, even though it was still daylight. She suspected he just didn't want her out of his sight yet. Sarah had been sure he had no idea how to drive the motor, but he had apparently been practicing in secret. Still, he was even more cautious than Maeve. Sarah had to bite her tongue to keep from making a joke about what a good thing it was that first babies usually took their time, since he seemed in no hurry to get her there.

The Robinsons' butler, Tom O'Day, answered the door. Usually, Tom was the picture of quiet dignity, but tonight he looked a little frazzled.

"We're very glad to see you, Mrs. Malloy," he said, sounding like he was, too.

"How are you holding up, Tom?" Sarah asked with an understanding smile.

"I'm holding up just fine, but I'm not too sure about Mr. Robinson," he said for her ears alone.

"I brought Mr. Malloy along to support him," she said.

"Is he in the parlor?" Malloy asked.

Tom nodded, and Malloy went off to find him.

"May I speak to Marie about the things I'll need?" Sarah asked.

Marie materialized instantly, having been waiting in the

shadows. Her usual dignity was a bit strained as well, although she seemed to be more excited than apprehensive.

"So nice to see you, Marie," Sarah said. "I know I can count on you."

"Yes, you can, Mrs. Malloy," Marie informed her. "I've already started heating some water."

"Good, keep it warm." She told her what else she would need, and Marie promised a maid would bring everything up very soon.

Then Sarah went upstairs, carrying the medical bag that had belonged to her late husband and which now contained everything she would need to deliver the baby.

Sarah knocked but didn't wait for a reply before entering the bedroom. She was pleased to see Jocelyn up and walking with a maid at her elbow, just as Sarah had recommended. The maid looked terrified, and she welcomed Sarah with almost pathetic gratitude. Everyone was always afraid the baby would just suddenly drop out, leaving them to deal with everything, when in reality, birth was most often a long, slow process.

"How are you doing?" Sarah asked.

Jocelyn rubbed her stomach. "The pains are coming about five minutes apart now."

"Things are moving along well, then. Can you lie down on the bed and let me take a look?"

FRANK HAD HOPED THAT GIVING JACK ROBINSON A DE-
tailed account of the case and how they had solved it would distract Jack from the fact that his wife was giving birth

upstairs. Unfortunately, Jack seemed to hear only about half of what Frank said and to understand very little of that.

"Who was this Princess Violet again?" he asked absently.

"It doesn't matter," Frank assured him. "The important thing is that Mrs. Norcross has been arrested for kidnapping, and I've spoken with the detective sergeant in charge of Hayden's case. I think she will soon be charged with killing Hayden and her husband as well."

"How long does it take to have a baby?" Jack asked, staring at the ceiling as if he could see through it to his wife. "Shouldn't it be here by now?"

"It takes as long as it takes," Frank said, trying to sound wise.

"What if something happens to Jocelyn?" Jack asked, his terror obvious in spite of his effort to conceal it. "Women die in childbirth, don't they?"

Frank had lost his first wife in childbirth, but he wasn't going to mention that to Jack. "Sarah is very good at what she does, Jack, and Jocelyn is young and healthy."

"I didn't know I could feel like this, you know? I wanted a wife who would help me socially. I thought it was enough that we liked each other and got along. I didn't expect to *care* so much."

"But you fell in love."

Jack sighed and ran a hand through his hair. "Not something I ever expected to happen to me."

"Count your blessings, brother."

They heard a groan, just audible from the second floor. Jack was on his feet like a shot, but Frank grabbed his arm when he would have run out. "That's perfectly normal, and there's nothing you can do to help."

"Normal?" he echoed incredulously.

"It's hard work having a baby. Sit down. Can I get you a drink?"

"I don't want to be drunk when the baby comes."

"I'll get you something," Frank said.

SARAH HADN'T SAID A WORD, BUT SHE HADN'T BEEN ABLE to find the baby's heartbeat. That didn't necessarily mean the baby was dead, but it wasn't reassuring. The baby's back should be right against Jocelyn's stomach, so the heartbeat would be loud and clear, but even though she'd moved the bell of the stethoscope all around, she'd found nothing. She wasn't going to say anything about it to Jocelyn, though. No sense panicking her.

Meanwhile, she had another concern. Jocelyn had been pushing for a while now, but the baby wasn't moving any farther along the birth canal. The baby was crowning, though, so Sarah was finally able to see and feel the baby's head. Her fingers found the baby's eyes, and they were facing front, which explained why Jocelyn hadn't been able to push the baby any farther.

"Jocelyn, the baby is not quite in the right position," Sarah said after examining her.

"What does that mean?" Jocelyn asked, instantly terrified.

"Nothing terrible. Baby is facing your front, but it's much easier for the baby to come out if he's facing your back."

"Why is he facing the wrong way? Did I do something wrong?"

"No, not at all. This happens to a lot of women."

Before she could go on, Jocelyn was gripped by another contraction. Her push didn't move the baby.

"There may be something you can do to turn him, though. It will be a little uncomfortable, but roll over on your side and pull your legs up. That's it." Sarah maneuvered Jocelyn's bulky body into the right position and ordered her not to push during the next contraction.

The effort made her groan ferociously, but Sarah praised her as she felt the baby stirring. "Once more," Sarah said. "I know it hurts, but it won't be long."

"I can't do it!" Jocelyn cried.

"Yes, you can," Sarah said. "I can feel the baby turning. Now, don't push!"

Another enormous groan, and Jocelyn's eyes grew round as they both felt the baby spin.

"Was that it? Did he move?"

"Yes, good work, Mother. It should be easier now."

Sarah helped Jocelyn roll onto her back and sit up. This time when the contraction came and she pushed, the baby slid closer as he should have. Sarah grabbed her stethoscope and pressed it to Jocelyn's stomach.

And there it was, a good strong heartbeat. Sarah wanted to weep with relief. She just hadn't been able to hear it before because of the baby's position.

"One more, and I think the head will be out. Come on, Mother. We're almost done here."

. . .

FRANK THOUGHT HE MIGHT HAVE TO KNOCK JACK UNCON-
scious to keep him from running upstairs after Jocelyn
groaned the second time. Luckily, there had been no further distressing sounds, and Jack had finally sat back down,
but only on the edge of his chair.

Then they heard it, the wail of a newborn infant carrying
faintly through the house. "What's that?" Jack asked in alarm.

"A sound you're going to hear a lot from now on. It's a
baby crying."

"Why is it crying? Is something wrong with it?"

"They get the baby crying to open up its lungs," Frank
said, happy to show off how much knowledge he had
gleaned through the years of loving a midwife. "It's perfectly normal. It will stop soon."

As if the baby had taken Frank's direction, the wailing
stopped as suddenly as it had begun. Jack continued to
stand, looking up at the ceiling and listening to the silence.
"Is that normal?"

Frank knew Sarah would have given the baby to Jocelyn
to nurse to help the afterbirth pass, but he decided Jack
probably didn't need to know about that. "Perfectly normal."

"Should I go up?"

"Not yet. They'll want to clean up. I'm sure Jocelyn will
want to look her best for you."

"I don't care what she looks like."

"Of course you don't, but she cares."

That seemed to make sense to Jack, who sat down again,

still on the edge of his chair. After what seemed a long time but was only about half an hour, Sarah appeared in the parlor doorway, holding a small bundle.

Jack was on his feet in an instant. "Is Jocelyn all right?" His voice was no more than a hoarse whisper.

"She's perfectly all right, although she's a little tired. I wanted to introduce you to your new daughter."

Jack stared at the bundle in Sarah's arms, having apparently just realized what it was. She walked over to him and pulled back the edge of the blanket to show him the baby's face.

"A daughter?" he repeated stupidly.

The baby's eyes flew open, and she stared at him in wonder.

"I didn't mean to wake her," he said, sure he'd done something wrong.

"That's all right. I think she just recognized your voice."

"How could she recognize my voice?"

"Because she's been hearing it for months, although I'm sure it's much louder now that she's out in the world."

"She could hear me when she was . . . ?"

Sarah didn't bother to answer. He probably wouldn't have heard her anyway. He was still staring at the baby in bemusement.

"She's so small." He tentatively reached out a finger to touch her cheek, and she grabbed that finger in her tiny fist.

Jack actually gasped.

"Would you like to hold her?" Sarah asked.

Jack looked up in alarm. "Oh no, I might hurt her."

"How could you hurt her? Just hold your arm like I'm doing."

"I don't know anything about babies," he protested.

"You soon will," Frank said, somehow managing not to laugh at his friend's discomfort.

"That's it," Sarah said, placing the baby into the crook of his arm.

"She's so light." Her head rested in the curve of his elbow and his hand supported her feet. She was still staring at him in fascination.

"Look at her. She knows you're her father," Sarah said.

Jack's surprise was almost comical, but then the baby smiled. "Look, she smiled at me!"

"I think you should tell Jocelyn. She'll be very happy to know it," Sarah said.

"Is it all right for me to go up?" Jack asked.

"Yes. I'm sure she'll be glad to see you both."

Jack wrapped both arms around the baby and took the stairs two at a time, making such a racket that Tom and Marie O'Day came rushing out to see what was happening.

"Is something wrong?" Marie asked.

"Not at all," Sarah said. "Jack was in a hurry to see his wife. They have a little girl."

Both of the O'Days smiled, and Marie dashed away a tear.

"I've been baking all night. You'll stay for breakfast," Marie said.

"I never miss an opportunity to eat your cooking, Marie," Frank said.

"I'll put some champagne on ice," Tom said. "We'll want to celebrate."

"And some beer for the new mother," Marie said. "It's good for the milk."

When they were gone, Frank led Sarah back into the parlor and sat down with her on the sofa. "Are you still feeling energetic?"

"I'm getting my second wind, I think. What time is it?"

"After four. The sun will be coming up soon. I think we just saw a man fall in love with a baby."

"I think we did."

"Why did you bring the baby down to Jack, though? Don't you usually take the father to see the mother and baby together?"

Sarah gave him a sad smile. "Jocelyn still wasn't sure how Jack would react. She wasn't even sure how she would react, if she'd be able to love the baby in spite of how she was conceived."

"And did she love it?"

"Instantly. But if Jack didn't or even if he was hesitant at first, she couldn't bear to see that. She wanted to give him a chance to have an honest reaction."

"That was the most honest reaction I think he's ever had," Frank observed.

"Yes, and thank goodness the baby had the sense to smile at him."

"I thought you said newborns don't really smile, that it's just gas."

Sarah's smile was real. "That's true, but don't tell Jack, will you?"

"Not on your life."

He slipped his arm around her and she laid her head on his shoulder. "Sometimes I wish . . ."

He sighed. "I know you'd like a baby of your own, but I

can't say I'm as disappointed as you are. I saw how scared Jack was for Jocelyn, and it brought Kathleen's death back to me. I don't think I could stand it if anything happened to you."

"And we already have two wonderful children," Sarah said. "We shouldn't be greedy. It's just that sometimes, I feel a *tiny bit* greedy."

"It could happen," he said. "You're still young."

But Sarah had been married to her first husband for three years and to Malloy for almost two, and it hadn't happened yet. Still, she smiled. "Yes, it could, but even if it doesn't, we have a wonderful life. Let's not forget that."

Malloy hugged her to him. "I won't."

"And in the meantime, I have to meet with Theda Ellsworth because she dreamed she lost some diamond earrings."

Malloy frowned in confusion.

"I'll explain later," she said. "Now I should go check on Jocelyn."

Author's Note

So many readers have asked when Jack Robinson would return, and I must confess, I wanted to see him again myself, so it was fun to visit with him and Jocelyn again.

Investment banking began during the Civil War era and continues to this day. I read a wonderful novel, *The Rich Are Different*, by Susan Howatch, which introduced me to this world and gave me the idea for this book. You can Google early investment banking, but Susan's book is a lot more fun if you want to learn more about it.

Opium was viewed as a wonder drug in early times, since it banished pain and calmed jangled nerves. It was often prescribed to ease female maladies. Too late people realized how addictive it was, but it was readily available at drugstores in the United States until it was finally banned in 1905. By then morphine had also come into common use, creating new addicts, and heroin was developed as a cure for morphine addiction. Modern readers will find this difficult to believe, I'm sure!

Readers of my earlier Gaslight Mystery *Murder in Chinatown* often wonder if it is true that Chinese men often married Irish girls. This is perfectly true. The government had allowed Chinese men to immigrate to the United States to help build the railroad, but they forbade Chinese women from immigrating because they wanted the men to return to China. Officials believed that the men would return to China if they didn't have any Chinese women to marry here. While most European immigrants arrived as family groups, immigrants from Ireland were often fleeing a famine, which meant that a lot of young women, sole survivors of their families, often arrived alone. These women had to make their own way, and some of them found that hardworking, successful Chinese men made very good husbands.

The idea for Theda Ellsworth's dream came from real life. Long ago, my daughter told me she thought she was pregnant because she had dreamed about losing a pair of diamond earrings. I was skeptical until I checked my dream interpretation book, which said it was "a common dream of pregnant women." It turned out she wasn't pregnant that time, although she's had three children since, but we all got a big laugh out of that dream, and I never forgot it.

People often ask if Frank and Sarah are going to have a child of their own. My answer is that they have not told me that yet. I can't help wondering how Sarah would investigate murders with a newborn to take care of, but if you've got some ideas on that, I'd love to hear them!

Please let me know if you enjoyed this book, and if you send me an e-mail through my website, victoriathompson .com, I will put you on my mailing list and send you a re-minder when my next book comes out. Or follow me on Face-book at Victoria.Thompson.Author or Twitter @gaslightvt.